HOW MUCH I CARE

MIAMI NIGHTS SERIES, BOOK 2

MARIE FORCE

How Much I Care
Miami Nights Series, Book 2
By Marie Force

Published by HTJB, Inc.
Copyright 2020. HTJB, Inc.
Cover Design by Kristina Brinton
Print Layout: E-book Formatting Fairies
ISBN: 978-1952793011

The Miami Nights Series

Book 1: How Much I Feel (*Carmen & Jason*)
Book 2: How Much I Care (*Maria & Austin*)
Book 3: How Much I Love (*Dee's story*)

CHAPTER 1

AUSTIN

I'm dead asleep after pitching a shutout against the
Mariners when my phone rings with the tone I
assigned to my parents. They'd never call me at this hour unless
something was up with Everly, so I pull myself out of a deep
sleep to reach for the phone on my bedside table.

"Hey." As I move to get more comfortable, the ice pack on
my shoulder falls off, making a squishing sound as it lands on
the bed. My arm aches like it always does after I pitch.

"I'm so sorry to wake you, Austin." Mom sounds frazzled.
"But Ev has a fever. We're at urgent care now, and I thought
you'd want to know."

I sit up, now wide awake. "What's her temp?"

"One-oh-three."

"Seriously? How long has she had it?"

"About eight hours now." Which means they waited to call
until after my start, knowing worries about Everly would mess
with my concentration. "We were giving her medicine, but
nothing was working, so we brought her in."

"I'll come home." I'm required to travel with the team, even between starts, but exceptions can be made. The team's management knows I'm a single father and are accommodating —to a point. Since I have four days until my next start, it shouldn't be a problem to fly back to Baltimore.

"We're so sorry to have to call with this news, but we thought you'd want to know."

"You did the right thing. I'll be there as soon as I can." I end the call with my mom and place another to my manager, Mick Danvers.

"Why aren't you asleep?" he asks, his voice gravelly with sleep.

"Sorry to bother you, Coach, but I've got a situation at home. My little girl has a high fever and is in the ER. I need to go home, and I'm hoping you won't mind if I catch up to you in Oakland." It'll be a bitch to add two cross-country flights to my week, but I don't care about that. Not when Ev is sick and needs me.

"Of course. Do what you've got to do. Let us know how she is."

"I will." I release a deep sigh of relief. Mick is fair but tough, so I wasn't sure if he'd let me go.

"Hell of a start tonight, AJ. Everyone is very pleased."

"Thanks, Coach."

"Keep me posted."

"I will." My next call is to book a flight home as quickly as possible.

Seven of the longest hours of my life later, my flight—on a plane without freaking WiFi— touches down at BWI. I fire up my phone to a string of new messages from my mother, each more frantic than the last. They've admitted Everly. Something isn't right with her blood.

My chest is so tight, I wonder if I'm having a heart attack as I run through the airport and grab the first cab I see, completely jumping the line. I don't care. I need to get to my baby girl. She's my whole world, and the possibility of anything being wrong with my angel is too horrifying to bear.

The thirty-minute ride to the hospital feels almost as endless as the flight did. By the time I join my parents in the pediatric ICU waiting room, I'm fairly certain I'm on the verge of a medical crisis of my own. How did she go from a fever to the pediatric ICU at Hopkins in the span of a few hours? My mother bursts into tears when I walk in. I drop my bag inside the door so I can hug her and my dad, who seems equally undone.

"Thank God you're here, son," Dad says.

As I look at them, I realize they know something I don't, and judging by their expressions, whatever it is will rock my world.

"Austin," Mom says tearfully, "Everly has leukemia."

MARIA

Fifteen months later...

I force myself to endure Sunday brunch with my boisterous extended family without checking my phone. I grocery-shop afterward and do a number of other necessary workweek preparation errands, while still ignoring my phone. Never has avoiding my phone been more painful than it is today, as months of anticipation have led to this day. I'm elated, excited, nervous and worried that the connection between myself and Mr. A, as I know him, won't be the same once we're no longer anonymous.

Just over a year ago, I donated bone marrow to save the life of a two-year-old girl who was battling leukemia in Baltimore. At the time, I knew nothing else about her or her father, except that my transplant saved her life.

As of six months ago, I know he loves her more than anything in his world, the child's mother isn't in the picture, and

3

he's thankful to me for giving his little girl a second chance. The child has since turned three, and her remission is holding, which is the most important part of this story.

But that's not the whole story.

It began with a call on a Tuesday night from Be the Match, an organization that'd done a registry drive at the clinic where I work in Little Havana more than three years earlier. Honestly, I'd forgotten all about having my cheek swabbed until I got the call that I was a match for a child battling leukemia. Would I be willing to undergo further testing?

Of course I was willing, and the testing was scheduled.

That call from Be the Match turned my life upside down for a few weeks. My parents had freaked out about me going under general anesthesia to donate bone marrow to a stranger. What if something goes wrong? they'd asked. Thankfully, Nona intervened with them, after seeing how hell-bent I was on saving the life of a child I'd never met.

"Maria is a nurse," Nona said. "This is what she does. You must trust her and have faith in her judgment."

I've always adored my Nona, but never more so than I did then. She dealt with my parents, which gave me the space I needed to mentally and physically prepare for the procedure. After we attended information sessions and my parents learned there was very little risk to the donor, they came around to supporting my determination to donate.

My cousin Carmen, who along with my sister, Dee, is my closest friend, accompanied me to the hospital and kept the rest of the family informed throughout the day.

Nona and Abuela, Carmen's grandmother and a third grandmother to me, cooked enough food to feed ten people and delivered it when we got home from the hospital. Really, it was more about confirming for themselves that I was truly fine than it was about food, but I appreciated their concern. Carmen spent two nights at my place, making sure I was okay before she went home.

I was stiff and sore for a couple of weeks after but went back to work a week later. I considered the entire thing a small price to pay to save a child's life.

Six months after the procedure, I received an anonymous email from the child's grateful father, through channels provided by Be the Match.

Dear Ms. M,

You saved my daughter's life. There's no way I can possibly tell you in mere words what you mean to my family and me or how much we appreciate what you did for us. I want to tell you about my daughter, E. She's a little spitfire with blond curls and big blue eyes. She loves to dance and play dress-up. I'm a single dad, and she's my whole world. When the doctors first told us she had leukemia, I thought I'd die myself from the idea of my precious love suffering in any way.

The next few months were pure hell. That's the only word I can think of to describe it. They tried everything but couldn't get her into remission. That's when they decided she needed a bone marrow transplant.

I'm going to be honest with you—the whole thing was terrifying. Thank God I had my parents with me through it all, or I might not have survived watching my baby go through hell. And E, she was such a trouper, so brave and strong. She kept trying to comfort me. Imagine that—a two-year-old comforting a twenty-eight-year-old man. But that's my girl. She's amazing and full of love, and now, thanks to you, she's in full remission and back to singing her nonsensical songs in her own particular language and dancing and playing and laughing. Her hair has grown back— curlier than ever—and her cheeks are pink again. Because of you. I've never met you, and I love you like a member of my family.

You are *a member of my family. And when the required one-*
year waiting period is up, I hope we can meet and talk and
share pictures, and you can see the life you saved for yourself.
Thank you. From the bottom of my grateful heart. Thank you.
We love you.
Mr. A

I must've read that email a thousand times after I first received it and sobbed my way through the first, second and third reading of it. I was so moved by how his love for his child poured off the page. I'm going to be brutally honest here. I fell a little bit in love with him based on how he talked about his daughter. How could I not?

When I showed the email to Carmen and Dee, they had the same reaction. Dee said she actually swooned a little. Both of them cried.

Carmen, who's madly in love with her pediatric neurosurgeon fiancé, Jason, didn't completely freak out the way Dee did, but even Carmen agreed that Mr. A sounds dreamy.

It took me a couple of days, and several hundred more rereadings of his message, to settle myself enough to write back to him.

Dear Mr. A,
Your email touched me deeply.
No, you can't say that! Why not? It did *touch me deeply, and*
he should know that.

Ignoring my own internal dialogue, I poured my heart onto the page, refusing to give him anything less than he had given me. Until the one-year mark, we aren't allowed to speak of anything more than the transplant and updates about the recipient's condition. I can't tell him, for example, that I'm from Miami with a large extended family or that I work at a free clinic in Little Havana. I checked, and I can tell him I'm a nurse, since it's relevant to the transplant.

Your email touched me deeply. Hearing about your wonderful E reduced me to tears. I'm so, so glad to hear she's doing well and is in remission. I'm a nurse, so I know what that means, and I share your elation that "our project" led to such happy results. I'm sure you're being very careful with her in this first tender year, when you have to limit her exposure to others, but when you're able to be out and about again, I'd love nothing more than to meet her and hug her and celebrate her return to good health. Thank you so much for sharing your joyful news with me, and I'll look forward to hearing more from you when the time comes.
Sincerely,
Ms. M

I debated whether I should sign it *Love, Ms. M*, but in the end, I went with *Sincerely*.

Two days later, he wrote to me again.

Ms. M,
I forgot to ask if you suffered any ill effects from donating. I really hope not. Please let me know that when you get the chance, and I will definitely reach out with more as soon as I'm allowed to.
Love,
Mr. A

Dear Mr. A,
Other than a few bruises and some stiffness for a week or two, the procedure was relatively painless for me. It was a small price to pay to help save your little girl. I'd do it again in a second. Thank you for checking on me.

7

Love,
Ms. M

Yep, you read that right. The second time I went with *Love.* Because I already love this father and daughter I've never met. I love the way he talks about her and how grateful he is for what I did for them. I've read the emails we exchanged so many times, I have them memorized.

His last email was short and sweet.

Ms. M,
I'm so glad to hear the procedure was almost painless for you.
I'll definitely write more to you the minute I can. Promise.
Love,
Mr. A

The transplant was one year ago today. For six months, I've been telling myself it's not possible to fall in love with someone because of a few emails. But try telling that to my overly involved heart. All I can think about is Mr. A and Miss E. My active imagination has spent hours wondering about them as I counted down to today. I've tried to keep as busy as I could, volunteering for extra shifts at the clinic and helping Carmen with her wedding plans, but there are still far too many hours in the day for my liking.

And yes, I'm fully aware of how ridiculous it is to get all spun up over a guy I've never even met. I don't even know his actual name, only his first initial. Is his name Alex or Anthony or Andrew? Is it possibly Asher, Adrian or Aidan? And little E, is she Emma or Emily or Emerson or Ellen?

I'm going to drive myself mad with the speculation. I want to know everything about both of them, and even realizing I might be setting myself up for a huge disappointment, I can't stop myself from wondering if A is really as wonderful as he

8

seems in his emails. Does he drink or party or chase women or—

"Stop it, Maria," I tell myself as I drive home from the grocery store. I live in a garage apartment that belongs to Aunt Francesca and Uncle Domenic, my dad's sister and brother-in-law. Thankfully, my aunt and uncle also rent out the main house, so they aren't around to clock my comings and goings.

I never would've lived here if they were right next door. Not that I don't adore them. I absolutely do, but I don't want anyone keeping tabs on me—or reporting to my parents about what time I get home or who I go out with. No, thanks. I love my cozy little place, but more than anything, I love the privacy. A couple of years ago, Dee moved to New York City with our cousin Domenic Junior, both of them eager to leave the clutches of the tight-knit family that spends far too much time minding each other's business.

I can't wait to see them both at Carmen's wedding, which is now just over a month away. It's been very difficult to stay focused on work and the wedding or anything other than hearing more from Mr. A as I counted down to the one-year mark.

It feels like ten years have passed since that first email from Mr. A, six months ago today. When I get home, I put my groceries away and fix myself a cup of tea before I allow myself to sit at my desk and fire up my laptop to check my email. Mixed into junk mail and a note from my sister with a link to an article on home decorating she thought I'd enjoy is a message from a name that's familiar to me, but I can't say why.

Austin Jacobs.

I click to open the message and gasp as I read the opening.

Dear Maria,
I thought today would never arrive.

CHAPTER 2

MARIA

*H*oly shit. His name is Austin. Austin Jacobs. Why do I know that name? It nags at me that I recognize his name, but I can't take the time to figure that out now when there's a whole email from him to be devoured.

I'm not sure why I've been so unreasonably excited to share more of our story with you, but over the last six months, I've thought of you every day, counting down until we could talk again, this time without limits. Bizarre, I know, but you saved my daughter's life, and I'm dying to get to know you better. I was so excited to get your actual first name and direct email, and I swear I'm not a creeper! LOL. Although, I wouldn't blame you for thinking that I am. This situation with Everly has taken over my life in every possible way, up to and including my obsession with her bone marrow donor.

His daughter's name is Everly! He's as obsessed with me as I am with him! Now I'm swooning.

*I guess maybe my unreasonable excitement has to do with the
bond we now share in the form of a wild little three-year-old
who's still here because of you. She's thriving because of you.
She has a chance to grow up and fall in love and have a life
because of you. I get very emotional when I think about what
you did and what it's meant to us. I'm just so freaking grateful.
I enclosed some recent photos of her so you can see her
adorableness for yourself.*
*Okay, enough about me being a weird, creepy, grateful, stalker
dad...*

I laugh at his summary, loving him more with every word I
read. I scroll down to look at the pictures because I've been
dying to see the face of the child I helped to save. And oh, my
heart. She's absolutely perfect.

About me—I'm a pitcher for the Baltimore Orioles.

That's it! That's how I know him! He's not just a pitcher,
though. He's a Cy Young Award-winning pitcher who won
twenty-one games two years ago, including a near-perfect game
that was scuttled in the ninth inning when one of his teammates
fumbled a routine grounder. I know this because I'm a huge
baseball fan. My dad and I have been following the Miami
Marlins since I was a little kid, back when they were known as
the Florida Marlins.

*My life is pretty crazy, and it became more so when my ex-
girlfriend and I had Ev. That turned into a bit of a nightmare
when I found out she was partying with other guys while I was
on the road. The wife of one of my best friends on the team was
able to prove that she was leaving baby Ev alone, sometimes for
a couple of hours, while she went out. I can't even think about
that without losing my mind. That led to me getting sole*

11

custody of my daughter just as my career was really taking off. Good times, those were. Fortunately, my parents decided to retire early and move to live next door to us. They help me with Ev while I'm on the road. I don't know what I'd do without them, especially since she got sick.

I lost almost all of last season due to her illness. My team was amazingly supportive, and I'm super thankful to them, too. Not only did they continue to pay me while I wasn't able to play, they made sure Ev had the best of everything—from doctors to private nurses and every form of support they could think to throw my way. It's funny how your priorities change when the person you love most is sick. Before her illness, I couldn't imagine missing a start, let alone most of a season.

I have a whole new relationship with gratitude after what we've been through. My mom thinks I have a form of PTSD since Ev's illness because I'm constantly worried about her relapsing or some other disaster striking. I hover over her to a ridiculous degree and overreact to every sneeze, sniffle and bruise. The team doctor hooked me up with a therapist, who's been a big help to me as we adjust to life after crisis. As you mentioned in your last email, we were VERY careful this year. No one outside our family was allowed to be with Ev, and yes, today is also the day when we can lift those restrictions and get back to living. We'll do so cautiously at first, of course, but we're both ready to get back to "normal," whatever that is. She can't wait to go to the playground and to eat out in a restaurant, which is one of her favorite things to do.

I'm not sure why I'm telling you all this. I guess it's because I feel such a connection to you, and not only because of what you did for Everly (and me), but because of our earlier emails. Okay, I've probably said enough. Too much, actually. Haha. I won't be offended if you decide to never respond to me again, but I'll be sad to not have the chance to get to know you. I'll stop now. Please write back.

Love,
Austin

I devour his every word and am smiling like a loon by the time I get to the end. I look at the photos of Everly again, and then I google him because I can't remember what he looks like.

When his picture pops up, I go stupid in the head as my eyes bug and my mouth hangs open. Thank God no one is there to witness my reaction to hot male perfection.

He has brown hair shot through with natural blond high-lights, gorgeous blue eyes, a great smile and a body to die for, with sleeve tattoos on his arms and diamond studs in both ears. I can't. I just can't. Look away, that is. I stare at pictures of him in and out of uniform, with and without shirts. He has intricate tattoos on his chest that stop just short of the base of his neck and cover most of the available skin on his torso. I've never been a big fan of that much ink, but on him it's just… Wow. My heart beats in a wild rhythm that has to be unhealthy.

Who cares about what's healthy at a moment like this?

I call Carmen and put her on speaker.

"Did he write to you?" She and Dee are the only ones who know today is the day I might hear from him.

"He sure did."

"What did he say?"

"Google Austin Jacobs, the baseball player."

I hear her clicking away on her laptop. "Shut. The. Fuck. *Up!*"

"*Right?*" I'm screeching, but I can't seem to stop any of this. It's complete madness, and I don't care. This is so not me. I'm always careful and reserved, especially since Scott, and here I am losing my mind over a man I've never met.

"He's the father of the child she donated to," Carmen says. "I'm filling in Jason."

"He's a superstar," I hear Jason say. "I saw him pitch against the Yankees, and he was lights out."

"Mari? Are you still there?" Carmen asks.

"I'm here."

"What did he say in his email?"

I read it to her, absorbing every delicious word all over again, and copy the pictures of Everly to text to her.

"Oh, wow," Carmen says on a long breath. "That's *amazing*! And Everly is so cute!"

"What do I do?"

"Write him back!" Carmen says, laughing. "You know you're dying to!"

"Ugh, I'm dying all right."

"Do it, Mari. You have nothing to lose. The man adores you. How could he not after what you did for him and his daughter?"

"I'm all... *invested*. At an unhealthy level."

"Of course you are! You *saved his child's life*. Before you exchanged a single word with him, you were at a whole other level with this guy."

How can I explain how his words have slayed me, the way he talks about his daughter, how big his love is for her... That's what's gotten to me the most.

"Are you going to write back?"

"Yeah, as soon as I calm the hell down and figure out what I want to say."

"Say this. Are you listening?"

"Yes, I'm listening," I say with a laugh.

"Dear Austin, I love you. I want to marry you and have more beautiful babies with you."

"That's not helpful, Car."

She loses it laughing. "Think of all the time it'll save you to cut straight through the bullshit."

"I'm ending this call." Mostly because my ovaries stood up to take a look around at her mention of having beautiful babies with him.

"I'm here if you need me."

"Thanks, but I think I'll be okay."

"This is so cool, Mari. Imagine if it turns into something, and you met him by saving his kid's life. God, that's so romantic! It's even more romantic than me falling for Jason when I helped to save his reputation."

"Hey," Jason says, "there's nothing more romantic than that."

"Will you guys please stop? It's not going to turn into anything. He's a nice guy who appreciates what I did for his child. That's all this is."

"Uh-huh. Okay."

"Gotta go."

"Invite him to the wedding!"

"Bye, Carmen." I press the End button and stare at my laptop screen, where the photos of Austin are in the background with his email front and center.

I read it again.

Dear Maria,
I thought today would never arrive.

Releasing a deep breath full of swoon, I click on the reply button and stare at the blank screen for a long moment before I begin to type, the words pouring straight from my heart.

Dear Austin,
I'm thrilled to know your name is Austin and that Miss E is Everly! I love that name. After seeing her pictures, I've decided her cute name suits her perfectly. She's beautiful. Thank you so much for sending the pictures. I appreciate them so much and am so happy to see her sweet, smiling, HEALTHY face. I've thought of you two every day over the last six months, and I, too, was counting down to today when we could finally talk freely. I'm so happy to hear that Everly's remission is holding and that she's bounced back from her ordeal.

15

Of course it'll take a while longer for you. There's nothing more difficult than seeing someone you love go through a serious illness. I can't begin to imagine what it must've been like for you to have to face such a frightening diagnosis and treatment with your precious little girl. It had to be terrifying, and I think you're wise to be in therapy to help you deal with the aftermath of that trauma. Everly is lucky that she probably won't remember any of it. Whereas you'll never forget it.

You asked about me... I mentioned I'm a nurse, but now I can tell you I work at a free clinic in Little Havana, which is the area of Miami where I grew up in a huge, loving, overly INVOLVED (haha) family. My parents, Lorenzo and Elena, own a firm that does accounting and legal work for tons of local businesses. My dad is an accountant, and my mom is a lawyer, so they make for a good team at home and at work. My aunt Vivian and uncle Vincent (my dad's brother) own a famous restaurant called Giordino's, which is my last name (without the 's). It's a hot spot in Little Havana, and everyone who is anyone has stopped in there at one point or another. I waitress at the restaurant on Saturday nights because it's fun, and it's a nice supplement to my salary at the clinic. My aunt and uncle host family brunch every Sunday at the restaurant, which features Italian and Cuban menus, and separate sides of the house for each. My Nona oversees the Italian side, and my cousin Carmen's Abuela is in charge of the Cuban side. They fight like cats and dogs, but Nona and Abuela are really the best of friends and would do anything for anyone. I refer to Abuela as my third grandmother.

I stop myself when I feel like maybe I'm rambling on with stuff that won't interest him. But he did say he wanted to know me, and to know me, you have to know my family.

I have a sister we call Dee. Her real name is Delores, but don't

*call her that unless you want her to punch you. She lives in
New York City with our cousin Domenic Junior, and yes, he's
always called the full name "Domenic Junior," to differentiate
him from his father, Domenic Senior. His mother is my father's
sister, Francesca, and they have three other kids besides Dom
Jr. I also have two brothers—Nico and Milo. Nico is older than
me, and Milo is younger. You following this? Haha! Carmen is
my best friend (and Dee's), and the three of us have always run
around together. Carmen is an only child, so she calls us her
sisters, and we love that. She's getting married next month to a
pediatric neurosurgeon named Jason, who we all ADORE. He's
such a good guy. I really got to know him when he volunteered
at the clinic, and I totally approve of him for my sweet cousin.
This is her second marriage, after Tony, her first husband who
was a police officer, was shot and killed on the job when they
were twenty-four. That was such a tough loss for all of us, and
to see her smiling again is just about the best thing ever.
I feel like I'm going on and on here, but hey, you asked...
True confession: I'm a huge baseball fan. My dad and I have
season tickets to the Miami Marlins, and I've definitely heard
of you. I think I might've seen you pitch a couple of years ago
when the O's played the Marlins in interleague play. Is that
possible? I'll ask my dad. He'll remember for sure.
Well, you asked for more about me, and I wrote a book! I guess
I'll just end by saying I'm so, so happy to hear from you, to
know your names and more about you both. Mostly, I'm so
relieved to know that Everly continues to do well. I have prayed
for her—and you—every night since the last time we talked.
Love,
Maria*

I send the email before I can second-guess every word of it. I
no sooner send it than I realize I didn't tell him to write back. I
really want him to write back.

I open a new email to him with the subject line: PS

The message reads: *Please write back.*

I press Send before I lose my nerve. And then I try to figure out what the hell to do with myself while I wait to hear from him. I could reread his email again. I do that. Four times, actually, before I make myself get up, take a shower, finish my laundry, make my lunch for tomorrow, set up my coffee for the morning and stop obsessing about Austin Jacobs.

My phone chimes with a text from Carmen. *Did you write back?*

I did. I regurgitated my whole life story to him.

All of it?

Most of it about the family and the restaurant and you and Dee and the others. It was probably too much.

I'm sure it was fine. He said he wanted to know about you. Are you ok??

Yes, of course I am. I'm trying not to go crazy over a guy I barely know.

How's that going!?!?! You already know him better than you knew Scott after a year.

Jeez, if that wasn't the truth. Austin showed me who he really is with the first message he sent. I saw his heart, and that's all I've been able to think about for six freaking months. And what I got from him today only confirmed my first impression.

I go to bed early and keep my phone handy. I try to only check my email for new messages every fifteen minutes, but in reality, it's more like once a minute. Okay, it's really every ten seconds, but don't judge me. You'd be checking, too. Who am I even talking to right now?

"You need to chill the hell out, girl. You're getting way down the road with this guy you've never met." Staring up at the ceiling I painted a pale pink, I try to talk myself down off the high I've been on since receiving the new message from him.

I force myself to close my eyes and breathe for five full minutes.

When I open them, I see it's actually only one minute later. Naturally, I check my email again.

Speaking of creepers.

A new message pops up from Austin, making me gasp as I give new meaning to the term *all thumbs*. I fumble to open the message without accidentally deleting it. Because that would be tragic.

Dear Maria,

I loved your message and hearing about your family. Is there a diagram you use to help new people keep them all straight?! If there is, I need it! Your family sounds amazing, and I love that you work in a free clinic. I imagine your work is essential to so many people in your community, and the restaurant looks awesome. (Is it weird that I checked out the menu online, and I want a Cuban sandwich like right now!?) I have two brothers as well—Asher and Carter. Ash plays for the Iowa Cubs, a farm team for the Chicago Cubs, and Carter is in college at Florida State, but he plays, too, and is hoping to go pro when he graduates next year. We grew up in Green Bay, Wisconsin, and as you might be able to tell, baseball was a big part of our lives. (Duh—haha.) My dad was our coach, and his goal is to see all three of us in the majors. So far, he's one for three, but my brothers have all the talent. Sometimes it's more about luck and being in the right place at the right time than it is about talent. I'm so hopeful they'll both get there eventually. And yes, I

*pitched in Miami three years ago. Were you there?! How cool
would that be?*
*I'm really close to my brothers, and they, too, were a huge
source of support when Ev was sick. We've also got an amazing
group on the O's. Many of them—and their wives—have
become like family to us since Ev was sick. They stepped up for
me and her in so many ways, big and small.*
*Anyway, see how it always comes back to Ev being sick with
me? That's the stuff I'm working through with the therapist.
She says it'll take time, and after a while, every road won't
automatically lead me back to the trauma anymore. As you can
tell, I'm not there yet. I keep telling myself how lucky I am, and
believe me, those aren't just words. I'm incredibly lucky, most
particularly because a wonderful woman named Maria
Giordino in Miami was a perfect match for my baby. I'm
thankful for that—and for you—every day. And I appreciate
that you prayed for us. That's so amazing to hear.*
*Couple of things you didn't tell me—are you married? Do you
have kids? Can you send me a picture of you since you can
google me? Did you google me? Tell me the truth. LOL.*
*Well, I need to hit the hay, as my coach says. We've got an early
flight to Detroit in the morning for a four-game series with the
Tigers, followed by three games with KC and four with Seattle.
I'll do the math for you—that's eleven days away from my
baby. My parents stay with her while I'm away, but I miss her
so much when I'm gone. Thank GOD for FaceTime!*
*Oh, and one more thing—if you write to me, I'll always write
back. Remember what I said the first time we "talked"? You're
family now. If you'd rather text me, that's cool. See my phone
number below. Feel free to use it.*
Love,
Austin

Oh my God, he gave me his phone number, which I

promptly program into my phone. I find the picture Carmen took of me when we were out shopping the other day. I don't always like pictures of myself, but I don't hate that one. My curly dark hair isn't huge from the South Florida humidity like it so often is, and we'd had our makeup done as a trial run for the wedding. I look as good as I ever do, so I set up a text with the photo before I can talk myself out of it.

Will write back more tomorrow, but this is me. Not married, no kids, and yes, I googled the hell out of you. I enclose the laughing and kissy-face emojis and send the message. I'm giddy off the high of talking to him.

He writes right back with the eyes-bugging emoji on its own, followed by another text:

WOW. You're BEAUTIFUL. But I already knew that. Write back to me tomorrow. I'll be waiting. Love, Austin

Drop the mic. I'm dead. How will I *survive* until I can talk to him again? Better yet, how will I *sleep*?

CHAPTER 3

AUSTIN

I'm glued to my phone from the second I take my seat on the ass-crack-of-dawn flight to Detroit. I'm pitching the third game of our series with the Tigers, so I've got a couple of days to chill and prep for my next start. In other words, I have time to obsess over that picture Maria sent me. I can't stop staring at her gorgeous face and sexy smile.

She said she's not married, but she didn't mention whether she's single.

I hope she is, because my obsession with her grows with every message we exchange.

Trust me, I know this whole thing is nuts. I can't fall for the woman who donated bone marrow to save my kid's life. Can I? No, I can't, but that's kind of what's happening, if I'm being honest.

The one good thing about an early-morning flight is no one is in the mood to chat, which is fine by me. I spend the first hour rereading the messages she and I have exchanged so far, getting the same high off the rereads that I got the first time around. She's a warm, sweet, beautiful woman, and the fact that I'm developing a world-class crush on her shouldn't come as any surprise to me.

She *saved my child's life*. How could I not love her? But aside from that momentous fact, I'm crushing on her, *Maria*, not my child's donor. It's almost like she's become two separate people to me. Sure, I met her *because* she donated, but after getting to know her a bit, I like her for a million other reasons.

I wonder what time she gets up and how soon I might hear from her, seeing as this is a workday for her. The ball is in her court, so to speak, but that doesn't mean I can't message her again in the meantime, does it?

No, it doesn't, and yes, I know this is starting to resemble middle school when the "should I or shouldn't I" debate over girls occupied ninety percent of my brain cells, thus my lousy grades.

I want to talk to her some more, so I call up the last message I got from her last night and hit Reply.

Hi there,
I know it's your turn, but I didn't want to wait to talk to you some more. I'm on the flight to Detroit, and rereading our messages. I gotta be honest—waiting to hear from you is a bit torturous.
I sound like such a pussy, and I don't even care. What does that tell you?
What time do you have to be at work? What are your days like at the clinic? Oh, and one more question... You said you're not married, but you didn't say whether you're single. Are you? Just in case you were wondering the same thing about me, I am. No girlfriend, no friends with benefits, no nothing since I broke up with Ev's mother. She kind of turned me off anything to do with women and dating.

I'm going to send this before I can talk myself out of asking
whether you're single. <grimace emoji>
Love,
Austin

I press Send on the message and realize my palms are suddenly sweaty, which happens only right before a start, when my nerves kick in. Ugh, does that mean I'm nervous about asking Maria if she's seeing anyone?

Well, yeah, kinda.

I put down my phone and rest my head against the back of the seat, closing my eyes and trying to chill the fuck out. I've let this thing with her become bigger than it should be, which is probably due to how completely fucked up I've been since Ev got sick. I cringe when I recall telling Maria about the therapy and the PTSD and all that.

It's not like it's a big secret, but did I really have to dump all that on her the first day I got to talk freely with her?

Like always lately, my own thoughts drive me crazy. I never used to be an anxiety-ridden disaster area, but seeing your child through a life-threatening illness has a way of turning even the most laid-back kind of guy into someone totally different than he used to be. And if I've learned anything in therapy, it's that I can't hide from the feelings Ev's illness has left me with. I can only try to cope with them.

Post-trauma, it would be impossible for me to get to know Maria, or anyone else, for that matter, without making that part of the equation. It's who I am now, for better or worse. And I can't hide from it, as much as I wish I could forget what we went through.

Sometimes it irks me that my parents have picked up and gone on like nothing ever happened. I'm aware that my hovering annoys them, but damned if I can help it. The fear of that beast of a disease coming back hangs over me like a dark cloud I can't shake no matter how hard I try.

I think that's why this flirtation or whatever it is with Maria is so exciting. For the first time since Ev got sick, I have something else to think about besides doom and gloom.

Writing to her and reading her responses have given me something I haven't had in far too long: hope. Of course I realize it's silly to be finding hope in someone I barely know. I've never even actually spoken to her, and yet, that doesn't change how she makes me feel. It's such a fucking *relief* to have something to think about besides baseball and health disasters.

I probably ought to refrain from sharing that thought with her, since I don't want her to think that's what she's become to me—something to relieve my anxiety—even if that's what she does for me.

My phone vibrates in my lap, and I grab it, fully aware that I'm worse than a fifteen-year-old girl in the throes of her first crush.

Morning!

Hope you're having a smooth flight. I hate to fly, and I could never have a job that required me to fly as much as yours does. They couldn't pay me enough! What do you do when you arrive in Detroit?

I get to work around eight thirty, and we open at nine. We try to close by four or four thirty if we can see everyone who's come in that day. Some days we're so busy, we have to give out numbers so people can take their place in line the next day. I check people in and record their vitals (height/weight, temperature, blood pressure and pulse). I handle all our patient charts and do a million other things to keep this place running smoothly. I'm at the clinic now, but this morning has been slow so far. I'm in the office sneaking this message to you. Not that anyone would care what I'm doing. It's a pretty cool place to work.

We have a nurse practitioner named Miranda (she and her husband founded the clinic thirty years ago) who sees all the patients, except for the days when Jason (my cousin Carmen's fiancé) comes in. He's been filling in while our regular doctor is recovering from injuries he sustained in a car accident, and Miranda was part-time for months while she recovered from knee surgery. We've been so slammed, and Jason has been a godsend to us over the last couple of months. He's arranged his schedule at Miami-Dade General Hospital, where he and Carmen both work, to be here on Thursday afternoons.

A lot of the people we see don't have insurance, so the clinic is truly a lifesaver for them. In fact, it's because of the clinic that I was in the Be the Match database. We did a registry drive here about four years ago, which is when I was swabbed. It's one of those things you do and then never give another thought to until you get a call that you're a match for someone.

About your questions... I'm also twenty-eight, completely single after a bad breakup a couple of years ago (although I think your breakup takes the prize for worst ever), and in case you're wondering, waiting to hear from you is torturous for me, too! Well, I'd better get back to work. If you think of it, text me when you land, so I won't be worried about you flying.

Love,

Maria

My heart does this weird fluttering thing when I read that last sentence and see that she's included her number. How long has it been since anyone other than my parents cared about whether I'd landed safely somewhere? Kasey never gave a shit where I was. Unfortunately, I didn't realize how little she cared until my teammate's wife told me what was going on while I was away.

I think it's cute that Maria says they couldn't pay her enough to fly the way I do. Would ten million a year get her on a plane every week or so for six months? I wonder, but I'd never ask her such a douchey question.

Hi again,
Flying isn't my favorite thing, either, but it's a necessary part
of the job for half the year. I've gotten used to it, but I can think
of a million other things I'd rather do.

Today, for instance, I'd much prefer to be visiting a free clinic in Little Havana... I'd love to have her check my vitals. I bet my blood pressure is up a little since I received that sexy-as-fuck photo of her last night. I've looked at it a hundred times, easily.

When we land in Detroit, a bus will take us to a hotel near the
ballpark. We get to chill until about three, when we go to the
park for batting practice and warmups. Sometimes a group of
us will go get lunch, but most of the time, we take the downtime
when we can get it. On game days, I usually sleep in, get room
service, watch TV and take it easy, especially the days when
I'm pitching. The season is a grind, and by the time September
rolls around, we've been battling annoying injuries and trying
to play through them for months. We're not in the running for
the post-season this year, so this is our second-to-last road trip.
Guess where we're going on the last one? Tampa and Miami!
That's the week after next, and the three games in Miami will
end the season for us. Maybe we can meet up while I'm in
town?

I toss that out there casually, as if the possibility of actually meeting her isn't the most exciting thing to happen in a really long time.

Your clinic really sounds like an amazing place. It's nice of your cousin's fiancé to volunteer at the clinic. I know way more about doctors and specialties than I ever thought I would. (And we're back to the trauma! See why I can barely stand myself? Not sure how anyone else can.) Anyhow, I'm glad to hear you're single. That matters to me more than it probably should, if I'm being honest. I'm almost twenty-nine, which makes me practically a senior citizen in this game.

Between everything with my ex and Ev's illness, I'm not the same guy I was a few years ago. My dad likes to say that life changes you, and that's certainly true in my case. It never occurred to me that Kasey would be unfaithful or that she'd leave our BABY home alone to party. You don't even want to know how ballistic I went when that happened. At first I didn't believe it, but there was video. The other wives suspected she was leaving the baby, and they set out to prove it. That video is the reason I was able to get sole custody of Ev. I told her if she fought me on that, I'd turn the video over to the cops. Not that I would've done that, because Ev would've ended up in foster care while they investigated us, but Kasey barely hesitated in signing away her rights. The whole thing was disgusting and upsetting and terrifying. When I think about what could've happened when my BABY was home ALONE... It boggles the mind. I knew it was over with her when I didn't even care if she was fucking other guys. She left my daughter home alone. Nothing says OVER like that!

"Who you texting, AJ?"

Startled out of my grim memories of Kasey, I glance across the aisle at Santiago, our starting catcher and my closest friend on the team. "No one." The last thing I need is for the guys to catch wind of the fact that I'm "talking" to someone. They'll turn it into a BFD, and I don't want them getting ahold of something that's become so important to me.

"Awful lot of words for no one," Santiago mutters.

I turn my back to him and continue typing. I wish I had my laptop with me. It's easier than typing on my phone.

Anyway, I was just starting to bounce back from that disaster when the next one hit with Ev. I told you about my epic breakup, so now you have to tell me about yours... If you want to, that is. No obligation. True confession? I've looked at your photo a hundred times since last night, and I'm really, really, REALLY glad you're single. Did I mention that?!
Love,
Austin

I send it before I can talk myself out of the super suggestive last bit. What am I doing exactly? She lives in Miami. I'm in Baltimore when I'm not in some other far-flung city. What do I think can become of this "friendship," anyway?

If I were to tell the team's media liaison that Everly's bone marrow donor lives in Miami, they'd want to do something with her when we play there in two weeks. Would she be up for that? Would I?

God, I'd love to meet her and to see if the attraction I've felt for her through pictures and words carries over in person.

And if it does? What then?

After this season, I'm a free agent, which means I can go anywhere I want—and more or less name my price. It's an exciting time that I've been looking forward to for a while now, except for the part about moving again. I love the O's. I love my teammates and their wives and kids. I love the management and the ownership, but playing in the AL East is tough if you're not the Sox or the Yankees. The thought of leaving the O's is heartbreaking, but there's almost no chance I'll sign with the O's again.

I haven't seriously considered any other team because my

agent has advised me to play it cool and do everything I can to finish this season strong. The goal is to ink a big deal that'll set me up for life and allow me to finish my career in the next city I end up in. The more wins I notch in these last few games, the higher my free agency price goes. After losing most of last season to Ev's illness, this season matters more than ever. I'm at nineteen wins, four losses and two no-decisions with three starts left.

This road trip is critical to finishing strong. It's not the time for distractions, even beautiful distractions like Maria.

I can tell myself that a thousand times, but I already know I won't stop talking to her regardless of what's at stake. Talking to her has made me feel better than I have in years, and I won't give that up for anything.

When we land, I send her a quick text. *On the ground in Detroit.*

We're on the bus, heading to the hotel when she responds.

Glad you arrived safely. Have a good game. I'll be watching.

I have butterflies in my stomach knowing she'll be watching, and I'm not even playing in tonight's game. Maybe we can Face-Time later. We just got here, and I'm already counting the hours until after the game when I can talk to her some more.

I can't wait.

CHAPTER 4

MARIA

J use my lunch break to write back to Austin on the computer in the office, because I hate typing on my phone. Hearing he's been staring at my photo since last night has made me super distracted. I've had to take more than one blood pressure twice this morning because I forgot the readings before I could record them, which is not like me at all.

Hi again,
How's Detroit? The story of how Jason came to volunteer here is a long one. I'll tell you that when I have more time.
Besides the added anxiety, which is totally understandable, by the way, how have you changed from before the breakup with Kasey and Everly's illness? And also by the way, anyone who'd leave an infant home alone so she can party is a MONSTER who doesn't deserve a child! I can't imagine how you must've felt to realize that was happening while you were away for work. I assume they pay you pretty well to play baseball. Why didn't she hire a babysitter if she needed to go out so badly?!? I

*feel bad judging someone I don't even know, but that's just
unforgivable. I'm SO GLAD you have sole custody of
Everly now.*

*I just looked at the schedule for the Marlins, and I can't believe
I'd forgotten that their last home stretch is against the O's! My
dad and I share our tickets with other family members, but I
already told him to save those three games for me. Are you
starting while you're here? And yes, we should get together
while you're in town. Is Everly coming with you, by any
chance? I'd love to meet her, too.*

*You said the guys are nursing lots of injuries by this point in
the season. Does that include you?*

*So my epic breakup was nowhere near the thermonuclear level
of yours, but it was still pretty bad. I'd been with Scott since we
were twenty-one. We met at the restaurant, actually, when he
worked as a prep cook while he was finishing college. We
moved in together after we graduated from college, and for a
few years, things were good. I got the job at the clinic, and he
was with a marketing company downtown. I wanted to get
married, but he dodged the subject every time it came up
(which I realized with hindsight—always 20/20, right?). I was
completely oblivious to any problems between us. I thought his
distance was just what happened when you'd been with
someone for a long time.*

*Then my sister, Dee, was home for a weekend and ran into him
in the grocery store with another woman. He introduced her as
a friend from work, but Dee said he acted super freaked out
about seeing her, which tipped her off there was more to the
story. So she told me what happened, I confronted him, and he
admitted he was in love with his coworker and had been for a
while. While I'd been talking about getting married, apparently
he'd been trying to find a way out of our relationship. I
remember being completely shocked. There were no signs he
was seeing someone else, at least not that I picked up on, and*

that made me feel stupid as well as heartbroken. I kicked him out of our place that day, and I've never seen him again. We'd been together five years by then, so it left me sort of reeling. The betrayal was the hard part, not to mention having to get tested for STDs in case he'd brought something home to me (he hadn't, but still...). That the person I trusted the most could do something like that was hard to take. Since then, everyone wants to fix me up with someone, but I've avoided that nonsense. I just do NOT want to deal with it, you know?
Ugh, people suck sometimes, don't they?
You asked about what happened when I got the call from Be the Match, and I never answered your question. They asked me to come to some information sessions about what was involved with donating. I'll admit I was scared it would hurt, and they made me feel more confident about it. My parents freaked out when I told them what I was going to do, but my Nona was really great and convinced them to trust my judgment as a nurse. They came to one of the info sessions with me, and they felt better about it after they knew more. It was all fine. No big deal in light of what it meant for you and Everly.
Well, I'd better get back to work. Have a great game! I'm going to say something I've never said for any team other than the Marlins: Go O's!
Love,
Maria

I force myself to concentrate on work during a busy afternoon. After work, I'm meeting Carmen for a final fitting for my bridesmaid dress. Dee and I are her maids of honor and their friend Betty, who played a big role the day they met, is the only other attendant. In our family, it's hard to limit anything to just "a few" people, so she decided to have only the two of us and one special friend so she wouldn't end up with twelve bridesmaids.

When I leave work, I'm rather proud of myself to realize I went three whole hours without checking my phone. Before I start my car, I check it and find a new message from Austin. Just seeing his name on my list of messages makes my whole system go batshit crazy.

Ugh. This is bad and getting worse by the minute, and I couldn't care in the least that I could be setting myself up for a huge disappointment by becoming so invested in a man I've never actually met. What if he smells or has bad breath or is rude to waitresses or—

"Stop, Maria. Just stop." Before I read the message from him, I close my eyes, take a deep breath and release it slowly. "Calm the hell down and stop being a crazy nutcase."

When I've managed to get things somewhat under control, for the moment, anyway, I read his new message.

Hi there,

I only have a couple of minutes before I have to be on the bus to the ballpark, but I just wanted to write back to say SCOTT IS A FOOL! You're better off without him. You know that, right? It took me a while to realize that about Kasey, but who needs someone in your life who'd do what he did to you or what she did to me? And yes, people do suck a lot of the time, but sometimes they don't. For example, I'd never do to someone what Scott did to you or what Kasey did to me. (I'd also NEVER leave my kid at home ALONE! In case you were wondering...) After having been through that crap, we both know what it's like to be treated that way, and it's not something I want in my life.

As for injuries, I've had some stiffness in the elbow of my throwing arm. I've been working with the team trainers to manage it, but my arm is ready for some rest.

Thank you for telling me about how it went after Be the Match reached out to you. I have so many other questions, but I can't

ask now. Any chance you might want to FaceTime after the
game? Oh, and thanks for rooting for the O's for the first time
ever. I'm honored. So FaceTime... Yes? No? Please say yes...
Love,
Austin

I write back with one word: *YES!*

And then I have to get my shit together so I can drive to meet
Carmen at the bridal shop in Coral Gables. Traffic is its usual
bitchy self, and I'm ten minutes late for our appointment. I rush
into the shop to find Carmen standing on the little stage in the
back of the store, wearing her wedding gown as the seamstress
examines her from every angle.

It's the first time I've seen it on her since the day she chose it,
and I'm surprised by the huge lump that suddenly lodges in my
throat.

She catches me looking at her in the mirror, her pretty face
lighting up with a smile. "There you are. What do you think?"

It takes me a second to fight back the wave of emotion that
comes from seeing her as a happy bride once again. "It's absolutely perfect."

"I'm so glad you think so. I love it even more than I did the
first time I tried it on."

The dress is a creamy off-white silk that manages to be sexy
and classy at the same time, just like Carmen. Her back is almost
entirely bare, and the front forms a snug V over her full breasts.
It's beaded and sleeveless and clingy. She decided to go without
a train, she said, because this is her second wedding, and trains
are for first-time brides.

I know how she's grappled with guilt about remarrying after
losing her first husband so tragically, but she seems to be
excited and looking forward rather than backward.

35

"What did you decide about a veil?"

"No veil," she says. "I'm doing a tiara that Tony's mother gave me."

"I like that." Carmen is like a daughter to her first husband's parents, who've been fully supportive of her in the years since they lost Tony. I loved Jason from the start, but when I heard he went to see Tony's parents before he proposed to Carmen, he earned the eternal love of our entire family. He's a class act.

"Josie wanted to do something, and when she offered her mother's tiara, I was happy to accept. She's been so amazing about everything."

"I'm so glad about that. Imagine if she hadn't been?"

Carmen cringes. "I can't even think about that." She rests her hands on her abdomen. "I get so nervous when I think about Jason seeing me in this dress."

"He's going to lose his shit."

"I think you're probably right," she says with a giggle. "Will you take some pictures for me? I had to threaten my mom, your mom, Nona and Abuela with restraining orders to keep them from coming tonight. I want the dress to be a surprise to everyone."

I laugh as I picture Nona and Abuela being told they couldn't come to the dress fitting. "You made a critical error making the appointment for the one night they're all off." Monday is the only day they occasionally turn the restaurant over to their competent staff so they can take a break.

"Believe me, I realized that. I told them they'll see it soon enough."

When the seamstress is finished, I take photos from every angle while Carmen vamps for the camera. I love seeing her smiling and happy after the grim years following Tony's tragic, senseless death. For a time, I wondered if she'd ever bounce back from that shock, but she rallied, putting herself through college and grad school, landing an awesome new job at the hospital and then falling in love with Jason. No one in this world is happier for her than I am.

"Your turn," she says, sending me off to the changing room to put my dress on.

I love the dress she chose for us to wear. It's dark navy silk and simple, which appeals to me. No crazy bridesmaid embellishments, just straight lines and a sexy, plunging neckline that does great things for my breasts, if I do say so myself.

"I love that on you," Carmen says as she has every time I've had it on since the day we chose it. Dee is having hers altered in New York.

I step up onto the pedestal, and the seamstress goes to work with her pins.

As we leave the bridal shop twenty minutes later, Carmen hooks her arm through mine. "Let's get a drink."

I'd planned to go straight home to find Austin's game on the MLB Network, but I never say no to time alone with my favorite cousin. We're both so busy and often surrounded by family members that time to ourselves can be hard to come by.

We find a table at a sidewalk café that's hosting happy hour and order drinks—vodka and soda for me and a gin and tonic for her. We'll each have only one because we're driving, so we sip them slowly to make them last. I show her the pictures I took at the shop, and she sends them to herself so she'll have them.

"I can't wait for the big day," she says with a dreamy smile. "I also can't believe Jason convinced me to pull off a wedding in three months."

"The man can't wait to be married to you."

"I feel the same way. Tell me the truth, Mari. Is it okay for me to be so crazy-happy again after losing T? Thinking about him, about how he'll never be anything but twenty-four... It just makes me feel so sad."

"It's okay for you to be happy again. It's what he'd want for you."

"I've been thinking about him a lot lately, more than usual."

"Which is only natural when you're about to marry someone else. There was a time when the idea of a second marriage would've been preposterous."

She nods. "We would've made it, Tony and me. We would've been together forever."

"No question. I have no doubt he's watching over you and fully supports you in everything you do. He'd love Jason."

"I think so, too. They would've been friends."

"Absolutely."

She shakes off the grief and makes an effort to rally. I've seen it happen so many times, I recognize the signs by now. "So, how's your baseball player?"

I sputter with laughter. "You're worse than Nona and Abuela."

"Why, thank you. I learned everything I know about prying from them."

"Including how to be subtle."

"Why bother being subtle when you're dying to talk about it?"

She's right about that. "He's awesome. We've been talking nonstop since yesterday." Has it been only since yesterday? It seems longer after six long months of waiting for the chance to have more of him.

"Really? That's fabulous. What've you been talking about?"

"Life and betrayal and trauma and baseball and life in Miami. That kind of stuff."

"Whoa, that's some heavy business. Did you tell him about Scott?"

I nod as I stir my drink. "And he told me about his ex, Kasey, who left their baby at *home alone* to go out and party while he was on the road with the team."

HOW MUCH I CARE

Carmen's expression goes completely blank. "Are you kidding me right now?"

"Nope."

"How did he find out?"

"Some of the other wives and girlfriends suspected she was leaving the baby alone, and they brought it to his attention— and they took video of her leaving the house without the baby. I'm not really sure of all the details, but the video was enough to convince her to give him full custody."

"Wow. That's horrible."

"I know. I couldn't believe it. Like I said to him, I assume he's paid well to play baseball. Why didn't she get a babysitter?"

"What did he say to that?"

"We haven't gotten back to that topic yet. We're going to FaceTime after his game tonight."

"Wow! I'm so excited about this guy!"

"Don't go all crazy. We're just talking." I venture a tentative glance at her. "But he's playing here in a couple of weeks."

"Oh my God! Are you going to see him?"

"I think so."

"I'm *dying*! This is *so* awesome."

"I don't want to get ahead of myself."

"But you like him?"

"Uh, yeah, I like him." That may be the understatement of my entire life.

Carmen lets out a squeal that has people at other tables looking at us.

"Shut *up*, will you?"

"I can't contain my excitement! Ever since you gave Scott the scumbag the boot, I've been wanting you to meet someone new. We all have. Imagine if something comes of this with Austin, the sexy baseball player!"

"Car, please... Don't go there. I just... I can't."

She shakes her head. "I hate that Scott did this to you."

"Did what?"

"Made you so cautious and afraid to risk anything out of fear of getting hurt again. Before him, you weren't like that."

"It's not just that. It's this whole thing... From the second I got the call about the transplant, to hearing from him for the first time, to the last two days. It's so..."

"What?"

"Big," I say softly. "It's so *big*. Like, how can I be halfway in love with a guy I've never even met?"

"Would meeting him change anything about what you already know about him?"

"No, but—"

"No buts. It's absolutely possible to connect with someone one email or text at a time. That happens all the time when people meet online. Why can't it happen for you, too?"

She makes a good point about online dating.

Carmen leans in so I won't miss a word. "Remember Becky, who I went to college with? She met her husband online and refused to meet him in person until her semester was over. They talked for *months* before they ever actually met, and by the time they finally hooked up, they both knew they wanted to be together forever. So don't tell me it can't happen."

I cover my belly, which is suddenly full of butterflies flapping their wings. I can't very well tell her that I've never felt a connection like I do with Austin to anyone, even Scott when things were good between us. This is so much *more* than that ever was. And that's what makes me so nervous. I'm already way too invested.

Carmen checks the time on her phone. "I'd better get home. Jason was in charge of making dinner, and by now, I'm sure my kitchen is a certifiable disaster area."

"It's cute that he tries, though."

"Everything about him is cute, except for the horrific mess he makes when he cooks. That is *not* cute."

She insists on paying for our drinks, and we part company with a hug on the sidewalk.

"I'm here if you need to talk about any of this, and I promise not to get ahead of where you are with him."

"Thank you."

"For what it's worth, though, I think it's okay to be a little bit excited about this guy."

"I'll take that under advisement."

Laughing, she waves as she walks away. I head toward my car, thinking about what she said about her friend Becky and how she fell in love with her husband before she ever met him in person. Knowing that's possible doesn't do much to calm the butterflies in my belly.

CHAPTER 5

MARIA

*W*hen I get home, the first thing I do is flip on the TV and find Austin's game. I keep half an eye on the game, which the O's are leading two to nothing in the third, as I make pasta and pour a glass of wine. I bring dinner to the sofa for a better view of the game. I've finished my dinner and most of the wine when the camera finds Austin in the dugout, watching the action on the field as the Tigers bring in a relief pitcher.

"All eyes are on Austin Jacobs as this season comes to a close and he enters the free agency market," the broadcaster says. "He came back strong this year after losing most of last season while his daughter battled leukemia. She's in remission and doing well now, thank goodness. What do you think, Tom? Is there any chance he stays with the O's after this season?"

"No chance at all," Tom says.

They go on to discuss the business of baseball and which teams will be able to come up with the money Austin will command.

"Bottom line," Tom says, "look for Jacobs to go somewhere that can a) afford him and b) has a chance at contending in the post-season."

"Would you call him the number one free agent prospect for this coming off-season?"

"Without a doubt. And he should command top dollar. He's that rare pitcher with more than one deadly weapon in his arsenal. His fastball is fire, and his cutter is almost unhittable."

"Not to mention, he can actually hit, too, which makes him attractive to National League teams."

"For sure. I'm looking forward to seeing where he ends up."

"Wherever it is, look for him to ink a deal that'll allow him to finish his career with the next team he plays for. He gave an interview a few months back, indicating that whatever happens after this season, he'd like it to be somewhere permanent for his daughter's sake."

I hang on every word, hearing some of this for the first time, especially the part about how he wants to finish his career with whatever team he signs with next. It's a testament to what kind of father he is that he's thinking of Everly and wanting to put down roots somewhere for her sake. The more I hear about him, even from broadcasters on TV, the more I like him.

He's hot as fuck in his uniform, and when he smiles while talking to his teammates, I freeze the frame for a closer look. I rewind and rewatch the part about him fifteen times, at least. And he thinks he's a creeper!

The game ends in an eight-to-four win for the O's. I wonder how long it'll take him to get back to the hotel and what time he'll call.

I rush through a shower, reapply a small amount of makeup while hoping it won't look like I tried too hard, put on pajamas and the pink robe my mom got me for Christmas. I make my lunch for tomorrow and fold a basket of clothes while becoming more nervous by the second. I'm rethinking the pajamas when my phone sounds with the FaceTime ringtone.

I grab the phone and take the call, holding my breath until he comes up on the screen, smiling as he reclines against a pile of pillows.

"Hi," he says.

"Hi."

For the longest time, we simply stare at each other. I don't blink for a full minute.

"Did you catch the game?" he asks.

"I did. Congrats on the win."

"Thanks, not that I had anything to do with it."

"The broadcasters were talking about you."

"They were? What did they say?"

"Speculation about free agency and your next move."

"Ah, yes, the big story in the off-season. I'm getting a lot of interview requests from baseball reporters, but I'm not saying anything until the time comes."

"Do you have any idea where you might end up yet?"

"Not really. Supposedly, there's interest from San Francisco, Seattle and Anaheim, as well as the Cubs and possibly the Red Sox. I'm staying out of it until after the World Series, when we can start to talk turkey."

My heart sinks as he lists all the faraway places where he might end up.

"How was the rest of your day?" he asks.

"It was good. I met my cousin Carmen after work for another fitting for her dress and mine for the wedding. We grabbed a drink after. Then I came home to watch the end of the game."

"When is Carmen's wedding?"

"Second weekend in October."

"Ah, not long, then."

"Nope. They'll have had a three-month engagement."

"Wow, that is quick. And you said this is her second marriage?"

"Right. Her first husband, Tony, was a police officer and was killed in a convenience store robbery when he and Carmen were twenty-four. They'd been married less than a year."

"Oh, God, that's terrible."

"It was. He was the best guy, and they were so happy together from the time they were in, like, ninth grade. The whole thing sucked so bad."

"I can only imagine."

"I'm so happy for her and Jason. They're great together."

"That's good."

I hate that it feels awkward to actually talk to him face-to-face. I hadn't expected that, and it's a little disappointing.

"Does this feel weird to you?" he asks, grinning.

"Yes," I reply on a sigh of relief that he feels the same way. "I was just thinking that I didn't expect it to be awkward after the way we've talked about everything by email."

"I couldn't wait to actually talk to you. I walked back to the hotel because I didn't feel like waiting for everyone else to get their shit together and get on the bus."

Hearing that, I relax a bit. "I couldn't wait, either."

"I was hoping the game wouldn't end up in extra innings."

"That would've sucked."

"Yep."

"What would you normally be doing after a game?"

"Maybe go out for a beer with the guys."

"Will they wonder why you didn't go tonight?"

"I don't think so. I don't always go."

"Did you get to talk to Everly?"

"Before the game. I tucked her in. That's our tradition when I'm on the road."

Swoon! "That's very sweet."

"I miss her so much when I'm away on these long stretches. It sucks."

"That's got to be so hard."

"It is. Eleven days without my baby girl is brutal."

"Could you bring her with you if you wanted to now that she's out of quarantine?"

"Sure, but that would be so disruptive for her. We've got her on a good schedule, and according to my mom, kids thrive off routine. Life on the road would mess that up, so for now, she's better off at home. Plus, I'm still super freaked out about exposing her to germs. It's not like something magical happens at the one-year mark. Her immune system is still compromised."

"You're a wonderful dad, Austin."

"Thanks. I try to be. She's my whole world. But enough about me. Tell me more about you. I want to know everything."

I laugh at the intense way he says that, in a gruff, sexy voice that sends shivers down my spine. "I've told you more than most people ever know about me."

"Same. Tell me something else."

"Let's see… I won the spelling bee when I was in eighth grade."

"That's so hot."

I lose it laughing. "Can I tell you a secret?"

"Please do."

"I wouldn't still be talking to you if your emails hadn't included proper spelling, grammar and punctuation."

He shivers and fans his face dramatically. "You're a stickler for proper grammar, then?"

"Not always, but people who don't know the difference between 'your' and 'you're' or 'there' and 'their' shouldn't be let out of school."

"I had no idea that ninth-grade grammar would one day be so important."

"Did you get good grades?"

"Hell no," he says, laughing. "I did the bare minimum to get the F out of there in both high school and college. I made it through two years of college and entered the draft. Best day of my life. No more school. What about you?"

"I did *very* well."

"Why am I not surprised?"

"I loved school. I still think about going back to get a master's in public health."

"Do you think you will?"

"I don't know. It is sort of nice to be able to do whatever I want when I'm not working. If I went back to school, all my off time would be about studying and homework."

"What do you do for fun?"

"I go to the beach every chance I get. I love to shop and have lunch with my cousin and sister when she's in town. We do that on a lot of Saturdays. I like to spend time with my family and go out dancing."

"Are you a good dancer?"

"I danced with a local studio from the time I was four until I was twenty-two."

"So that's a yes, then."

"I do okay. What about you?"

"Um, well… I've never broken anyone's foot, but I'm a bit of a hack when it comes to dancing."

"So proceed with caution?"

"Something like that," he says, laughing.

He's sexy and sweet and everything perfect. But he lives hundreds of miles from me and could end up thousands of miles away if free agency goes well for him, which it will. My sense of self-preservation overrules my desire to spend more time with him.

"I should probably get to bed. I'm working in the morning."

"I wish we could talk all night. I like talking to you."

"I like it, too."

"Will you email me from work tomorrow?"

"Do you want me to?"

"Hell yes, I want you to. I love your emails. I've read them so many times."

I love that he's not shy about admitting that he's reread my emails. A lot of guys wouldn't confess to that. "If I get a quiet minute, I will."

"I hope you do. Sleep tight."

"You, too."

"Night, Maria."

"Night, Austin." I hit the red button to end the FaceTime call. For a long time after I get in bed, I stare up at my pink ceiling, processing everything I know now. Anaheim, Seattle, San Francisco, Chicago and Boston are all a very long way from Miami. I've never had any desire to live anywhere but right here. Dee couldn't wait to go somewhere else. She moved to New York for college and never came back. Domenic Junior was the same way. They both wanted out of here as soon as they could. Not me. I love my hometown and don't want to move, even for a guy as great as Austin seems to be.

I feel deflated after our FaceTime call. It was a big heads-up that getting wildly excited about a man I barely know could turn out to be a huge mistake. I need to take a step back from him and find some perspective.

Knowing there's no way I'll sleep for a while yet, I scroll through our messages again, starting with the first one six months ago, through the ones from yesterday and earlier today, experiencing the same magic I felt the first time I read them.

The next day, I force myself to resist all temptation. I don't write an email to Austin, and I don't check my personal account to see if he's hit me up. I spend the whole day trying to get my head on straight where he's concerned, but by the following morning, I'm no closer than I was the day before.

While I'm eating lunch with my coworkers, my phone dings with a text from him. *I'm pitching tonight, and all I can think about is you and why I haven't heard from you since the other night. I'm not trying to be a creeper. I swear. But I'm worried about you, and there's no one else I can ask if you're okay. I need to get my head in the game, but first I need to know you're all right. So can you tell me that much?*

I melt reading that text, and all the resolve I've built up over the last two days disappears in a matter of seconds. I write back to him right away, because he has other things to be focused on today, and I don't want him to worry. *I'm sorry. I needed to take a breather and get my head on straight about you.*

Did you?

Not really.

Me, either. Call me after the game if you want to talk. In the meantime, I'll just say this: I miss you. He includes the heart and kissy-face emojis.

I stare at his message thinking the same thing. *I miss you, too.*

AUSTIN

I'm so relieved to hear from Maria. I was beginning to worry that something awful had happened to her, which is part of the legacy of Ev's illness. I'm always anticipating worst-case scenarios.

"Did you hear from your friend?" Larry, the pitching coach, asks. I told him I was worried about a friend who went silent.

"Yeah, I did. All good." I stash my phone in the locker, still thinking about what she said. She tried and failed to get her head on straight about me. I need to hear more about that, but it has to wait until later.

"Great, now maybe we can talk about this game you're starting in an hour?"

"Let's do it."

By the time we take the field in the bottom of the first, I'm in my zone, laser-focused on the task at hand. I've pushed everything else to the back of my mind so I can do my job. That's how I've managed to get back to playing after Ev's illness, by visualizing everything else in the far back corners of my mind when I'm pitching. My therapist has really helped with that. She's taught me about visualizing the immediate goal and focusing only on that so I can function when necessary.

Since focus and concentration are so critical to successfully doing my job, the visualizations have been extremely helpful. This is the first time I take the mound with Maria stuffed into one of those corners along with Ev and my career and free agency and all the other things occupying my attention between games lately.

I wonder if Maria is watching the game, or if getting her head on straight means she's avoiding anything to do with me.

I pitch four three-up-three-down innings and take the mound in the fifth, with a perfect game going more than halfway through. That means we've retired every batter we've faced. Speaking of things that need to be stuffed into the back corners... Pitchers never allow themselves to think about throwing perfect games, especially in the midst of such a possibility. I've come really close in the past and have learned not to get excited about the possibility, especially after the near-miss two seasons ago that was scuttled by a routine grounder gone wrong in the ninth.

No one says a word about it, and I certainly don't think about it as I stare down the top of the Tigers' order. The lead-off batter smokes one to center field, and I hold my breath waiting for Donny to grab it, which he does. I retire the next batter on strikes, and the third one pops up to the infield. I wave everyone off and dispose of him on my own before trotting back to the dugout.

Everyone leaves me alone between innings, which is how I want it. It's chilly in Detroit, so I put on a jacket to keep my arm warm while our guys put three runs on the boards. More than forty minutes later, I return to the mound for the sixth. My pitch count is still low, so there's no talk of taking me out, especially since I've got a perfect game going in the seventh.

I glance behind me and note the fierce concentration on the faces of my beloved teammates. They know what it would mean to me—and my free agency bid—to pull off a perfect game, and none of them wants to be the one to mess it up. Knowing they've got my back, I square off with the batter, who connects with my first pitch, sending a grounder to short, which Jose handles smoothly, throwing the batter out at first.

One down.

An hour later, we enter the bottom of the ninth with three batters between me and my first career perfect game. The tension in the dugout and the ballpark has risen with every inning, making it a huge effort to stay cool and focused and not get ahead of myself. I take one second to again wonder if Maria is watching. I really hope she is and that she knows what's happening. The thought of her cheering me on makes me happy for reasons I can't begin to think about right now.

Three more outs. You've got this.

I bring everything I've got to those first two batters, putting them away with fastballs they never see coming. Six strikes in a row. Lights out.

With one batter standing between me and a perfect game, my palms are sweaty. How many times have I seen a pitcher blow it on the last batter? Too many to count. *Don't be that guy, AJ. Get it done. Make the close.*

I shake off the signal from Santiago. He wants another fastball. By now, the batters will be expecting that. I go with the cutter. The batter swings and misses. I need two more strikes.

Santiago again calls for the heat.

I shake my head and throw a curve ball that lands outside the strike zone for a ball. I regroup and throw another slider, which the hitter fouls off into the third-base seats. Two strikes.

Santiago calls for a time-out and approaches the mound. The infielders join him in a circle around me. We hold our gloves over our mouths so the other team can't read our lips. "Send the heat, man," my catcher says. "They can't touch you tonight."

"Go for it," Carlo, the first baseman, says. "You're on fire with that fastball. That's what I'd do."

"All right." They're right. I'd be crazy not to use the pitch that's gotten me this far to get the last strike.

One strike away from adding my name to a short list of pitchers who've thrown perfect games. I've got this. I hope...

CHAPTER 6

AUSTIN

*W*ith everyone back in place, I stare down the target Santiago's catcher's mitt provides, take a deep breath and release it as I go into my rotation and fire off my signature pitch. The sound of the bat connecting stops my heart as the ball sails toward the left-field wall. I'm almost sure it's going to be a single until Rodrigo launches and grabs that fly ball right out of the air—and manages to hold on to it when he lands hard.

My teammates go wild, surrounding me and freaking out.

Grinning widely, Rodrigo jogs in from the outfield and hands me the ball he caught.

I hug him. "Thanks, man."

"I was shitting my pants when that ball headed my way."

Laughing, I smack him on the back and hug him again. I'll get credit for the perfect game, but I couldn't have done it without him and my other teammates backing me up with offense and defense.

Even the Tigers' fans give me a warm round of applause,

which I acknowledge with a tip of my cap as we finally head toward the dugout.

"Holy shit, AJ," Mick says when he hugs me. "That was fucking awesome."

"Thanks, Coach."

While the others celebrate, Larry straps an ice pack to my arm that encompasses my shoulder and elbow. It's almost unheard of these days for a starter to throw a complete game, and I'll pay for it later. But for right now, all I feel is elated. Throwing a perfect game is a rare feat and one that's always been a goal of mine.

I want to find my phone, call my folks and see if Maria texted, but right now, I need to give my full attention to the teammates who helped make it happen.

The Tigers send over champagne, which is a classy move. We celebrate for at least an hour before they let in the media. Reporters swarm me. I answer all their questions while trying to be patient with them. Baseball reporters were so good to me when Ev was sick, and I keep that in mind when it starts to feel like they're going to trap me all night.

"That's enough, people," Mick says. "The trainers are waiting for AJ."

"Thanks, everyone," I tell them as Mick extracts me from the scrum and leads me into the training room, where Mary Ellen, the trainer assigned to pitchers, will rub down my arm.

"How're you feeling?" Mick asks.

"Pretty good right now." We both know that won't last. "What was the final pitch count?"

"Ninety-two. Eleven strikeouts."

"Haven't thrown that many in a while."

"I was gonna pull you at a hundred."

"You'd a had to take me kicking and screaming."

"Whatever it took," Mick said, grinning. "Glad you got it done before it came to that."

"Me, too." We both know I just made myself even more valuable in the free agency market with that performance, but we don't talk about it. Everyone involved with the O's is aware that I'll be hitting the road after the season, and there're no hard feelings that I know of. Any of them would do the same thing in my shoes.

Mary Ellen's rubdown feels damned good on my tired arm and shoulder. She uses what I refer to as her magic balm as she also works on the tense muscles in my neck until I'm limber and feeling no pain. "Ice it periodically for the next twenty-four hours," she reminds me.

"Will do. You're the best, ME."

"Congrats. It was thrilling to watch."

"Thanks." I head for the shower and let the hot water rain down on my arm and shoulder before I wash up and head for my locker, a towel knotted around my waist. I reach for my phone and take a quick look to find hundreds of texts from friends, family, former teammates and coaches sending their congrats. I scroll through the long list, looking for one name in the sea of texts.

Maria.

I'm almost through them all when her name pops up. Her text is the only one I read now. *That was AWESOME! I'm so happy for you! I was afraid to breathe in the 9th. I can't imagine how you felt. Amazing. CONGRATS!!*

I respond to her right away. *Thanks! Surreal. You going to be up for a while?* I feel a little guilty asking her to wait up when she has to work in the morning, but after the biggest night of my life, she's the only one I want to talk to.

It's crazy. I know it is, and yet... There you have it. I should be on the phone with my dad, who made me the pitcher I am today, and I will call him. But she's the one I most want to talk to.

I get dressed and give a quick call to my parents, who'll be waiting to hear from me.

"Austin," my dad says when he answers on the first ring. "That was fucking fantastic!"

His enthusiasm is always entertaining. "Thanks, Pops. It was a good night."

"You were on fire, son. I was beside myself."

"He was," Mom says. "He drove me crazy with his pacing and his swearing and his praying."

I laugh, picturing the scene. "I can only imagine."

"Congratulations, son," Mom says. "We're so proud."

"Thank you." Making them proud has always been important to me.

"How's the arm?" Dad asks.

"Good right now. We'll see what later brings. I gotta run. The guys want to celebrate." The last thing I feel like doing is going out drinking, but I'd never deny my teammates the celebration after a frustrating season in which not much of anything went our way. If nothing else, we've got this perfect night that none of us will soon forget. "How's Ev?"

"She's wonderful," Mom says. "Dad only had to read four books before bedtime tonight."

I hate that I'm not the one reading to her, but my dad is the next best thing. "Thanks, guys. You know… For everything." I have no idea what would've become of me after Kasey if they hadn't rearranged their lives to be there for me and Ev.

"We love you, Austin," Mom says.

"Love you, too." I end the call and check to see if Maria responded to my text—she hasn't—and then stash the phone in my back pocket. I'm the last one on the bus back to the hotel, and when I board, everyone goes crazy cheering and whistling and high-fiving as I make my way to the seat in the back they saved for me. We end up at a pub down the street from the hotel. I start a tab and insist on buying for everyone.

An hour later, I check my phone to find the text I've been

waiting for.

I'll be up for a bit.

"I've got to make a quick call," I tell Santiago. "Be right back."

"Are you calling the one you've been writing to every chance you get?"

"Blow me."

"Say that to her," he says as I start to walk away. "It might move things along."

While he laughs at his own joke, I flip him the bird and push through the crowded bar, stepping into the cool September evening to call Maria.

"Hi there," she says when she picks up. "Is this Mr. Perfect?"

"It is."

"How you feeling?"

"Thrilled and relieved. The last couple of innings were tense."

"You'd never know it. You were so cool and composed."

"On the outside, maybe. Inside, I was saying to myself, 'Don't fuck it up.'"

Her warm, rich laughter makes me shiver as I look up at the sky, wishing she was here to help me celebrate. Maybe it's the beer and champagne that loosens my tongue and my inhibitions, but I want to share that thought with her. "I wish you were here."

"You do? Really?"

"Yeah, I really do."

"Austin…"

"I know." I close my eyes, tip my head back against the brick exterior of the pub and sigh. My arm is beginning to ache, but there's a new ache in my chest that has nothing to do with baseball. "Believe me. I get it. I've got my own list of reasons why this is a bad idea for both of us, but you want to know what?"

"What?" she asks, sounding breathless, or maybe that's just wishful thinking on my part. "You were the only one I wanted to hear from after the game. I got, like, two-hundred-something texts, and yours was the only one I read."

"I don't know what to say to that."

"I'm sorry to put you on the spot."

"You didn't. This has been so…"

"What?"

"Exciting, thrilling, fun…"

"But?" Why do I ask questions I don't want the answers to?

"You're looking at San Fran, Seattle, Anaheim, Chicago, Boston… I live in Miami. I'm happy here. My life and my family are here. I really like you. I've loved our emails and everything we've talked about, but I can't set myself up to be hurt again. I just can't. And I don't want that for you, either."

"In four days, talking to you has become the best part of my day."

"Same here, and that's why I have to stop it while I still can. Tell me you understand."

Now she sounds tearful, and I hate that. "I do, but, Maria… Please, tell me we can still meet while I'm in Miami. If I were to mention to the team that Ev's bone marrow donor lives in Miami, they'd want to do something… I'd only arrange that if you were up for it. I want the whole world to know what you did for us."

"I'd be happy to meet you both and do something at the game, but that's it, Austin."

"Fair enough." The pain in my chest intensifies as I realize I'm not going to be talking to her anymore. "I just want you to know that you've done way more than save my daughter's life. You've also restored my faith in humanity. Knowing there're people like you out there… You're the best, Maria. Don't let anyone ever make you feel otherwise. You hear me?"

A sound that might be a sob comes through the phone. "Yes.

I hear you."

I don't want to end the call or sever the connection to her when all I want is more with her.

"I'm sorry, Austin."

"I'm not. I'm so glad we got to know each other, and I'll always, *always* love you for what you did for Ev. Call me any time. I'll always want to hear from you."

"I'm... I'm going to go now."

I can hear that she's crying, and I hate this. "Bye, Maria."

The line goes dead, and my chest hurts so bad, I have to rub the ache. I feel like I've lost one of the most precious things in my life, which is a ridiculous way to feel about someone I've never actually met. I'm out there a long time, breathing the cool air and trying to get myself together.

It quickly becomes clear to me that I can't go back inside. I've lost the desire to celebrate and party. I text Santiago, telling him to sign the tab and grab my card. *I'm going back to the hotel.*

What's up?

My arm is hurting. I need to get some ice on it.

Everything else ok?

Yeah.

It will be. I've certainly survived worse than losing someone I never had in the first place. I walk back to the hotel and accept the congratulations of the man working the main door.

"That was some kind of amazing to watch," he says.

"Thank you so much."

When he asks for an autograph, I give it to him, even though I desperately want to be alone. I take the elevator to my floor and go to my room to grab the refillable ice bag I use after games. Following the signs to the ice machine, I fill the bag and screw on the cap. I should be on top of the fucking world tonight, but the game feels like a distant memory after the conversation with Maria.

I return to my room, lock the door and sit on the bed staring at my phone, which is still racking up the congratulatory texts hours after the game ended.

I open a new text to my agent, who sent his congrats earlier. I look at the screen for a long time before I start typing.

Put Miami in the mix for next season.

I look at it for a long time before I press Send.

MARIA

The day after Austin pitches a perfect game and we agree it'd be best if we didn't continue talking every day, I do something I've never done in all my years of working at the clinic. I call out sick.

"Are you okay?" the receptionist, Angie, asks.

"I will be. I woke with a fever and headache, though."

"Take it easy, and let me know how you are tomorrow."

"Thanks, Ang. Sorry to leave you shorthanded."

"We'll be fine. Feel better."

I feel so guilty for not going to work, but my eyes and face are swollen from crying, and I feel like complete shit. The part about the headache wasn't a lie, and I feel as if I might have a heartache-induced fever. I just want to burrow into my bed and never come out. That's exactly what I would've done if it weren't for my family showing up later that afternoon with enough food to feed an army.

My mom, Aunt Vivian, Nona and Abuela have come to find out "what's wrong with Maria."

And how do they know I'm "sick"? If I had to guess, Jason arrived for his regular Thursday shift, told Carmen I called out, and she filled in the others. I'll get her for that when I see her. For now, I've got to contend with four very savvy women who can take one look at me and see all the way through me, or at least that's how it always feels to me.

"What's wrong?" Mom asks as she leads the parade into my apartment, bringing an array of mouthwatering smells that have my stomach growling to remind me I haven't eaten all day. I even skipped coffee, which hasn't helped my headache. Mom takes me by the chin and examines me closely.

She's a tiny dynamo with hair kept dark thanks to the magic of color, and shrewd brown eyes. I'm about six inches taller than her, but that doesn't stop her from overpowering me the way she always does. "Did you get a strep test?"

"I don't have a sore throat."

"It might be strep," Viv says. "One of the prep cooks had it last week." Carmen's mom lays her hand flat against my forehead. "You're a little warm. Did you take your temp?"

"I did earlier, and it was normal. It's just a bad headache. I'm fine." I catch Nona studying me, and I *know* she can tell I'm lying. "What's up with you guys?"

I'm treated to all the gossip from the restaurant and the neighborhood, as well as a plate of chicken marsala that makes my taste buds go crazy no matter how many times I have it. They sit with me while I eat, which I know is critical to getting them to move along. I want to tell them there's nothing to see here, but I keep that thought to myself.

"Thanks, guys," I say when they finally make the move to leave, probably when they realize I'm not going to tell them anything more. "I appreciate the house call."

Nona is the last one to go. She hugs me and whispers in my ear, "I'm a phone call away if you want to talk about it."

I squeeze her tighter. "Thanks."

MARIE FORCE

She kisses the top of my head. "Love you, sweet girl."

I blink back new tears, refusing to give in to them until I'm alone. "Love you, too." I close and lock the door, lean my head against it and let the tears roll down my face. How can I miss a man I've never met? How can I want more of someone I barely know? How can I be heartbroken when nothing even happened?

If it feels this bad after four days of talking to him, I did the right thing pulling the plug when I did. It's not going to get better from here. That much is certain.

Since I've given myself this day to wallow in the sadness, I devour everything written online about his perfect game. I give my iPad a workout as I scroll through every story about his amazing accomplishment. It's easy to tell that the baseball reporters like him, because of the glowing way they talk about him.

One of the *Baltimore Sun* baseball reporters wrote an opinion piece about how Austin has sealed his one-way ticket out of town with the amazing performance in Detroit. "O's fans knew this day was coming, but it won't make it any easier to say goodbye to a player who's worked his way into our hearts, on the field and off. We won't soon forget the epic battle he and his family waged to save the life of his little girl or the sense of victory we all felt at hearing she was in remission.

"Bad things happen to good people all the time. Austin Jacobs would tell you that. But sometimes, the good guys finish first, and I, for one, will continue to root for our 'AJ' no matter where he lands next season.

"Well done, No. 10. Very well done."

I collapse into tears and body-jarring sobs. I hate this so much. It's the worst feeling ever, even worse, somehow, than after Scott cheated on me. Maybe because I never got to have *anything* with Austin, and yet somehow, I know it would've been *everything*.

CHAPTER 7

MARIA

I cry myself to sleep and wake quite a bit later to someone knocking at my door. Moaning, I drag myself out of bed, run my fingers through my rat's nest hair and open the door to Carmen and Jason.

"Oh, Lord," Carmen says as she brushes past me on her way in. "It's worse than I thought."

"I only came because she made me," Jason says. "I can wait in the car if you want."

"It's fine. Come in." What does it say about my mental state that I could care less if my cousin's smoking-hot fiancé sees me looking like shit? He's blond, handsome and sweet. I adore him for her, and he's been a damned good friend to me, too.

"Nona called me. She said you're heartsick."

"A little maybe." I sit on the sofa and curl my legs under me, hugging a pillow that Dee gave me with a Marilyn Monroe quote embroidered on it: "Sisters make the best friends in the world."

"What happened?"

"Nothing happened."

"And yet you look like death warmed over."

She is one person I can't avoid, no matter how much I might wish I could. "We decided it would be better to put the brakes on before we get more involved."

"Didn't you just really get to talk to him for the first time on Sunday?"

"Yeah, but it got intense very quickly, and we were..." I shake my head. "Doesn't matter. It's the best thing to stop it before it gets worse."

"Hmmm," Carmen says, making her contemplative face.

"What?"

"I'm just wondering why you'd stop something that makes you happy."

"Because! He's looking at teams *nowhere near here* for next season, and I don't want to move somewhere else and... It's just not what I want."

"But you really like him."

"Yes, I do," I say, sighing, "but what good is it if we live thousands of miles from each other? That's not what I want."

"I understand that," Jason says. "I didn't want to live thousands of miles from Carmen, so I changed my life for her."

"And I appreciate that more than you could ever know," Carmen says with a smile for her fiancé. "But are you saying Maria should change her life for Austin?"

I have to stop this train before it leaves the station. "I've never even met him! I can't be thinking about things like changing my life for someone I've never met just because I like talking to him. I'd feel the same way if this was you, Car. I wouldn't let you lose it over a guy you've never met in person."

"Thank you for that," Jason says.

I smile for the first time since Austin pitched his perfect game. "I've got you covered, J. Don't worry."

Carmen seems to sag at the realization that I've done the right thing by putting some distance between myself and Austin. "I hate this," she says.

"I hate it, too, but reality is what it is, and I refuse to set myself up for a disaster by becoming more involved with a man who doesn't live here. Remember how it was for Dee when she and Marcus tried to do long-distance? How long did that last?"

"Six months," Carmen says, "before they realized it wasn't feasible."

"Exactly, and remember how crushed she was when they finally broke up? Why would I put myself through that knowing how it's going to end?"

"I hear you," she says, her expression as dejected as I feel. "But it sucks."

"It totally sucks."

"What can we do for you?" Carmen asks.

"Nothing. I'm okay. Really. I just needed a day." To Jason, I add, "But we need to train you on gossip containment within this family." I smile so he knows I'm joking. Kinda.

"Sorry, but in my defense, I only told Carmen you'd called out sick. What happened after that was out of my control."

"My bad," she says. "I was straight out at work and knew I couldn't get here until tonight, so I asked Nona to check on you." She doesn't have to spell out how it spiraled from there.

"It's fine. I got some awesome marsala out of it and enough other stuff to last me the rest of the week."

"Was your mom extra?" Carmen asks tentatively.

We love my mom, but she can be, as Carmen says, extra at times.

"Not too bad. She thinks I have strep because one of the prep cooks at the restaurant had it last week."

"Good," Carmen says. "Let's run with that. They don't need to know the truth."

"Nona knows it's not strep."

65

"She won't say anything. She's a vault with stuff like this."

That is certainly true. Nona is awesome that way.

"There's nothing to tell. It was a thing, and now it's not." As I say those words, the ache inside me intensifies once again. I figure that's going to be with me for a while as I go back to the life I was leading before Sunday. I can do that. I *will* do that. After Scott, I promised myself I'd never let another man become so important to me that he had the power to crush me the way Scott did. I was doing pretty well with that vow until Austin came along.

Jason glances at me. "If I can just say one thing… That was *one hell* of a game he pitched last night."

"Wasn't it awesome?" And then I'm crying again, sobbing all over Carmen when she wraps her arms around me.

"I'm sorry," Jason says. "I didn't mean…"

"It's not you." I wipe away tears with the sleeve of my sweatshirt. "That's been happening a lot since last night. Why couldn't he have just turned out to be an asshole?"

Carmen nods, in sync with me as always. "Right? That would've been so much better."

"I'll never understand women," Jason says, making me laugh for the first time all day.

"We could've hated him that way," Carmen explains. "This sucks more because Mari knows he's a good guy and she can't have him."

I use my thumb to point at Carmen. "What she said."

"Ah," Jason says. "Strangely enough, that actually makes sense to me."

"There may be hope for you yet," Carmen says, smiling at him.

"We should go and let Maria get some rest," he says.

"I'm glad you guys came over. It helped to see you."

Carmen hugs me tightly. "We're here if you need *anything*."

"I know. Thanks." I walk them to the door, hug them both and see them out.

"Call me tomorrow," Carmen says.

"I will." I close and lock the door, shut off the lights and take myself off to bed without doing any of the stuff I normally do on work nights. Maybe I'll take one more day to myself tomorrow before rejoining my life to work Saturday night at the restaurant. I can't afford to miss a waitressing shift.

Before I can guilt myself out of it, I text Angie. *Still feeling shitty. I'm going to take tomorrow, too, but I'll be back Monday. Sorry about this.*

No worries. Feel better.

I shut off the alarm on my phone and snuggle into bed, wishing I could shut off my brain as easily as I turned off the alarm. Wouldn't that be awesome? To be able to slide something on a screen to shut off any thoughts you no longer wish to have. I'd pay good money for that ability right now. But since that's not possible, I wallow in my thoughts of Austin, the confidences we shared, the love he showered me with and the happy feeling I got every time I read one of his heartfelt messages.

It'll be a very long time before I stop thinking about any of it, and I'll never forget him or Everly.

AUSTIN

Everything goes to shit after Maria and I decide to quit while we're ahead. We haven't won a game since Detroit, and I got shellacked on my next start in Seattle. Mick pulled me in the fourth after I gave up five fucking runs. I couldn't find the strike zone to save my life, and everything I threw was pure shit. I'm one hundred percent certain it's Maria's fault. She's all I think about, even when I should absolutely be thinking about other things, such as why I suddenly can't throw a strike.

It's always been this way for me. When my personal life is in an uproar, I suck on the mound. That's why I didn't even try to come back last year after Ev's diagnosis. I knew there'd be no point.

"I don't know what the fuck has happened to you," Mick rants at me at a meeting he requested on our first day back in Baltimore. "But whatever it is, *work it out*. You haven't gotten this far to fuck up your chances now."

That's the first time he's so much as hinted at what's ahead for me in the off-season. Since the O's aren't really in the running to keep me on their roster, he and I have gone out of our way to avoid discussing the elephant in the room.

"I hear you, Coach."

"You're a good guy, AJ. One of the best pitchers I've ever seen come through this game. The sky's the limit for you, and you fucking *know* it. Get your head out of your ass and finish this goddamned season, will you, please?"

"I will."

"Good. Now get the fuck out of here."

I leave Mick's office and nearly run into Santiago outside the door.

"Ouch," he whispers.

"Nothing I didn't already know."

"What gives with you, anyhow? You were on fire in Detroit and then shit in Seattle. How does that happen practically overnight?"

I know exactly how it happened, but I'll be damned if I can figure out a way to fix it in time to pitch once more here in Baltimore and then for the last time in an O's uniform in Miami, Maria's hometown, where I'll get to meet her in person.

That ought to make everything better. *Not.*

"I'm working it out," I tell Santiago. "I'll see you tomorrow."

"Later."

I head home after practice and the meeting with Mick, eager to see my baby girl. She always makes me feel better, no matter what's getting me down. On the drive across the city to my condo in Fells Point, I realize I totally lied to Santiago. I'm not working out shit, because I can't talk to the one person who could fix what's wrong with me. She's off-limits, and I miss her something fierce.

Trust me, I know it's insane to be grieving the loss of something I never really had. I feel worse about losing Maria after four days than I did about breaking up with Kasey, who I was with for three years and is the mother of my child. This hurts in a way that never did, probably because I connected more with Maria without ever having touched her.

It wasn't like that with Kasey, who was fun and funny and sexy and all about having a good time.

Maria is all substance and depth, which is just what I needed after the ordeal with Everly's illness.

There's really no comparing the two women, except to note that Maria filled a need in me I didn't realize I had until her. And now she's gone, and I ache for her. I'd give anything to be able to pick up the phone and hear her voice and listen to her laugh and be able to tell her all my first-world problems.

I park in the garage under the building and take the elevator to the fifth floor, where my parents and I have side-by-side units I bought after the breakup with Kasey forced me to reengineer my entire life. Having my folks next door has been a lifesaver in every possible way. I knock on their door and wait, even though I have a key. We're considerate of each other that way, which is critical to the success of our arrangement.

Mom comes to the door with Ev in her arms.

Everly lets out a screech when she sees me, launching herself in my direction.

I grab her before Mom can drop her.

"Honestly, Ev," Mom says. "I've told you not to do that." To me, she adds, "I'm afraid I'm going to drop her."

I should chastise her for misbehaving for Mom, but I can't do that, having just gotten home after eleven endless days. I'm so damned glad to see her. When I got home from the airport late last night, I crawled into bed with Ev at Mom and Dad's and slept next to her all night. I woke up when she plugged my nose and startled me awake, which is one of her favorite tricks. She laughs and laughs and laughs, which of course makes me laugh, too.

I follow Mom into their condo, which looks out on Baltimore's scenic Inner Harbor, like mine does, too. My mom has short blond hair and a trim, athletic figure she maintains through regular tennis matches at a local club. I'm the one who looks the most like her, and I joke about being her favorite, but duh, I am. I tell my brothers all the time that she loves me so much, she needed to move in next door to me. They know I'm full of shit, that without my parents to help with Ev, I'd be totally fucked.

Everly has wrapped herself around me, clinging to me the way she always does for days after I get home from a road trip. While I love the way she welcomes me home, I hate being away from her in the first place.

"How's my baby girl?"

She squeezes my neck with her chubby arms.

"Did she nap?" I ask Mom.

"Briefly."

Lovely. That means she'll be a bear by bedtime.

"I'm making spaghetti and meatballs for dinner if you guys want to join us."

"Sure, thanks. That sounds good—and it smells good, too. Where's Dad?"

"In the study."

"Let's go say hi to Papa, Ev."

"Papa," she says, which is one of her favorite words, along with *Dada*, *Gamma* and *no*. That last one is her most favorite. She's a late talker, and the doctors have said to relax and let it happen when she's ready. They say the delay isn't due to her illness, but I suspect it's directly related since she went mostly silent during the worst of it.

I walk into the study where my dad is seated at his desk, poring over the day's papers while he puffs on one of the cigars my mom has been trying to get him to give up. He's allowed to smoke only in the study because she hates the smell. When he sees Everly is with me, he extinguishes the cigar. He never smokes when she's in the room. His wiry gray hair is standing on end, and he hasn't shaved in a couple of days, which is something that never would've happened before he retired.

My brother Ash looks just like him, only he has the dark hair my dad had as a younger man. Dad's hair turned gray while Ev was sick. He can be tough as nails, but when it comes to Everly, he's like pudding. Her illness took it out of all of us.

"How was the meeting with Mick?" Dad asks, cutting straight to the day's headline.

"He ripped me a new one, which I expected." I take a seat in one of the plush leather chairs Mom picked out, rubbing Everly's back as she snuggles me. She's always so relieved to see me that I feel guilty for days after I get home. I give her as much of me as she wants while I'm here.

"What the hell happened in Seattle?"

My parents don't know that I've been in touch with Ev's donor or that I fell halfway in love with her over four unbelievably awesome days. "I'm not sure. It was just an off night."

"Tell that to someone who doesn't know you as well as you know yourself. What the hell *happened*?"

I should've known Dad wouldn't buy my shit. I never have been able to pull one over on my first coach and the man whose voice is always in my head. "I've been dealing with some stuff… It's nothing to worry about. I'm working it out."

"You've got two more games to seal the deal with your next team. You gotta get your head on straight. Don't give them any reason to hesitate pulling the trigger on signing you."

"I know. I get it. I'm working on it. Had a good practice today. Seattle was a fluke."

"I sure as hell hope so."

As we talk, I rub circles on Ev's back until I realize she's fallen asleep in my arms. "She's out. I'm going to take her in to rest for a bit before dinner."

I carry her into the room my parents put together for her so she'd feel at home in either condo. I stretch out on her bed, keeping her on my chest while she sleeps. I love the feel of her warm, sturdy body in my arms, and the fragrant scent of her baby shampoo. There's no question that the crap start in Seattle rattled me, but after what I've been through, I keep it in perspective. The only freaking thing that truly matters is that Everly is healthy and thriving.

I doze off, too, waking when Mom comes in to let me know dinner is ready.

I kiss Everly awake, knowing that if she sleeps too long at this hour, bedtime will be a nightmare. Like always, she's cranky when she first wakes up, but she's so happy to have me there that she rallies for dinner. Afterward, we go home to our place, where I give her a bath and read five stories at bedtime.

I stay long after she's asleep for the night, because I love being with her again after the days apart. I finally drag myself out of her bed and go in to take a shower, standing under the rainforest showerhead for a long time, letting the hot water work out the tension I've been carrying with me for a week now.

I haven't felt this shitty since Ev was diagnosed, even though that was way worse than anything else has ever been. I keep telling myself I can't let four days of correspondence and conversation with a woman fuck me up this badly, but really, it was much more than four days. It was six months of thinking about her after that initial exchange and counting down to the day when I could contact her under my real name and share my real self with her.

I ended up sharing more with her than I have with anyone other than my family. The connection we built through words was among the most powerful things I've ever experienced, and I'm lost without it now that I don't have it any longer.

But my dad and Mick are right. I have to get my head on straight before my last start in Baltimore two days from now. I want to give the fans my very best after the way they've supported me over the last six years, especially when Ev was sick. When I returned to start on opening day this year, they gave me a ten-minute standing ovation that reduced me to tears. I want to leave on the best possible note, which means I have to bring my A game.

I change into sweats and a T-shirt and grab a beer from the fridge before making my way to the sofa to watch *SportsCenter*. I check my phone for the first time in hours and see that Aaron, my agent, has responded to an earlier text. He doesn't agree that Miami ought to be in the mix and has been giving me all the reasons why for days now.

I still want to give them a look.

He writes me right back, which is rare for him. *So you said. What you haven't said is WHY.*

Personal reasons.

Let's talk on the phone tomorrow.

He'll call and try to talk me out of Miami, but I'm serious about considering the Marlins. They're a young, dynamic team with a real chance of being competitive. They check most of my boxes, except for one. I'd be the number two starter there, behind their ace, Joaquin Garcia, the Dominican phenom who's in the running for the National League Cy Young Award.

I'd be the ace with any of the other teams we're considering, and that's why Aaron is freaking out about me adding the Marlins to our list.

It's funny how things that would've mattered a few weeks ago don't now. I call up my email and scroll through the messages until I find the stream from Maria. I go all the way back to the first messages and read them all again, like I have every night since the last time I talked to her. I'm not sure why I keep torturing myself this way, but I can't seem to break the habit where she's concerned.

My phone chimes with a text from Erica, the team's promotions manager, about the event we're going to do before the first game in Miami. *Hey AJ, I talked to Maria tonight, and we're set for a brief ceremony at 12:50 on the field before the 1 p.m. start of the first game in Miami. Can you please confirm that Everly and your parents will be available to attend as well? This will be AMAZING. We're all excited about it.*

I write back to confirm the time is good and everyone will be there. *Thanks for arranging it.*

My pleasure!

My heart is all fired up at the reminder that I'm going to see Maria, in person, in just over a week. I feel better in that minute than I have since the last time I talked to her. But another thought occurs to me that stops me short. I'm going to meet Maria, for the first time, in front of thousands of people, my

whole team, my family and probably hers, too. That feels wrong
on every level to me.

I don't like it at all. Long after I turn in, I stew about that,
tossing and turning and trying to figure out what to do. I'm no
closer to a solution in the morning when Ev crawls into bed
with me and goes back to sleep for a while as I stare out at the
Inner Harbor, trying to decide whether it would be okay to ask
Maria if we could meet privately the night before the ceremony.

I hate the idea of meeting her for the first time in front of all
those people, and by the end of that day—a game day—I've
convinced myself that I have to reach out to her and at least ask
if we can get together on our own before then.

We win the game in extra innings, but I don't get home until
after midnight, so I wait to text her until the next morning.

Ev eats her cereal while I stare at my phone, hoping I'm
doing the right thing as I type a text to Maria. *Hi there, Erica let
me know we're set for the ceremony before the game, but I was
wondering if it might be okay if we meet up the night before? I hate the
idea of having thousands of people watching the first time we meet in
person…*

And I hate this message almost as much. I have so much I
want to say to her, that the words on the screen just look stupid
and inadequate to me. Before I can talk myself out of it, I send
the message.

Everly and I spend the next hour playing in her room, which
basically consists of her dressing me up in her princess attire
and putting pretend lipstick on me. We have a tea party, and I
sit still while she pretends to paint my nails the way my mother
does for her. "Dada pwitty."

That's a new word I welcome with nearly painful relief. "Not
as pretty as Everly."

"Dada silly."

Make that two new words. I hug her and kiss her and annoy
the hell out of her with my effusive response.

"No, Dada." She pushes me back and grabs my hand to finish the manicure.

My phone chimes with a text, and though I'm dying to check it, I give Ev my full attention until she tires of playing manicure. Then I lunge for the phone and see the message is from Maria.

I devour her words. *I'd really like that, too. I was sort of worried about what it would be like to meet in front of all those people.*

She has no idea that she's given me a new lease on life with that message.

I respond right away. *We land around four on Friday.* We're playing Saturday, Sunday and Monday in Miami, which is an odd configuration, but that happens at the end of the season sometimes. *Could I take you to dinner?*

I stare at the phone for what feels like an hour, waiting for her to reply. It's really only five minutes, but they seem like forever.

Sure, we can do that. Or I can cook at my place.

That sounds good, too. I like the idea of meeting her in private and having the chance to spend time alone with her. Ever since I threw the perfect game, I've been getting a lot of national press, and there's a possibility of someone recognizing me if we go out in public. I'd hate that, and I'm almost sure she would, too.

Everly is coming, right?

I'm coming with the team from Tampa. She and my parents are flying in on Saturday morning.

Ah, I see. So just us, then.

Is that ok?

Yes, of course. Looking forward to seeing you.

Same. I want to tell her I miss her so much, but I don't say that. I can't say that, even if it's true. Maybe I'll tell her when I see her next Friday night.

God, how will I stand to wait another week?

CHAPTER 8

MARIA

*a*fter a torturously slow week, I leave work on the Friday of Austin's arrival and drive to the restaurant to pick up the takeout meal I ordered earlier. I'm an okay cook, but there's no way I'm risking disaster tonight, even if it means answering a million questions from my family about who I'm having over.

It's bad enough that everyone is coming to the game tomorrow, after my dad spilled the beans about the team's plans to honor me.

"As if we'd ever miss it," Abuela said when I told them they didn't have to come.

Even though Dee, Nico, Milo and I aren't technically her grandchildren, Abuela has never missed an important event in our lives. Why would I expect her to start now?

I park in the back of Giordino's and duck in through the back door, going directly to the kitchen, where I find my uncle Vincent packing up a to-go order.

"Hi there."

"Oh, hi, honey. This is yours. Just waiting on some fresh bread out of the oven for you."

"Thank you so much." I pull out my wallet.

"This one's on me, sweetie."

"You don't have to do that!"

"I know I don't, but I want to, so you have to let me."

"Thank you, but next time, I'm paying."

"We'll fight about that then."

I go up on tiptoes to kiss his cheek. "You're the best."

"How you feeling?"

I've been asked that question a hundred times by every member of my family since I took two days out of work last week. "I'm fine. Back to normal." That isn't true, but it's what he needs to hear.

"That's good news. We were worried about you." One of the prep cooks brings over the bread wrapped in foil. Uncle Vin adds it to the brown bag. "And with that, my dear, you're all set."

"Thanks again, Uncle V."

"I hope you have a lovely evening, honey. I'll see you at the game tomorrow."

I grimace at the reminder of what I agreed to do, questioning the wisdom of that for the nine hundredth time since Austin first asked me if I'd be willing. "I'll be there."

I'm on my way to a clean getaway when Abuela comes in the back door, eyes my takeout bag and lifts her gaze to my face. "Who you buying dinner for?"

"A friend from out of town."

"What friends do you have from out of town?"

Amused, I kiss her cheek as I breeze by her. "No one you know. See you tomorrow!"

Hurrying, I stash the food in the back seat and get in my car, eager to get out of there before anyone else can try to figure out my plans. Yes, I could've ordered from somewhere else, but I wanted the best for Austin, and to get the best, I had to come to

Giordino's. I pull out of the parking lot and breathe a sigh of relief that the inquisition wasn't worse.

My phone rings, and I take the call from Carmen on my Bluetooth. She's the only one I've told about my plans for tonight. I assume Jason knows, too, but he didn't say anything when I saw him at the clinic yesterday.

"How you holding up?" she asks.

"I'm doing all right. Just picked up dinner from your dad, and I'm headed home now."

"Did you decide what to wear?"

"I'm doing jeans with the black off-the-shoulder shirt."

"I like that shirt. You look hot in it."

"I'm not trying to look hot."

"Why the hell not? You're having dinner with a hot guy who you really like."

"Do we need to go through this again?"

"No, we don't," she says, sounding defeated. I know how she feels. "What time does he land?"

"Around four."

"What time is he coming over?"

"We haven't set a time yet. He said he'd text when they land."

"I want you to know that I heard what you said about all the reasons this can't happen. I heard you, and I understand why you feel the way you do. It's just that if this guy is 'the one,' Mari, do whatever it takes to make it work. Just go for it."

Her sweet words go straight to my overcommitted heart. "Easier said than done."

"Of course it is, but what's worse? Taking a gigantic risk or spending the rest of your life wishing you'd had the balls to try?"

The question cuts straight to the crux of the torturous dilemma that's grown and multiplied with every passing day since I cut things off with him. It hasn't gotten easier with time. It's gotten much, much worse, and I'm actually terrified about what'll happen when I meet him in person.

"I hear you, and I appreciate what you're saying."

"Good luck tonight. Text me later if you need me."

"You guys have the thing at the hospital tonight." Carmen and Jason are attending a black-tie benefit that Carmen has been working on for weeks.

"I'll have my phone close by. If you need me, text. I mean it."

"I will. Thanks. Love you."

"Love you, too."

I disconnect the call and pull into my driveway a few minutes later. When I get inside, I transfer dinner to casserole dishes and put them in the oven on warm. Then I hit the shower and redo my makeup, using waterproof mascara because I expect this could be an emotional evening.

Austin texts me at four fifty. *Just landed and headed to the hotel. What time do you want to get together and where am I going?*

Do you want me to pick you up?

No need. I can grab a car.

I send him my address. *I'm in the garage apartment in the back. Come whenever you want. I'm home.*

Sounds good. I'll text when I'm on the way.

I send a thumbs-up emoji, but only because they haven't yet created the combo swoon, top of head blowing off, blushing, bug-eyed emoji to sum up how I'm feeling right now. I finish getting ready and strap on chunky-heeled, open-toed black sandals and check myself in the full-length mirror on the back of my bedroom door. If you ask me, I have way too much ass and a cup size more boob than I'd prefer, but guys seem to like what I've got going on. And besides, this night isn't about impressing anyone.

"You're so full of shit, it's not even funny," I tell my reflection.

Disgusted with myself and sick of my own thoughts, I go into the kitchen and pour a glass of Chardonnay. If there was ever a time for liquid courage, this is it.

An hour later, Austin texts that he's on his way, and Uber is saying he's twenty minutes away.

It's a good thing he'll be here soon, because I'm almost through my second glass of wine. I turn on the outside light and go to the bathroom to pee and brush my teeth so I don't get him drunk with my wine breath.

I wish I could calm the hell down, but every part of me is on full alert as twenty minutes becomes ten and then five, and then I see headlights in the driveway, and he's here. I go to the door to wait for him and watch him come up the stairs. He looks up, sees me waiting for him and smiles. In the two seconds before he reaches the top step, I realize I've made a huge mistake allowing myself to meet him.

AUSTIN

This has been the longest day. Hell, it's been the longest *week* I've had since Ev got sick and time seemed to stand still for months on end. Counting down the days until I could see Maria reminded me of being a kid waiting for Christmas. Only, finally seeing her is way, way, *way* more exciting than any Christmas I've ever had.

Of course I already knew she was beautiful, but she's even more so in person. She opens the door and greets me with a shy, tentative smile that tells me I'm not the only one who's nervous about tonight.

On the short flight to Miami from Tampa, I gave myself a talking-to about staying cool when I meet the woman who saved my daughter's life. But all that is forgotten when the moment is upon me, and all I can think about is the amazing gift she gave me—and Everly.

"Could I, um, hug you?"

Again with that shy smile that does wonderous things to her gorgeous face. "Sure."

We come together in a hug for the ages. It's smooth and easy, as if we've been hugging for years, and she fits in my arms like she belongs there. Everything about her appeals to me, but the physical attraction is secondary to what I know about who she is on the inside.

Neither of us is in any hurry to let go.

"I know I've said it a hundred times already, but thank you. Thank you, thank you, *thank you.*"

"You're welcome."

Such simple words to represent the greatest gift anyone has ever given me.

When we finally pull back, we both have tears in our eyes.

She laughs as she contends with hers. "We're a mess."

"You could never be a mess." I can't stop staring at her. I'm so damned happy to finally see her, to be with her. I want to bury my face in that mane of dark curls and just breathe in the rich scent of her until I satisfy my craving. I suspect that'll take a while.

"Come in," she says.

That's when I realize I made it a foot inside her door before hugging her. *Way to play it cool, AJ.* I follow her into the big, open room that serves as a combined living room and kitchen. "Something smells good."

"I cheated and picked up dinner from the restaurant. I wasn't sure what you liked, so I ordered a few things to share if that's okay."

"Of course. I hope you didn't go to too much trouble."

She glances at me, still seeming adorably shy. "I made a phone call to my uncle."

I laugh, and she seems to relax a little. At least I hope so. I don't want her to be nervous around me.

"What can I get you to drink? I have beer, wine, soda, water."

"I'll have a beer, please."

She gets a bottle of Sam Adams out of the fridge and opens it for me. "Glass?"

"Nah, it comes in one."

"True."

Maria refills the wineglass she already had going and sits next to me at the bar, where she's put out some crackers and dip. "Giordino's famous spinach and artichoke dip," she says. "You have to try it."

"Don't mind if I do." I dip a cracker into the dip and take a bite. The rich flavor explodes on my tongue. "Holy crap, that's good."

"Right?"

I have another cracker full of the amazing dip. "Did you take one for the team by going to the restaurant to pick up dinner for two?"

"How'd you guess?"

"I'm honored that you took such a big risk for me."

"I wanted you to have the best of Miami, and to do that, I had to go home to Giordino's. But it wasn't too bad. I only saw Uncle Vin and Abuela."

"That's Carmen's dad and her grandmother, right?"

"Yes," she says, seeming impressed.

"I've reread our emails a thousand times. I think I have them memorized by now."

"Me, too," she says softly.

I'm not sure what compels me to reach for her hand, to link my fingers with hers, but the need to touch her is overwhelming.

She looks down at our joined hands, her face flushing with

color that only makes her more adorable—and sexy. She's curvy and sweet and beautiful and...

Slow your roll, AJ. She put a stop to this for reasons that still exist.

"Is this okay?" I ask.

"It's okay, but I have to be honest that I'm a little freaked out by all this."

I turn on my stool to fully face her. "All what?"

"You. This." She squeezes my hand, and that's all it takes to make me hard for her. "It's a bit overwhelming."

"For me, too. I don't want you to think this is something I do all the time. It isn't. I've never talked to *anyone* the way I've talked to you."

"Me, either."

Hearing that settles something in me, and I begin to relax, too.

"You can't eat the dip if you're holding my hand," she says.

"Watch this." I put down my beer and use my right hand to take another cracker full of the delicious dip and then chase it with a sip of beer before waggling my brows at her suggestively. "I'm good with my hands."

The comment succeeds in making her laugh and blush again, both of which are quickly becoming my favorite things to do.

"What happened in Seattle?"

I wince. "You saw that, huh?"

"Yeah."

"*You* happened."

"*What?* What does that mean?"

"After we talked that night when I was in Detroit and agreed we shouldn't continue this, I was really screwed up."

"I was, too." She looks up at me with beautiful brown eyes. "I called out sick to work the next two days. I've never done that before."

With my free hand, I reach out to cup her face. Her skin is silky soft, and I want so badly to kiss her, I burn from the need that overtakes me in a tsunami of emotions I've never experienced before. Not like this. "Maria…"

"I, um, I should check on dinner."

I pull back from her and release her hand, even though it's the last thing in the world I want to do. But more than anything, I don't want to hurt this sweet, precious woman who did such a big thing for my daughter. So I let her go, take a deep breath and try to get myself settled. I have to follow her lead. She's the one who said this couldn't happen, and I have to respect her wishes.

Even if I want her with every fiber of my being.

MARIA

I'm *dying*. He was going to kiss me just now, and I wanted him to. I wanted it more than I've ever wanted anything in my life. So much for calling a halt to this thing between us. Ten minutes in his presence, and I'm holding his hand and trying not to kiss him.

I can't kiss him. Hugging him was bad enough—in the best possible way.

When I open the oven, a blast of heat hits me in the face and forces me to think about something other than how much I want to kiss Austin Jacobs. And you know what's really not fair? That he's even hotter in person than he is on TV. I thought he couldn't get any hotter than he is in his uniform, but wearing an untucked dress shirt with sleeves rolled up over muscular forearms and jeans that hug all the right places, he's a thousand times sexier in person.

Not to mention the groove that appears in his right cheek when he smiles or the subtle hint of cologne that makes me want to get closer so I can further investigate the appealing scent or the tattoos that cover his forearms. The whole package —from how he looks, to how he dresses, to how he smells, added to what I already know about him—is almost more than I can handle.

The cheese on the lasagna and chicken Parm is bubbling, which means it's ready. I grab pot holders and hot pads and remove the dishes from the oven, placing them on the bar. My place is too small for a table and chairs, so the bar is my table. Serving dinner gives me something to do besides want to kiss Austin.

You can't kiss him, no matter what, because if you do that, this is going to get worse than it already is. Remember those two days you were in bed crying because you couldn't talk to him? How will you feel when you can't kiss him anymore because he's gone home to Baltimore, *which is hundreds of miles from here?*

I grab the bread, salad and another beer for Austin and bring everything to the counter.

That's when I realize I forgot plates and silverware. Some kind of waitress I am. I fetch what we need and join him at the bar.

Serving spoons. We need them, too. I jump back up to get them. "You'd think I've never done this before."

"I'm not thinking anything but how good that looks—and smells."

"I should warn you that this meal will ruin you for Italian anywhere else. People come from all over for this."

"Wow, now I really can't wait."

I serve him some of both dishes and divide the salad into bowls. "The house Italian dressing is my favorite."

When he takes a bite of the lasagna, his moan travels all the way through me to land in a throb between my legs.

Awesome, I think as I cross my legs. *Now I'm getting turned on by him eating. Think of something else to focus on, will you, please?* My better judgment is turning out to be a huge pain in my ass. "Is Everly excited about her trip to Miami?"

"So excited."

"Does she know why you guys are coming?"

He takes a sip of beer, wipes his mouth and nods. "I told her we're going to meet the wonderful lady who helped her get better. And that we're very happy to meet her because she did such a nice thing for us."

"Do you think she understands?"

"Not really. She's been on airplanes before and loves to fly, so that's the headline in her world. But I hope you know—"

I put my hand on his arm. "I know. I get it. She's three. Thankfully, she'll never remember any of it."

"I'm grateful for that every day, among many other things."

I know he means me and what I did for them. "Try the chicken. It's even better than the lasagna."

"I'm not sure that's possible."

"Trust me on this."

He cuts a bite of the chicken, and again with the moan.

Jesus, Mary and Joseph. I can't handle that moan. "Told ya. I think half my ass is accountable to the chicken Parm at Giordino's." And I can't believe I said that out loud. *Have some more wine, Maria.*

Austin chokes out a laugh. "Is that so?"

I'm mortified. "Uh-huh."

"And you're thinking you shouldn't have said that, am I right?"

"You're right."

"If you ask me, your family's chicken Parm has helped to build a rather spectacular ass."

CHAPTER 9

MARIA

I choke on the sip of wine that was halfway down when he said that.

Austin pats me on the back. "You okay?"

"Yeah, sorry."

"You're so cute, you know that?"

"When I'm blowing wine out my nose?"

"All the time. It's all I can do not to completely stare at you now that you're sitting right next to me. So if I'm staring, let me know, and I'll try not to. But I won't try too hard."

"I'll do that. If you promise to do the same."

His face lifts into a small smile. "Deal."

We eat in silence while I try to nurse my third glass of wine. Based on the ass comment, I've already got more than enough liquid courage on board. It wouldn't take much for me to throw caution to the wind and forget why kissing this man is a very bad idea. I put down the wine and focus on eating, but that's not easy, either, with my whole system in an Austin Jacobs-induced uproar.

"You were right," he says after polishing off most of the lasagna and a good portion of chicken.

"About what?"

"I'm ruined for any other Italian after this."

"Told ya." I'm always so proud of how much people love the Cuban and Italian food at Giordino's. "My aunt and uncle have worked so hard and made their restaurant into such an institution around here. Lots of famous people come in whenever they're in town."

"Like who?"

"Justin Bieber, Gloria Estefan, Taylor Swift, George Clooney, to name a few."

"No way. That's awesome."

"You should bring your family in tomorrow night. They'll love it."

"Isn't it hard to get reservations?"

"It can be, but I know people." I lean in closer to him. "I can hook you up."

"I won't say no to hooking up with you."

I sputter with laughter. "That's not what I said."

"Can you blame a guy for trying?"

"Yes, I can." I try to hide my over-the-top reaction to everything he says and does. I've never been so attracted to a man in my life. Figures it would happen with someone who doesn't live anywhere near me, not to mention he's looking at moving even farther from me than he is now. It's rather depressing, actually.

"What's wrong?"

And that he *sees* me so clearly doesn't help anything. I could be in a full-on rage for days and Scott wouldn't even notice. I already know Austin wouldn't let me get away with that. "Nothing's wrong."

"Something is. I can tell by that little frown you do when you're bothered or upset. I noticed it on FaceTime."

"You're too much for me. That's the problem."

He draws back as if I slapped him. "What do you mean?"

"I keep telling myself I can't do this. I can't see you and talk to you and be with you, because of all the reasons we've already discussed."

"Do you want me to go?"

"No, I don't want you to go, and that's also a problem."

"You're going to have to help me out here," he says, looking as confused as I feel.

I push my barely touched plate aside and look down at my hands, trying to find the words I need to tell him how I feel. Since I can barely explain it to myself, that's harder than it should be. "When I told you we couldn't talk anymore, it wasn't because I don't like talking to you. I like it too much."

"I feel the same way."

"Being with you in person..."

"Is amazing."

"Yes." I force myself to look at him, and what I see coming from him is everything I could ever want in one sweet, sexy package. I'm drawn to him by something more powerful than anything I've ever felt, and my resistance crumbles like a sand-castle taken down by an incoming tide.

He raises his hand to cup my face as he stares at me intently. "I heard what you said when you called it off while I was in Detroit. Hell, I even agreed with you that it was the right thing to do. But ever since then, I've felt like complete and absolute crap because I can't talk to you anymore. I kept asking myself how I could feel so bad about losing something I'd never had in the first place. But what I realized is I've had more with you in emails and phone calls and FaceTime chats than I've ever had with anyone else, and all I want is *more* of that. *More* of you."

Now, you tell me how I'm supposed to remember all the reasons this is a bad idea when the hottest, sweetest guy I've ever met is saying those words to me. I can't resist him, and in the second before I do something that can't be undone, I recall what Carmen said: *If this guy is "the one," Mari, do whatever it takes to make it work.*

In what will surely go down as the most perfect moment of my entire life, we both lean in at the same instant, our lips coming together in a needy, hungry kiss unlike any other first kiss in the history of first kisses. There's nothing awkward or fumbling about it. Like everything with him, it's utter perfection.

Without missing a beat in the best kiss ever, he puts his arms around me, compels me to stand and brings me in tight against his muscular body. He makes no effort to hide the fact that he's hard for me, which only makes me want him more. Is that even possible? I wind my arms around his neck and moan when he rubs his tongue against mine. All thoughts of self-preservation are gone. I don't care about anything other than more of this, more of him. Even though I'm one hundred percent certain this is still a bad idea, I don't care anymore.

"Tell me to stop," he says.

For all I know, days, weeks and years have passed since we started kissing. I've lost track of everything that isn't him. I can barely form thoughts, let alone words. And *stop* is the last word on my mind.

He leans his forehead against mine, his breathing uneven and his face flushed.

I love that he seems as undone as I feel after the best first kiss ever.

"You're not telling me to stop."

"You noticed that, huh?"

"Mmm. I told myself this wasn't going to happen when I came here."

"I told myself the same thing."

"Is lying to ourselves a bad thing?"

"Not if it feels this good."

"Maria?"

"Yes, Austin?"

"I want to kiss you some more."

"I want that, too."

"You're supposed to say no and tell me to go and remind me of all the reasons why we're not doing this."

"I can't remember any of those reasons." I move my hands from his shoulders and slide them down his arms to take hold of his hands. Giving him a gentle pull, I walk backward toward my bedroom.

"Where're you taking me?"

"Somewhere more comfortable."

"You should be kicking me out."

"Believe me, I know."

"I'm really glad you're not."

"I am, too." I release my hold on his hands and remove my shoes before stretching out on my bed and inviting him to join me.

He kicks off his shoes and stretches out next to me, turning on his side to face me. "Hi."

"How's it going?"

"Best first date of my whole life."

"Mine, too. Except this wasn't supposed to be a date, remember?"

"I remember everything." He twirls a length of my curly hair around his finger. "Except I can't seem to remember why this is a bad idea."

"Me, either. I can't recall a single reason."

I love his smile, the groove that appears in his cheek and the way his eyes sparkle with silent laughter. "That's not what you said a couple of weeks ago."

"I know, but that was then, and now... Now, I just don't care. From the first time you ever contacted me, I've felt a connection to you that goes so far beyond me donating to Everly. I can't explain it."

He continues to play with my hair. "I've felt more connected to you than I have to almost anyone I've ever known. I'd ask myself how that was possible when we'd never met, but it's the truth. And now that I've met you…"

"What?"

"I want more." He reaches for me, and I go willingly because I want the same thing.

I wouldn't have thought it possible to top that first kiss, but the second, third and fourth ones get progressively hotter, sexier and needier. My world is reduced to this room, his lips and tongue and the tight press of his body against mine. I can't get enough, and even knowing this road could be paved with ruin, I simply don't care.

AUSTIN

Her kisses destroy the resolve I brought with me when I came to her house. I was determined to keep things platonic, like she wanted, and to go on with my life after having met the woman who saved my daughter's life. Even if I knew that would be one of the hardest things I've ever done, I was willing to do it for her. But then I kissed her, and all bets were off. After the way we connected through words, it's no wonder our physical connection is so hot.

I want her so much, but not just like this. I want her in every way I can have her, and after being so badly burned by Kasey, I honestly thought I'd never want that with anyone again. But Maria has been different from the first time I ever talked to her through anonymous emails when I barely knew her. How else to explain why I couldn't wait for the one-year mark when we could finally talk freely?

Only when I need to breathe more than I need to kiss her do I shift my interest to her neck, leaving kisses all the way down to the deep neckline of the sexy-as-fuck shirt she's wearing. "You're still not telling me to stop."

"What's that? Can't hear you."

Laughing at her witty reply, I kiss the plump slopes of her full breasts while working a hand under the hem of her top.

Her fingers slide through my hair, sending a shiver of need straight to my balls. Christ have mercy, I'm on fire for her. "Tell me what you want."

"I want you. I've wanted you from the first time you emailed me, before I even knew your name."

Her direct response is a refreshing change of pace. "I want the same thing."

I feel her hand on my chest and look down to see that she's unbuttoning my shirt. "I, uh, I'm kinda unprepared for this."

She offers me a smile that manages to be sexy and shy at the same time, a combination I didn't know I loved until her. "I'm not."

Okay, then, so this is going to happen, and... *Ugh.* "I can't." I place my hand on top of hers. "But it's not because I don't want to." I look down at her and try to find the words I need to share something with her that I've never told anyone. "I didn't bring condoms because I didn't want you to think I was planning something like this. I wasn't."

"Neither was I. But I have them."

"Which is awesome, but the thing is... When I was with Kasey..." God, there's no way to say this without making it seem like I don't trust Maria, when that's not the case at all. And Kasey is the last freaking thing I want to talk about right now, but I have rules for these things thanks to her, rules I can't break no matter how much I might want to with Maria.

She massages my back with a gentle touch that makes me want to wallow in her sweetness. "Tell me what's wrong."

"I think she might've messed with the condoms, and that's where Everly came from."

"Oh God, Austin. Really?"

I give a short nod, and my whole body goes tense the way it does any time I think about that time in my life. "I've never said that out loud to anyone before."

"I promise no one will ever hear it from me."

I believe her, and I already trust her more than I've ever trusted any woman I dated. "We passed it off as an oops to everyone else, but I was always careful. I didn't make those sorts of mistakes. I already knew that things with Kasey were tentative at best, and there was no way I was looking to have a child with her. So imagine my surprise when she tells me she's pregnant."

"It must've been shocking."

"It was. I know it takes two to make a baby, and I have no regrets about having Ev. But there's always been something kind of fishy about how it happened, especially since she was the one who bought the condoms. Ever since then, the only condoms I use are the ones I buy. Which is a shit thing to say to you, because it makes it seem like I don't trust you, when that isn't the case at all."

"I get it. I'd feel the same way if I were you."

I appreciate that she understands, even if I'm disappointed. "I'm sorry."

"I appreciate that you came here intending to honor my wishes."

"I did. I swear I did. Even if I wanted to kiss you from the first second I walked in the door."

"I wanted that, too," she says with a reassuring smile. "And there's lots of other stuff we can do that doesn't require condoms. If you want to, that is…"

"Uh, yeah, I want to."

Laughing at my hasty reply, Maria goes back to what she was doing, unbuttoning my shirt and pushing it off my shoulders.

I help her by removing it and tossing it aside. Then I tug on her top, "Fair is fair."

Without hesitation, she sits up and removes her shirt, revealing a sexy black bra that barely contains spectacular breasts.

When she reclines on the pillow, I cup her cheek, running my thumb over the softest skin I've ever felt. "I'll never forget the first time I saw your face in that picture you sent me. I thought you were stunning, and now... Now I know that's not a big enough word. You're beautiful."

She reaches for me, and we come together in a frenzy of lips and tongues and hands moving over bare skin.

Her touch sets me on fire.

We kiss for hours, or so it seems. I have no idea what time it is, and I couldn't care less. The team has curfew on game nights, but with three games remaining in the season, no one is enforcing it. Just as well, because I'd take the fine before I'd leave her right when things are getting even more interesting.

"I want to touch you everywhere," I whisper against her lips.

"I want you to."

With every kiss and stroke of her tongue against mine, I fall deeper into this thing with her. Soon I won't be able to find my way out, and that's completely fine with me. I release the front clasp of her bra and feast my eyes on full, gorgeous breasts with sweet pink nipples that require my immediate attention. I look down at her face, flushed with color, as I cup her breasts and run my thumbs over the tight tips. "You're still not telling me to stop."

"What? Still can't hear you."

I love this woman. I know it's ridiculous to feel that way about someone I just met in person a couple of hours ago, but I loved her before I ever knew her name. And everything I've learned about her since we were able to communicate freely has only added to the huge feeling I have for her. This, however, has nothing to do with the amazing gift she gave my daughter and everything to do with what she's come to mean to me separate from that.

Dipping my head, I take her left nipple into my mouth and tug gently. As I move from one side to the other, I could spend days right here and never get bored. She's so sweet and responsive and sexy. So fucking sexy, I almost can't bear it.

This night will go down as one of the best of my entire life, and all we did was kiss and touch and hold each other until we finally fell asleep sometime long after midnight. I have no idea what time it is when I wake up with her in my arms, her breasts pressed against my chest and her hair wild on the pillow. I check my watch and see that it's nine o'clock. I've missed curfew by nine hours. Ask me if I care.

I kiss her forehead.

She stirs, and the heat of her body against my hard cock is a torturous reminder of how badly I want her.

"I have to go."

"I'll take you to the hotel."

"I can get a car."

"No need. I don't mind. Just give me a minute to get ready."

When I release her, I notice how she covers her bare breasts with her arm as she gets out of bed and ducks into the bathroom wearing only the underwear we both ended up in when our jeans came off. We were in silent agreement that if we went any further, we wouldn't stop.

I sit up, run my fingers through my hair and reach for my jeans and shirt, both of which are on the floor where they landed last night.

I want to ask her—what now? What happens after the best night ever? I'm afraid to ask, because I don't want to hear her say this was a one-time thing that can't happen again.

She comes out of the bathroom wearing a robe. "I left you a new toothbrush if you want it."

"I want it. Thank you." I take my turn in the bathroom, hoping I'm giving her enough time to get dressed. As I splash cold water on my face and brush my teeth, I'm full of questions. My plan is to take this day a minute at a time and follow her lead.

When I emerge from the bathroom, she's dressed in leggings that hug her sexy ass and a tank that showcases her gorgeous breasts. I wish I had time to coax her back into bed, but I don't. I need to get my ass back to the hotel before someone figures out that I never came back last night.

The dishes still sitting on her bar are a reminder of how fast the game changed last night.

"I feel bad leaving you with a mess to clean up."

"It's no problem."

I follow her out, closing the door behind me while wondering if I'll ever be at her home again. The not knowing is a little crazy-making, if I'm being honest. I get in the passenger seat of her silver Honda Civic and tell her which downtown Miami hotel the team is staying in.

Neither of us says much on the fifteen-minute ride into town, and the quiet only makes me feel more desperate to know what happens next.

"Do you want me to see about getting you a reservation for dinner tonight?" she asks as she takes a downtown exit.

"If it's not a problem, that'd be great," I tell her, relieved to know there'll be more.

"My uncle always holds a few tables for friends. It's no problem."

"Can you join us?"

"I'm working, but I'll ask for your table."

I'm not sure how I feel about her waiting on us, but I keep that thought to myself. If it's that or nothing, I'll take it.

She pulls up to the main door of the hotel a few minutes

later. "I guess I'll see you at the game," she says with a comical grimace.

"It'll be great. Thanks for doing it."

"No problem. I can't wait to meet Everly."

"I can't, either. My mom is apt to cry when she meets you..."

"That's fine. I understand."

"I, um... Last night was awesome." I reach for her hand because I need to touch her. Bringing it to my lips, I kiss the back of it. "Thank you."

"You'd better get in there before you get in trouble."

"I won't get in trouble, and if I do, it was one hundred percent worth it." I lean across the center console, hoping she'll meet me halfway.

She does, giving me a quick kiss that's nowhere near enough.

When I pull back, I notice her cheeks are flushed. "I'll see you in a couple of hours."

"See you then."

I get out of the car and watch her drive off, wishing I had nowhere to be today so I could've spent the day with her. I check my phone on the way into the hotel and see a text from my mom, letting me know their flight is on time, and they'll land around eleven.

I can't wait to see Ev, and I'm counting the hours until I can see Maria again.

CHAPTER 10

MARIA

*A*s I drive away from Austin's hotel, I call Carmen on the Bluetooth.

"What happened?"

"Good morning to you, too."

"Come on! I've been dying waiting to hear from you. How was it?"

"It was... Car..."

"Bad? Was it bad?"

I'm so emotional, I can barely speak. "No. It was *so* good."

"Oh my God! This is *awesome!*" When I don't reply, she says, "Isn't it?"

"It sure as hell felt good in the moment."

"Did you, you know..."

"No, but he spent the night, and it was... *everything*."

"Where are you now?"

"I just dropped him back at the hotel in town."

"Come over. Jason isn't here. He's on a ride with his cycling club this morning."

Since the last thing I want to do is be alone right now, I find myself agreeing. "You want coffee?"

"When do I say no to that?"

"I'll be there soon." After a brief detour to pick up cortaditos from Carmen's favorite ventanita, I head to her place in Brickell and park in one of the visitor spaces. She buzzes me in, and I take the elevator to the seventh floor. Carmen is standing in the open doorway to the incredible condo that looks down on Biscayne Bay. I'd be green with envy if I didn't know how much Carmen deserves every good thing she's found with Jason.

She hugs me, ushers me into their sleek, spacious, modern home and closes the door. "Let's sit outside. It's so nice."

We take our coffees to the huge deck and take seats on the double lounge chair that Jason bought her for Christmas.

"Tell me everything. Leave nothing out." She leans in for a closer look at me. "Um, is that a *hickey?*"

My hand flies up to cover my neck. "What? No."

Her raised brow tells me otherwise.

"No way."

"Way."

I close my eyes and lean my head against the back of the lounge.

"That good, huh?"

"Better."

She lets out a squeal that probably wakes every dog in a one-mile radius. "This is so, *so* cool!"

"It's all your fault that it got so out of control."

Her brows furrow with confusion. "How is it my fault?"

"You told me to throw caution to the wind and go for it, so I did."

"And now you regret it?"

"No, not at all, but I will... When he goes back to Baltimore, and I'm stuck here with memories of an amazing guy I can't have."

"Maria, you *can* have him. You absolutely can. Will you have to make some changes? Probably, but maybe that wouldn't be so bad."

"How can you say that when you were no more willing to move for Jason than I am for Austin?" Just saying his name out loud gives me a thrill. That's how far gone I am over him.

"I've thought a lot about that since Jay and I figured things out. I think if he'd been forced to go back to work in New York, I probably would've ended up there. Maybe not right away, but eventually."

"And you think you could've been happy there?"

"I think," she says in a measured tone, "I would've been happier there with him than here without him."

"I'm getting so far ahead of myself even talking about this. It was one night."

"Why're you downplaying it?"

"Because! I'm freaking out! The only reason we didn't have sex is because he has a thing about condoms—"

"What kind of thing does he have about condoms?"

"If I tell you this, you seriously can't tell anyone else. It's a big deal."

"I swear."

Because we've kept each other's secrets all our lives, I tell her what he suspects about Everly's mother and how she ended up pregnant.

"Wow." Carmen blinks. "Can you imagine doing that to someone?"

"No, I can't, but she was probably hoping to trap the rich baseball player, and now he's super cautious."

"I think it's pretty great that he didn't come there last night prepared for that possibility. It says a lot about how he heard what you said and respected your wishes."

"Yeah, I thought so, too."

"What's the plan for tonight, after the game?"

"He's bringing his family into the restaurant." Which reminds me, I need to text my uncle to ask if he can get them a table. I take care of that before I forget.

He writes right back. *Consider it done, honey.*

Thanks, Uncle V! xo

"Aren't you working?"

"Yeah, but I'll wait on them so I can spend some time with them."

"That's not happening. I'll take your shift and give you the money."

"Stop it. You're not doing that."

"Why not? You'd do it for me. He's only in town for this weekend, Mari. I'm more than happy to work for you, and I don't need the money. Let me do this for you."

"You guys must have plans."

"We don't. We had the hospital thing last night, and we purposely didn't plan anything for tonight."

"I don't feel right about it."

"Too bad. It's happening. Tell my dad to make your reservation for one more."

"You're a bossy pain in the ass."

"Yep, but you love me. Now, do what you're told."

I text her dad and then glance at her, by my side where she's been all my life. "Thanks, Car."

"Anything for you."

I arrive at the ballpark at twelve thirty and park in the VIP lot where I'm greeted as if I am, in fact, a VIP. It's so weird to be coming here under these circumstances, when I'm at the park at least once a week for six months a year. I've never been a VIP, however, and the treatment is a bit heady.

Valentina, a perky young woman from the Marlins promotions department, meets me and walks me in through a special entrance where we meet up with Erica from the Orioles.

"It's great to meet you," Erica says when she shakes my hand. "We're so happy to have the chance to thank you for what you did for AJ's daughter."

As I follow them deeper into the stadium, I hope I've done enough to hide the hickey "AJ" left on my neck last night. I covered the mark with foundation and left my hair down. I'm wearing a V-neck Marlins shirt with black shorts and the same shoes I had on last night.

Ah, last night... I've relived the hours with Austin a thousand times today, and I already know I'll never forget a minute of it. I can't wait to see him, to meet Everly and his parents, and...

Judging by the way my heart goes into a crazy gallop, I'm getting way ahead of myself again. I'm apt to hyperventilate, or something equally embarrassing, in front of thousands of people if I don't get things under control—and fast.

"Have you met either of them yet?" Valentina asks.

"Only Austin." *I've definitely met him,* I think, resisting the urge to descend into nervous hysteria. "I'll meet Everly for the first time today."

"Aw, that's so sweet. It's amazing what you did for her."

"I did what anyone would do."

"I don't think that's true," Erica says. "A lot of people wouldn't inconvenience themselves for someone they've never met, let alone undergo a scary medical procedure. What you did is pretty damned heroic. Everyone thinks so."

"Oh, well, thanks." It still seems weird to me to be treated like a hero for something that was a no-brainer to me. Of course I'd try to save an innocent child's life if I could.

The Marlins offered seats to whoever I wanted to invite to the game. My parents, brothers, aunts, uncles, cousins and grandmothers are planning to be there. My sister, Dee, had to work in New York, so she couldn't come home for the weekend. I'll join my family in the stands after the pregame ceremony.

I stand with Valentina and Erica in one of the stairways that leads onto the field and listen to the announcer talk about the special treat they have in store for today's attendees.

"Fifteen months ago, Miami's own Maria Giordino donated bone marrow to save the life of a child she'd never met. That child is the daughter of Orioles pitcher Austin Jacobs, and today, we're so pleased to bring Maria and the child whose life she saved together for the first time. Please help us give a warm Marlins welcome to Maria Giordino, Austin Jacobs, his daughter, Everly Jacobs, and his parents, Jeff and Deidre Jacobs!"

Valentina and Erica walk with me onto the field, where I'm due to meet up with Austin and his family in the infield. The crowd provides thunderous applause.

As they approach the infield, Austin leans down to say something to Everly.

She pulls her hand free of his and runs to me.

I scoop her up and hug her, amazed that she came to me, a perfect stranger, without hesitation. Closing my eyes against a rush of tears, I hold the child whose life I saved and absorb the thrill of this amazing moment. Her sweet little body against mine, the scent of her baby shampoo and her soft arms around my neck fill me with gratitude for her good health.

The applause goes on for a long time.

Austin joins us and hugs us both. "There you are," he whispers in my ear. "I've been missing you."

His words fill me with unreasonable elation.

The three of us hug as if we're alone and not in the middle of a crowded baseball stadium.

Eventually, he takes Everly from me so I can receive hugs from his tearful parents.

"Thank you so much, Maria," his mom says. "We'll never have the words…"

His dad hugs me next while Austin holds Everly.

"Thank you for saving our little girl," his dad says.

We're all a mess by the time the announcer asks for one more round of applause for "our own local hero, Maria Giordino."

We pose for the team photographer, who wants pictures of the group, one of me with Austin and Everly and then just me and Everly.

The whole thing is surreal, to say the least.

"I'll text you after the game," Austin says when we have no choice but to go our separate ways for now.

I nod to let him know I heard him and walk with Valentina and Erica back the way we came.

"Thank you so much for that," Valentina says, wiping up tears of her own. "That was one of the coolest things we've ever gotten to do."

"Thanks for having me."

"Let me get you to your family in the VIP section."

She walks me through more winding tunnels to an elevator that takes us to the top of the stadium, where I'm shown to one of the deluxe boxes that I've certainly heard about but never experienced for myself.

"I hope you and your family enjoy the game," Valentina says.

"Thank you for everything."

"Our pleasure."

The box is full of family members who hug me and congratulate me and thank me for inviting them to partake of the VIP suite, which includes a buffet and open bar.

"So proud of you, honey," my dad says when he hugs me.

"Thank you, Dad."

"It's gonna be tough to go back to the cheap seats after this," he adds.

We love those cheap seats, as well as the people we see at

every game. The season ticket holders are like a family after years of sitting near each other.

"Pretty cool, sis," my brother Nico says. "This is the life."

It's not easy to impress my brothers, and it gives me pleasure to see them enjoying something I made possible.

Jason and Carmen hug me next.

"You looked good out there," Carmen says. "I loved the way Everly ran to you."

"I know! That was amazing."

"Well done, kid," Jason says when he hugs me. He was the first person I reached out to after I got the call from Be the Match, and his support was instrumental to me as I navigated the sea of information and questions. I didn't know him all that well yet, but he jumped right in and helped to put my mind at ease about the whole thing.

"Thanks for all you did for me during that time."

"My pleasure."

The game is a blur of people and food and beer as the home team runs away with the lead in the fourth and holds on to win, six to three. My dad is bitter that he has a birthday party for a close friend and can't come back tomorrow to see Austin pitch his final game as an Oriole. We're reluctant to leave the fancy box, but as we file out, I end up between Nona and Abuela.

"Thank you for a lovely day, honey," Nona says. "We're so very proud of you."

"Thank you guys for coming."

"We wouldn't have missed it," Abuela says. "Cried my eyes out when that little girl ran to you."

"I know! Me, too. She's so cute."

"The dad's not exactly hard on the eyes, either," Abuela adds.

"He isn't? I didn't notice."

She pokes me in the ribs. "Liar."

"I hear you're bringing them in tonight," Nona says.

"I am."

"We can't wait to meet them."

I hope I'm not making a huge mistake by bringing Austin and his family to the restaurant, where my eagle-eyed grandmothers are going to take one look at us and see everything I'd like to keep private. But it's too late to change our plans now.

I head home to shower and change and end up taking a nap that leaves me feeling refreshed and ready to see him again. At least I hope I'm ready. After I got home from Carmen's earlier, I finally cleaned up after our dinner from the night before. It was funny to realize how things went from hot to bothered in a matter of minutes, and how dishes and cleaning up became the least of my concerns. I even forgot to worry about having almost-sex with him and then possibly never seeing him again.

I emerge from the shower to find a text from Austin. *Today was incredible. Thank you again for letting us celebrate you. Today has gone by SLOWLY since you dropped me off earlier. Can't wait to see you.*

Can't wait to see you, either. Guess what? Carmen heard you were coming in and insisted on covering my shift, so I can eat with you guys.

That's great news. I didn't like having to share you with others. Is it seven yet?

Almost.

Did I mention I can't wait to see you?!?!

I love that he's as excited about this as I am and doesn't even try to hide it. I drive to the restaurant where we're due to meet, again thinking about his texts and last night and wondering how it'll go with his parents and Everly with us. Will it be awkward or weird or... Once again, my nerves have gotten the better of me, and I'm a bit of a wreck by the time I arrive at Giordino's. I park in the back lot and go in the back door. Aunt Viv is the first one I see, and she greets me with a hug.

"There's the star of the day. Thank you for such a fun afternoon."

"Thanks for coming."

"We wouldn't have missed it. We're so, *so* proud of you. I've got your table ready." She leads me to the Cuban side of the house, to a table that's set back from the action in the main part of the dining room. "Is this okay?"

"It's perfect, Auntie V. Thanks."

"I wanted you to be able to talk and hear yourselves think."

Carmen joins us, wearing the waitstaff uniform of white dress shirt, black skirt and black apron that I haven't seen very often on her since she moved in with Jason. Other than occasionally filling in for a sick waitress or waiter, she hasn't worked at the restaurant for a while now.

"Thanks again for this," I tell her.

"I'm happy to do it, and Jason is glad to have an excuse to come in for dinner. Dad's going to give him more bartending lessons."

"In case neurosurgery doesn't work out for him?" I ask, amused.

"Dad tells him it's good to have a backup plan."

My witty retort dies on my tongue when I see Austin coming toward me, tall, impossibly handsome, smiling at me and carrying Everly, who has her curly blond hair in pigtails. She's wearing a pretty yellow dress, and the sight of her backpack dangling from Austin's fingers is just so sweet. His parents are behind him as Abuela leads them to the table.

Somehow, I manage to introduce them to Viv, Carmen and Abuela without tripping over my words or making a fool of myself.

I can feel Austin's eyes on me the whole time we're talking to the others. Viv and Carmen make a big fuss over Everly, who seems to eat up the attention. And when it's time to be seated, I love that Austin arranges things so he's next to me in the booth, his leg pressed against mine.

And when I feel the heat of his hand on my leg, it's all I can do to hide my reaction from the others.

This is going to be a very *long* dinner.

CHAPTER 11

AUSTIN

*M*y parents adore her. I can tell by the way they're completely themselves around her, but that's Maria for you. It's impossible to be anything other than genuine with her. Ev likes her, too, and sits with Maria for a long time, coloring with the placemat and crayons Maria's Nona brought over.

Everly loves to color, and Maria is super patient with her, giving her undivided attention that impresses my parents—and me. Who am I kidding? Anyone who is all about my daughter has my attention, but Maria already had it. Seeing her with Ev only makes me like her more than I already do.

After a delicious meal, Everly curls up in Maria's lap with her thumb in her mouth, a sure sign that she's winding down for the day. I desperately want some time alone with Maria, but I'm not sure that's going to happen tonight.

I'm pitching the one o'clock game tomorrow, and I need to sleep, especially after hardly sleeping last night. But I'm wired from sitting next to her for hours and having to behave myself.

I'm pretty sure my parents are on to me, though. I've gotten a couple of looks from each of them that lets me know I'm doing a shit job of hiding my over-the-top attraction to the woman who saved my daughter's life.

"We can take Ev back to the hotel if you want to hang out for a bit, Austin," Mom says.

Have I mentioned that my mom is the best?

"Um, sure, that'd be great, if you don't mind."

"We don't mind," Dad says. "It's been a long day with the early flight."

"Thanks again for being here," I tell them.

"We wouldn't have missed it for anything," Mom says as she reloads the backpack we brought with a few toys and books to keep Everly entertained during dinner. Turns out we didn't need most of what we brought because Everly has been entertained mostly by Maria. "This has been a lovely evening, Maria. Your family is delightful, and the food was outstanding."

"I'm so glad you enjoyed it."

Her uncle wanted to treat us, but I insisted on paying—and I leave Carmen a huge tip.

I take Everly from Maria and follow her out of the booth, my daughter snuggled into me the way she does when she's ready to sleep. She'll go down easy tonight after the long busy day with no nap.

My mom orders up an Uber with a car seat, and while we wait, we chat with Nona, Abuela, Vincent and Vivian.

Carmen comes over with a man she introduces to us as her fiancé, Jason Northrup. "My dad would love a picture with you for the wall, Austin, but he won't ask, so I'm asking for him," Carmen says.

"Of course. I'd be happy to." I transfer Everly to my dad and pose for the picture with Vincent and Vivian.

"Thanks so much." Vincent shakes my hand. "Let us know any time you're back in town. I'll always have a table for you."

"I'll definitely be back. You've ruined me for anywhere else."

When the car my mom ordered arrives, Maria and I walk them out. I load Everly into the car seat, making sure she's securely belted in. I kiss her forehead and hug both my parents.

"Thank you for such a wonderful day, Austin," Mom says. Then she hugs Maria for a long time. "You're family to us. Forever."

I can see that Maria is overwhelmed by what my mom said. "It was such a pleasure to meet you both."

She hugs Dad, too.

"We'll see you at the game tomorrow," Dad says.

"See you then."

I've arranged for them to sit together tomorrow. My parents and Everly will be flying back to Baltimore tomorrow night while I stay for Monday's final game of the season.

We wave as they drive off in the Uber.

"They're great," Maria says.

"They are. I got very lucky, especially when they ditched their whole lives to move to Baltimore after everything went down with Kasey. I don't know what I'd do without them."

I take a step toward her, needing to hold her after this endless day. As I put my arms around her, the tension I've carried with me since I left her earlier disappears, and there's only her. "They loved you."

"I saved their granddaughter's life. They have to love me."

"Not just because of that. They loved *you*."

We stand on the sidewalk, hugging each other for a long time.

"You want to get out of here?"

"And do what?" she asks.

"Anything you want."

"Don't you have to pitch tomorrow?"

"Yep."

"So you have to be back at the hotel pretty soon, then, right?"

"Not until midnight. So we've got two and a half hours."

"Are you allowed to have guests at the hotel?"

"Not really, but I don't think anyone will hold me to it at this point."

"You need to win tomorrow, so we probably shouldn't do anything to mess with that."

"Being with you will ensure a win."

She pulls back, her expression skeptical. "How do you figure?"

"I get a natural high from being with you, and I'll take that with me to the mound tomorrow. I'll be on fire after spending this time with you."

"That's a lot of pressure to put on me."

I shrug, feeling shameless. "If you want me to win tomorrow, you need to come with me and do all you can to make it happen."

She smiles as she rolls her eyes. "Does that actually work for you?"

With my hands on her shoulders, I look her dead in the eye. "I've never used that line before."

"If you say so."

"I swear! Come with me. I need more time with you."

"All right. As long as you promise you'll sleep when I tell you to."

"I'll do whatever you tell me to. I promise."

She takes my hand and gives a subtle tug, and I follow her to her car in the back lot. As she drives me to the downtown hotel, I hold her hand between both of mine.

"You were great with Ev at dinner."

"She's sweet and so well behaved. A lot of times, kids want to run around in restaurants, which is tough on the waitstaff. I'm always afraid I'm going to drop scalding-hot food on them."

"We've been taking her out to eat since she was a baby. She knows the rules by now."

"You'd never know she'd been sick to look at her now."

"I try not to think of the images of her bald and sick and bruised from all the needles. It was a horror show."

"I can't imagine what you all went through."

"It's in the past now, or so I hope. We still have to do blood work every three months for the next few years. I try not to think about the possibility that it could come back."

"I'm sure that's the worst kind of fear."

"It's horrible. They say she won't be officially cured for five years. That's a long-ass time to worry about it coming back."

"I'm sorry you have to worry about that."

"It's a small price to pay to have her healthy again. Her being sick changed me in every possible way. Everything is different now."

"How do you mean?"

"Before, I felt like I was sort of bulletproof, you know? Other than the thing with Kasey, I'd had a pretty easy go of it. Things tended to work out for me. All I ever wanted to do was play baseball, and that happened—and it was even better than I ever could've hoped for. Even if the team wasn't winning, I was kicking ass. I won the Cy Young three times, was American League MVP a couple of times... And then it all went to shit when Ev got sick and I was forced to confront the fact that none of that other stuff matters at all. The only thing that matters is that the people we love are healthy and safe."

"The other stuff matters, too, Austin. It's okay to be proud of your career."

"I am, but I don't care about it the same way I used to. Everly's illness was a huge wake-up call, and it realigned my priorities. I know what's really important now, and in case you're wondering, you're at the very top of the list."

"I'm not sure what to think of that."

"What do you mean?"

"Well, this weekend has been incredible, but nothing has

really changed since the night we talked when you were in Detroit."

"*Everything* has changed."

"How so?"

"I met you, I kissed you, I slept with you in my arms. You're all I can think about."

"Austin..."

"I know what you're thinking, and trust me, I'm thinking all the same things. But I want you in my life, Maria, and I refuse to believe that two reasonably intelligent people can't figure out a way to make this work, if it's what we both want."

She has no reply to that, but I can tell by the set of her jaw that she's thinking about what I said.

At the hotel, we valet-park her car and walk inside together. I really, really don't want to run into anyone from my team when I have so little time with her. We get lucky in the lobby and in the elevator. But when the doors open on the sixth floor, Santiago is standing there. He takes one look at me and Maria, and in a matter of seconds, he puts together what's been going on with me.

"Maria, this is Dante Santiago. Dante, this is Maria."

"So nice to meet the woman who saved little Everly's life," he says when he shakes her hand.

"Thank you. Nice to meet you, too."

"I, ah, was just going to get a beer." Santiago steps onto the elevator. "I'll see you in the morning, AJ."

"Later."

I walk with her to my room at the end of the hallway and send her in ahead of me, thankful we didn't encounter anyone else on the way in.

"Will he tell everyone you brought me here?"

"No, he won't. He's my best friend on the team."

She walks over to look out the window. "Oh, well, I guess that's good."

I follow her, placing my hands on her shoulders, which feel tense. "I don't care if anyone knows you're here, Maria." I kiss the top of her head. "Tell me what you're thinking."

"My thoughts are all over the place."

"I can help you organize them."

She laughs. "No, you can't. You're the reason they're jumbled in the first place."

I gently turn her to face me. "We're going to figure this out. Maybe not today or tomorrow, but we *will* figure it out. If you want to be with me the way I want to be with you, then we will find a way."

"I do want to be with you—"

Before she can qualify that statement or add a *but*, I kiss her the way I've been dying to since I left her this morning.

It takes a second, but she kisses me back, and the same intense desire that erupted between us last night is back again, burning even brighter than it did then, if that's possible. I want this woman in a way I've never wanted anyone before, with every part of me. Mind, body and soul. She can have it all.

We end up on the bed, arms and legs intertwined, our kisses as hot and crazed as they were last night and into this morning. My lips actually hurt from last night, and I wonder if hers do, too. Easing back from the kiss, I gaze down at her gorgeous face and kiss-swollen lips.

"Do your lips hurt from last night?"

"A little. Do yours?"

"Uh-huh." I kiss her more gently this time, sliding my lips over hers in the sweetest, softest of caresses. It sends a shiver through me as I try to contain my desperate need for her. "I have to pitch tomorrow, so I need to take it easy tonight," I tell her between kisses. "But tomorrow night... Tomorrow, I want to see you after the game and be with you. Can we do that?"

She nods, but I still see the hint of hesitancy in her eyes.

"I promise you, we'll work this out, and everything will be

okay." As I hold her close to me and breathe in the scent that drives me so crazy, I really hope that's a promise I can keep.

MARIA

I didn't intend to spend the night with Austin, but we fell asleep at some point, and when I woke up, it was morning and he was gone.

I find a note on his pillow. *Morning, beautiful. I had to leave early, but feel free to stay as long as you like, have room service, relax and enjoy. I'll see you after the game. Love, Austin.*

Usually, I'd be getting ready to head for Sunday brunch at the restaurant, but I'm going to skip it this week so I can go home, shower and change before the game. I text Carmen to let her know I won't be there.

I'll make excuses for you, she replies. *Did you hang out with Austin again last night?*

Yeah, I ended up sleeping at his hotel.

And???

Kissing and snuggling and other good stuff, but he's pitching today, so we crashed early.

And he has one more night in town?

Two.

My phone rings, and I take the call from my cousin.

"How're you doing?"

"I have no idea. I've been acting all weekend like I have nothing to worry about, and he's so sure we'll figure something out, but I just don't know what the hell I'm doing in his hotel room."

"You like him, Mari, and he's crazy about you. We all saw that last night."

"What did you see?"

"Everything you see. He's fantastic, a wonderful father and not exactly hard on the eyes. And speaking of eyes, he never takes his off you."

"You noticed all that, huh?"

"Yep."

"I like him more than I ever liked Scott."

"Of course you do. He's a million times the man Scott was, and you're smart enough to realize that."

"I just wish it wasn't so complicated."

"I hate to tell you, pal, but stuff like this is always complicated because it matters. *He* matters to you, or you wouldn't be so undone by the complications."

"I try to picture myself chucking my whole life for a man, even one I like as much as I like Austin, and I just don't see it."

"That's because the one time you took a chance on a guy, he let you down big-time. Austin isn't like that. He's been screwed over by a woman. He knows what that feels like, and he's not about to do something like that to you, especially in light of what you did for his daughter. I think you're safe with this guy, Mari."

"I'm starting to think so, too."

"Then you just have to relax and let it happen."

"I want to."

"Do it. You won't regret it."

"How do you know that?"

"Well, I don't know for sure, but I have a good feeling about you two. And so do you. From the first time you ever talked to him, you said it was different with him. You should put some faith in that. You connected with him long before you ever met him. What does that tell you?"

"It tells me he's special, and I'm being silly for being worried about things that don't matter."

"That's my girl. Enjoy the ride. Let it take you where you're meant to go. I think all the time about what I would've missed if I hadn't taken a chance on Jason, even when everything was a mess in his life. Look at what I would've missed."

She makes a good point. "I never expected any of this."

"Do you think I expected to meet my second chance at love when he pulled up to the hospital in a black Porsche with a bottle blonde riding shotgun?"

I laugh at the way she describes her first meeting with Jason. "Nope."

"You never know how it's going to happen. The secret to success is being smart enough to know a good thing when you have it."

"I hear you, oh wise one. I'm trying to chill and enjoy it and not think about him leaving."

"He's no fool. He'll be back."

"I guess we'll see."

"When I look back at everything with Jason, I wish I'd been more able to enjoy the ride rather than worrying about all the obstacles. They work themselves out when something is meant to be. Remember that."

"I will. Thanks for this, Car. It helps."

"Have fun at the game."

"I'm looking forward to watching him pitch."

"I'll be watching on TV after brunch. Text me if you need me."

"I will."

"Oh, and I'm sending you last night's take by Venmo. We had a good night."

"Thank you again for doing that. I really appreciate it."

"It was fun to see everyone. I'll talk to you later."

As my phone chimes with a payment for three hundred and twenty dollars from Carmen, I realize I also need to update my sister on everything that's happened this weekend so she won't feel left out. I decide to call her when I'm in the car. As I leave Austin's room, I check the corridor and don't see anyone out there—thankfully. I don't want his teammates to catch me leaving his room after having spent the night.

I make a clean escape and am waiting for my car at the valet stand when my mom calls.

"Maria! You're on national TV!"

"What?"

"The ceremony at the game! They showed it on the Sunday *Today* show!"

"Oh. Wow." I'm not sure how I'm supposed to feel about our story going national.

"You look good on TV, sweetheart. And that Austin Jacobs is one handsome man."

I couldn't agree more.

"His little girl is so cute," Mom says without taking a breath. "I heard you were at the restaurant with him and his parents last night. How was that?"

"We had a nice time."

"You can tell me all about it at brunch."

"I'm skipping brunch today. I'm going to the game."

"Oh, all right. Well, I'm sorry I won't get to see you today."

"Dee is calling. I'm going to grab it. Talk to you later."

"Love you."

"You, too." I take the call from Dee, who's screaming.

"You're on the *Today* show!"

"I heard. Mom just called me."

"Holy smoking-hot baseball player, Batman!"

I smile at my sister's description of Austin. "You noticed that, huh?"

"You'd better start talking right now. I talked to Car yesterday, and she deflected, which means there's stuff to tell."

I spend the first part of my ride home filling my sister in on what's transpired since Austin arrived in Miami.

"Whoa," she says when I finish with the note he left me this morning, which is now tucked into my purse. "I love this so hard."

"Easy, cowgirl. It's early days yet."

"No, it isn't. You've been crazy about this guy from the first time you ever heard from him."

I can't deny that, so I don't bother to try. "I'm just trying to maintain a semblance of sanity while Car is telling me to go all in."

"I can see both sides of that, for sure. But damn, it's got to be exciting."

"It is."

"Speaking of excitement, Marcus's sister called me yesterday. Apparently, the skank left him." We have no idea if Marcus's ex is a skank or not. We only call her that because she's not Dee. And yes, we know that's wildly unfair, but the name has stuck.

"No way! When did that happen?"

"A week or so ago. Bianca said he hasn't left his house since. He's been calling out to work and is a hot mess. She asked me to talk to him."

"Come on. No way. How is that your problem?"

"I think she's feeling desperate since she's never seen him go off the deep end this way."

"It's not your problem, Dee. Tell me you know that."

"I do," she says with a sigh. "What does it say about me that I still love him so much that I hurt because he does?"

"I'm sorry you're hurting for him. Text him if you must, but don't get sucked in. It took you so long to get over him. I don't want you going backward."

"I hear you."

"I've got to run. I'm going to the game today. Austin is starting for the O's for the last time. He's a free agent after this season."

"That's exciting. He's going to cash in."

"I suppose so." Of course, I already know he's got to be worth millions after six years in the majors, but free agency is next-level money. I can't think about that. It's too much on top of a lot. "Talk to you later? And keep me posted on what's up with Marcus."

"I will. Love you."

"Love you, too." The reminder of Dee's situation with Marcus is a cold dose of reality for me as I get more involved with Austin. Long-distance relationships are almost always a difficult mess, and that's exactly what I'm setting myself up for with him. Even knowing the potential for disaster, I can't seem to stop myself where he's concerned.

I pull into my driveway and dash up the stairs to my place, where I rush through a shower and blow dry. I can't wait to watch Austin pitch, and I'm excited to see Everly and his parents again, too.

If I've lost all perspective in this out-of-control situation, well, I'll have plenty of time to rediscover my perspective after he's gone.

CHAPTER 12

AUSTIN

I hated leaving Maria sleeping in my bed, but my agent, Aaron, flew in last night to take this highly unofficial meeting with the Marlins ownership and management. We're at the palatial home of one of the team's owners for a friendly breakfast meeting before today's game.

There are all kinds of rules about how and when we can talk to the teams who've shown an interest in me, and this conversation is so far "off the record" as to have not happened. I'm sitting back and letting Aaron do the talking, which gives me the chance to think about Maria and our night together.

It's crazy how much of my awake time lately is devoted to thoughts of her, and how badly I want to spend more time with her. After today, my season is over. The team has one more game in Miami tomorrow, but I'm done, and I have the next few months "off." Other than daily workouts and pitching practice, I can do whatever I want.

And what I want is to be with Maria—and my daughter.

How can I make that happen? Adrenaline speeds through my system as the idea takes shape.

"AJ," the team owner says, "we were surprised but happy to hear of your potential interest in playing in Miami, and we're looking forward to talking to you boys this winter."

"Thanks for considering me."

"I gotta be honest," the manager says. "I was surprised to hear we were in the running."

"The climate here agrees with me." We can't talk details or specifics or anything other than things like the weather, which is spectacular. It's getting chilly in Baltimore, but not here in Miami, where the sun is bright and warm for most of the year. I could get used to that.

Aaron still isn't sure what the hell we're even doing at this meeting, but that's okay. He doesn't need to know why I'm considering Miami. Besides, it's a long shot at best. A lot of things have to fall into place for me to end up here, and I don't want to get up my hopes—or Maria's—until we're able to talk specifics with the various teams in the running. I'd be an absolute fool to accept a less-than-ideal contract so I can be closer to her.

Things are a very long way from settled, but for the immediate future, I can do whatever the hell I want. And what I want is her.

After the meeting, Aaron drives me to the ballpark. "I wish you'd tell me what the fuck this is all about with Miami."

"It's about covering all the bases."

"That's bullshit. Tell me the fucking truth, will you?"

Because he's always been straight with me, I decide to give him the same courtesy. "There's a woman. She lives here."

"The bone marrow donor?"

"Yeah."

"Seriously?"

"Dead seriously."

"Didn't you just meet her this weekend?"

"In person, but we've been talking for weeks."

Aaron doesn't say anything as he processes that information. At nearly forty, my agent is one of the sharpest people I know. He's been my friend, advocate and sometimes my savior during my MLB career. When Ev was sick, he called in his considerable army of contacts to connect me with some of the best doctors in the world and was tireless in his efforts to help me in any way he could.

He's got dark hair going gray around the edges and is wearing aviator sunglasses over shrewd dark eyes that don't miss a trick.

I have no doubt he's got something to say, and when we park in the players' lot at the ballfield, he shuts off the engine of his rental car and turns to me. "I want you to know... Everly's illness was a fucking nightmare for me, and she's not even my kid. I can't imagine what it was like for you. I admire the hell out of the way you handled it, on and off the field."

He's never said any of this to me before. "Thanks, man. You were a rock for me through it all."

"I also understand completely why you'd feel an attachment to the woman who saved your child's life."

What I feel for Maria goes so far beyond the word *attachment*, but I don't share that with him. He needs to have his say, and I need to listen. I pay him to oversee my career, and he's only doing his job, which is to keep me from doing something epically stupid.

"Of course you feel something for her. Anyone would after what she did for you and your daughter. But, AJ, this is your *moment*. This is what you've worked so hard for. You can't let the deal of a lifetime slip away because of a woman. I like the Marlins. They're a first-class organization. But you, Austin Jacobs, don't need to be second to anyone. You're an *ace*."

"I hear you."

"But?"

"But nothing. I hear what you're saying, and I don't disagree."

He pulls off his sunglasses and turns his formidable stare on me. That stare has helped him make a shit-ton of money for his clients, including me. "What aren't you saying?"

"Nothing. I hear you, I agree with you, and my mind is wide open to all the many possibilities that we'll encounter this off-season. I simply want to consider Miami as one of the possibilities. That's all."

"That's not all. What are you up to?"

"Honestly, Aaron," I say, laughing. "You're far too suspicious. I'm not up to anything."

"I understand why your head is turned around by her, AJ. She's a beautiful woman who did the most incredible thing for you and Everly."

You don't know the half of who she is.

"Tell me you aren't going to base the most important decision of your life on a woman you barely know."

I stare out the window at the players' entrance to the ballpark.

"AJ."

Glancing at him, I smile. "I'm keeping all my options wide open. Including Miami." I reach over to shake his hand. "Thanks for coming down for the meeting."

He shakes my hand, but I can tell he's got more he wants to say. A lot more. But I get out of the car and head inside to prepare for my start. That's what I need to be focused on today. I'll have time after the game to figure out what's next.

MARIA

Austin's parents greet me warmly when I join them in yet another VIP section near the third-base line. We have a perfect view of the mound, which is the only thing any of us want to see today. Everly lets out a happy squeal when she sees me, and Austin's dad hands her over to me.

I'm moved by the greeting as I take her into my arms and kiss her chubby cheek. "Hi, pumpkin. How're you today?"

"Dada play."

"That's right. Dada's pitching today. Are you excited to watch him?"

Everly nods, making her blond curls bob adorably. She's wearing a Baltimore Orioles sun hat and a tiny jersey with *Jacobs* on the back. She settles on my lap and stays there through the top of the first while the Orioles are at bat.

She lets out a squeal when Austin takes the field for the bottom of the first. "Dada!"

"There he is," Deidre says, standing to clap for her son.

He finds us in the stands and blows a kiss to Everly.

She blows one back, and I'm slayed by their cuteness.

Everly wants to sit on her grandpa's shoulders to watch Austin pitch, so I pass her back to him and give Austin my full attention. I love watching his intense concentration, the silent communication with his teammates and the way he uses his entire body to power his fastball. Even though I'm a huge Marlins fan, I find his domination over the Marlins hitters sexy as hell.

In the seventh inning, the O's are up five to two, when the manager comes to the mound to pull Austin from the game.

As he leaves the field, probably for the last time in a Baltimore uniform, the Orioles fans in the crowd give him a warm ovation that he acknowledges with a tip of his cap and a smile that seems directed right at me.

On the way into the dugout, he blows a kiss to Everly.

"Dada!"

"He's working for a little while longer," Deidre tells her granddaughter. "And then we can see him."

That seems to pacify Everly, who decides she wants to sit with me again. First, her grandmother insists on applying more sunscreen, and then she can come sit with me. As I hold Everly in my arms, it occurs to me all over again that this child is alive today because of me and the miracles of modern medicine.

To look at her now, you'd never know that she was so terribly ill just over a year ago. As I hold her sturdy little body in my arms, I pray that she'll continue to grow and thrive and that her remission will hold indefinitely. The thought of the disease coming back is terrifying to me, and I only just met her. How in the world do Austin and his family cope with that possibility?

"Tomorrow's supposed to be a total rainout," Jeff says after scrolling through his phone. "The game's canceled, and this'll be the season ender for both teams." A groan goes through the crowd as the news hits about tomorrow's game being canceled.

I immediately wonder if that means Austin will leave tonight rather than Tuesday morning. And why does the thought of him going sooner make me feel me so flattened? *Because you knew he was here for only the weekend, and you let yourself get caught up in the craziness. And now you're going to pay for that when he leaves and you're right back where you started—alone and falling for a man who doesn't live here and probably never will.*

I watch the last two innings of the game, making conversation with Deidre and Jeff and helping to keep Everly entertained, while trying to hide my turmoil from them. All Everly wants is to see Dada, and we must explain to her a hundred times that Dada is still working. She can't see him on the field, so she doesn't like that explanation.

By the time the game ends with a win for Austin and the O's, we're all ready to get out of there.

"We're going to get this cranky girl back to the hotel to finish packing before our flight," Deidre says. "It's been so lovely to meet you and spend this time with you, Maria. I hope we'll see you again sometime."

I hug her. "I hope so, too."

Jeff is holding Everly, so I give her a kiss on the cheek. "Be a good girl for Gamma and Pop," I tell her.

She reaches for me, so I take her from Jeff and give her a hug. "Take care, sweet girl."

I hand her back to her grandfather, wondering if I'll ever see any of them again. We walk out of the stadium together and go our separate ways. Everly waves to me until I'm out of sight. I navigate post-game traffic on the way home, my emotions all over the place. I haven't done any of my Sunday stuff, so I take a detour and hit the grocery store to get what I need for lunches this week. When I return home, I change into a T-shirt and leggings and curl up on the sofa to watch the *SportsCenter* break-down of Austin's last outing in an O's uniform, all the while wondering why I feel so heartbroken.

Nothing has really changed, I tell myself, even as I know that everything changed when he came to my home on Friday night and turned my world upside down even more than he already had prior to that.

I can't help but wonder what happens now.

AUSTIN

After the game, we're told that tomorrow's game is canceled. My high from notching a final win for the season quickly becomes a low when I realize the team will be flying back to Baltimore tonight rather than Tuesday morning.

Just that quickly, I make a decision. "Guys, could I have a minute?"

The usual uproar in the locker room that follows a win takes a second to die down. One of the other guys whistles sharply to get the attention of those who didn't hear me.

"Shut up," Santiago says to two of the younger guys. "AJ wants to say something."

I smile at my friend, who rolls his eyes. "Listen, I just wanted to say thank you for six great years in Baltimore. I have no idea what this off-season holds for me, but we all know I probably won't be back with you next year. Even though this is the end of the road for us as a team, I hope you'll all keep in touch. I'll be rooting for you guys from wherever I end up."

I see Mick, the rest of the coaching staff, the trainers, front office people and one of the owners have stepped into the room. I nod at them as I look around at the others, allowing my gaze to land on each of my teammates. "For the rest of my life, I'll never forget the way all of you, your significant others and this organization stepped up for me and my family when my daughter was sick." My voice wavers on the word *daughter*. I need to quit while I'm ahead. "Thank you seems so insignificant, but it's all I've got. That's it. That's what I wanted to say."

After a rousing round of applause, each of the guys hugs me, slaps me on the back, wishes me good luck with free agency and promises to keep in touch. I hug the coaches, trainers, Erica and others from the front office. Mick is the last one left, and he gives me a gruff one-armed pat on the back.

"Thanks for everything, Coach."

"Been a pleasure, AJ."

"I'm gonna hang here for a couple of days, so I won't be on the flight."

"Thanks for letting me know. Talk to Erica if you need the hotel room extended."

"I will. Thanks again, Coach."

"Take care of yourself and your little girl, AJ. We're all pulling for her."

"Means the world to me. I'll definitely be in touch."

The guys file out of the locker room, headed to catch the bus to the hotel, where they'll grab their stuff before continuing to the airport to go home early. By the end of the season, we're all ready to get home to our families and be off the travel grind.

Under normal circumstances, I'd be the first one on the bus, ready to get home.

However, nothing about my circumstances is normal right now. I huff out a laugh at how quickly everything has changed. It took one hour in Maria's presence the other night to upend my plan for the off-season. I toss my equipment bag in the pile to go back to Baltimore and head out to get on the bus for the ride to the hotel. I take the elevator to the suite I reserved for my parents and Everly after it was decided we'd be doing something with Maria at yesterday's game.

Everly lets out a scream when I walk in. "Dada!" She runs across the room and launches herself into my arms, knowing I'll always catch her.

The greeting I get from her every time I come home to wherever she is makes me feel ten feet tall. I scoop her up and lift her over my head, her smile revealing sweet baby teeth. I never gave much thought to how cute baby teeth are until she had them. Every part of her is perfect to me. I give her a squeeze that has her wrapping those pudgy arms around my neck in the stranglehold that tells me I'm home. I love her unreasonably.

"Miss Cranky Pants is all smiles now that Dada is here," Mom says. "She's been a bear since they took you out of the game. She put on quite a show for Maria."

My heart skips a happy beat at the mention of Maria. "My baby isn't a bear." I make a face that has Everly giggling. "Are you a bear, Pooh?"

"No bear."

"The words are coming fast and furious all of a sudden," Mom says.

"Thank goodness for that." Her developmental delays have been a source of grave concern to me and my parents. The doctors haven't been as worried, so we've tried to chill and let her come around to talking on her own time, but we're all thankful that time seems to have finally arrived.

"Is the team heading back to Baltimore tonight, son?" Dad asks.

"Yep."

"What time do you guys fly out?" Mom asks.

"They're leaving around seven thirty."

"You're not going with them?"

"I was thinking Ev and I might hang out here for a few more days."

"And do what?" Mom asks.

"Enjoy the pool and the beach and the time together."

Mom raises a brow the way only a professional mother can do. "And that's *all*?"

As the son of a professional mother, I'm wise enough to know when I'm cornered by the expert. "I'd also like to spend some more time with Maria."

Mom claps her hands and then fist-pumps the air. "*Yes!* I *knew* it!"

I glance at Dad, who shrugs. "You know how your lovely mother can be when she catches the scent of romance with any of her sons."

"I know all too well." Mom *despised* Kasey and never tried to hide it, and that was some kind of fun, let me tell you. That she's so happy I'm staying to spend more time with Maria is a good sign, and one I don't take lightly. It was horrible being involved with someone my mom actively disliked, and that she turned out to be so right about Kasey is another thing that still rankles all these years later. I should've listened to her concerns, but if I had, I wouldn't have Everly. So there is that...

"She's absolutely lovely," Mom says of Maria.

"Is she? I haven't noticed."

"Oh, please, Austin, tell that to someone who doesn't know you the way I do. I told your father last night after dinner that there's something brewing between you two, and you know how much I *love* to be right."

Dad and I share a long-suffering eye roll. My mom had to become scrappy, being the only woman in a family full of men, and she more than holds her own with us.

"Why don't you let us take Everly home with us so you two can have some time alone together?" Mom says.

As much as I'd love to be alone with Maria, I can't do that to Ev after all the time we've spent apart during the season. "Thanks for the offer, but I want to be with Ev, too."

Everly squeezes my neck, which is her way of voicing her approval. "Dada."

"Are you sure?"

I can't bear the thought of being separated from her so soon after the last road trip. "Yeah, I am."

Mom pats my face the way she used to when I was little. "You're a wonderful father, Austin. You make me so proud—on and off the field."

"I love her."

"I know, son."

"Let me ask you this…" I take a deep breath and let it out, hoping they're going to go for my other idea. After all they've done for me and Ev, I'd never remove her from their daily lives for months on end if I can avoid that.

"What's up?" Dad asks.

"What would you guys think of spending the winter here in Miami?"

Mom looks at Dad and then back at me. "Like *move* here?"

"Temporarily. We're going to be moving somewhere by spring. Why not spend the winter in the warm sunshine?"

"Everly's doctors are in Baltimore," Mom reminds me, as if I need the reminder.

"I'm aware of that, but she could have checkups here in consultation with them. We could work something out."

"Is this because of Maria?" Mom asks.

Though my inclination is to keep my private life private, this involves them, too, so I look her in the eye and tell her the truth. "Yes."

She does the clapping thing again, and while I want to be exasperated with her, I feel the same way she does. "I love this *so* much."

"So you'll think about winter in Miami?"

"How do you see this working?" Dad asks.

"I find a house to rent with room for all of us, we drive down and spend the winter." Could it really be that simple? I've got a few months off, they're retired, so why not?

"When did you decide to do this?" Mom asks.

"Uh, over the last couple of days?"

"Since you met Maria in person," Mom says with a knowing nod.

"Something like that." I'm amused by her when I'm normally super resistant to anything that smacks of maternal prying into my love life. But I can't deny that Maria is the reason I'm making a whole new plan for the off-season from the one we had a few short weeks ago. We'd talked about spending part of the winter with my brother Asher in Arizona.

"We promised Ash we'd spend a few weeks with him," Dad reminds Mom.

"We can still do that," Mom says. "It'd help Austin to have us here with him so he can spend time with Maria when Everly is in bed at night."

"I like how you think, Mom."

"Whatever we can do to help you spend more time with that wonderful girl. Have I mentioned that I absolutely *love* her?"

"You might've said something to that effect."

"Dad and I will go home and start packing."

"Just like that?" Dad asks, seeming amused. I knew I wouldn't have to try hard to convince him. He'd love nothing more than to spend the winter playing golf, and he doesn't care where that happens. As long as Everly is part of the package, I figured he'd be on board.

"Just like that," Mom says.

When she makes up her mind about something, there's no point in arguing with her. I love when that works to my advantage. "I know I say it all the time, but you guys really are the best."

"Are you *kidding*? Our friends back in Wisconsin will be green with envy that we're spending the winter in Miami while they're buried under two feet of snow. We appreciate that you made it possible for us to retire early and enjoy this ride with you and Ev." Mom goes up on tiptoes to kiss my cheek. "Does Maria know you're staying or thinking about spending the winter here?"

"Nope." I can't wait to surprise her.

Mom smiles. "I love this. I can't wait to hear how she reacts."

"You and me both."

CHAPTER 13

MARIA

I don't hear from Austin after the game, but I watch the extensive coverage of his twenty-second and final win for the season, including the perfect game in Detroit. I absorb the speculation about where he might end up next year like a crazy stalker.

"My money's on Seattle." The commentator goes into a lengthy explanation about why he feels the Mariners would be the best fit for Austin and how they're likely to make the most lucrative offer. "I'll tell you one thing, Mike. It's a *very good time* to be Austin Jacobs."

"For sure. I hear Vegas is taking odds on where he'll end up in what's sure to be the big story of this off-season."

I'm stunned to see footage of myself on the field from yesterday's ceremony.

"This time last year, things were anything but certain for the ace pitcher. His little girl was battling a life-threatening illness, his career was on hold, and it was anyone's guess as to whether we'd ever see Austin Jacobs take the mound again. Thanks to

Maria Giordino in Miami, Everly Jacobs received a life-saving bone marrow transplant and achieved full remission. Her dad was back to work with a vengeance this season and is a shoo-in for another American League Cy Young Award. We'll be following AJ's story this off-season, and we'll be sure to keep you posted."

I hang on their every word. It's surreal to me that I could have any stake in where he ends up playing next season.

I check my phone, surprised there's still nothing from him.

I think about texting him, but I don't want to bother him while he's with his teammates, preparing to return to Baltimore.

Knowing he's on his way out of town leaves me feeling empty and depleted. It's the lowest of lows after the highest of highs. "This is what you get for allowing yourself to be carried away by a man who *doesn't live here*." I get out the leftover salad from Friday night, add some grilled chicken and use the last of the house Italian dressing from my takeout order. Sitting at the counter, I try not to relive the momentous kiss that occurred right here about forty-eight hours ago, but that proves impossible.

I relive that stupendous kiss a thousand times while forcing myself to eat food I don't really want, pushing lettuce around on my plate until it's wilted and inedible. I wash the small amount left down the garage disposal, put the plate in the dishwasher and tear up at the sight of our plates from Friday night still waiting to be run through.

"Now you're going to cry over dirty plates? I'm starting to actively hate you." I turn on the dishwasher, angry-clean the kitchen until it's sparkling and make my lunch for tomorrow. It's time to get my shit together and return to my workweek routine.

I'm on my way to an early bedtime when someone knocks at my door. Figuring it's Carmen coming with wine therapy, I throw open the door and blink a couple of times before my brain catches up with the fact that Austin is there with Everly on his shoulders.

"We were wondering if you know where we can get some ice cream around here."

MARIA

"Wh-what're you doing here? I thought you were gone."

"Nope." He's smiling and clearly pleased with himself because he can tell he's completely shocked me by showing up at my door.

"Rie!" Everly says.

"That's her name for you," he says. "The words are starting to come. Ev, tell Rie what we want for dessert."

"Scream!"

"That's right. What do you say, Rie?"

Could they be any cuter? "I say scream sounds good, and I know just the place." I step back from the doorway. "Come in. I need to change."

"Hey," he says.

I glance at him, trying to ignore the light-headed, breathless way I feel when he's around—and even when he isn't.

"This is okay, right?"

"Of course. I'm thrilled to see you guys. I just thought…"

"I know, and we'll talk about that. After scream."

"Make yourselves at home. I'll be quick." I run into my bedroom and try to figure out what to wear for *scream* with Austin and Everly. I've got folded laundry in the basket that I rifle through, finding shorts, bra and a T-shirt. Once I'm dressed, I go into the bathroom to brush my hair and teeth, put on mascara and lip gloss.

I wish I had another hour to prepare, but they're waiting for me, so I put on flip-flops and rejoin them in the living room.

Austin is wearing a Nike T-shirt and shorts, and to look at

him, you'd never know he's an award-winning professional baseball player. Right in this moment, he's just a dad with a little girl who wants scream.

"Ready when you are."

He picks up Everly and leads the way out of my place.

I'm so rattled, I nearly forget my keys. The last thing I want to do tonight is call my uncle to come let me into my place. I grab the keys, go down the stairs and find Austin buckling Everly into a car seat.

"Where'd you get the car?"

"Rented it earlier."

"Where're your parents?"

He checks his watch. "About to take off for Baltimore."

"So wait… They left, and you…"

After closing Everly's door, he leans in to kiss me. "We stayed."

"Oh."

Grinning, he opens the passenger door and holds it for me. "Madam."

Completely frazzled by this unexpected bonus time with them, I get in the car and put on my seat belt.

He gets in and does the same. "Where to?"

I direct him to Azúcar on 8th Street, which is only a few blocks from my house. We actually could've walked, but I'm so rattled that I never thought to suggest it. "We can park at the restaurant lot and walk from there."

A few minutes later, he pulls in behind Giordino's, and we walk the short distance from there.

"Cute place," he says when he sees Azúcar.

"They have the best scream in Miami."

"You're the boss." Austin, who's got Everly in one arm, places his free hand on my lower back to guide me inside.

"What's your favorite?" he asks when we contemplate the menu.

141

"Café con leche, which is their Cuban coffee and Oreo flavor."

"Yum. That sounds good to me. Ev, what do you feel like? You want to try the s'mores or the birthday cake?"

"Cake!"

"Cake it is." Austin orders for all of us, and when he reaches for his wallet, I take Everly from him as if it's the most natural thing in the world to hold her while he pays.

She comes to me, but she keeps her gaze fixed on him as if she's concerned he might get away.

With cones for us and a cup for Everly, we make our way to a table on the sidewalk. It's a warm early-autumn night, and I'm thrilled to be spending it with them.

Everly is focused on her ice cream as Austin keeps a close eye on her to make sure it doesn't end up all over her.

"I thought you guys were going back to Baltimore tonight."

"The team took off an hour ago, but I decided to hang out here for a bit."

"For how long?"

He shrugs. "Haven't decided yet." Nodding at my melting cone, he says, "Eat your scream."

Everly pipes up. "Rie! Scream!"

I love the name she's given me and how cute she is in a pink-and-yellow-striped shirt with pink shorts and her blond curls in a ponytail.

"Do what the lady tells you, Rie, and eat your scream!"

Everly giggles at the way he mimics her.

I'm captivated by how cute they are together, by the way he mops up the ice cream on her face without missing a beat and by the obvious love they have for each other. They make me want to be part of them, part of what they have with each other. So much for protecting my heart in the face of their crazy cuteness.

"So…" I raise a brow, hoping he will fill in the blanks for me.

"So... I decided to hang in Miami for a while since the season is over, and I can do what I want."

"How long is a while?"

He shrugs as if he hasn't a care in the world, which he probably doesn't since he's on vacation for the next few months. "We haven't decided yet."

Is he being intentionally vague, or is it just my imagination? "What do you guys have planned for your time in Miami?"

"Lots of hotel pool time, right, Ev?"

"Rie! Pool!"

His smile lights up his handsome face and makes him even dreamier than he is when he's not smiling. He is inordinately blessed when it comes to sexiness. And watching him lick that cone is making me wonder what it would be like...

Stop! There's a child present!

"We've been a little concerned about her speech delays," Austin says softly while Everly is fixated on her ice cream. "All of a sudden, it's like a door opened, and the words are coming fast. Pool makes ten new ones today alone."

"That's wonderful."

"Pool, Dada."

"Tomorrow, pumpkin. First we sleep, then we swim."

Everly isn't sure she likes that answer.

"I have a feeling I'm in for some early morning swimming tomorrow. What else should we do while we're here?"

"You should check out the zoo, the Seaquarium, Jungle Island, the children's museum and the Venetian Pool in Coral Gables, which is the pool of pools. You could take a picnic to Crandon Park in Key Biscayne, and of course, I'm partial to Little Havana, but I'm not sure that would hold Everly's attention. Oh, and don't forget the beach."

"That all sounds fun. I wish you could join us."

"Me, too, but alas, some of us still have to work."

"Maybe we could save the picnic and the beach for the weekend if you're free?"

"I'm free other than work on Saturday night and brunch on Sunday, but you guys could come to brunch if you'd like to."

"We'd love to."

"Except..."

"What?"

"My whole family comes to brunch, and if I bring you guys, that's kind of a big 'statement.'"

He looks me in the eye. "I'm fine with that statement if you are."

"I, uh, well..."

Laughter on Austin is the sexiest thing I've ever seen, hands down.

"Dada funny," Everly says.

"Make that eleven words, and it's Rie who's funny, baby."

"Rie funny."

It's official. I'm on cuteness overload. And then Austin tugs a pack of wipes from his pocket and efficiently cleans Everly's hands and face, and I'm just sunk. He's just...

Ugh. I can't. I just can't.

As we walk back to the car, I fall deep into my thoughts, wondering what he's doing here and trying to make sense of him staying after the team left. It's because of me, right? Duh, of course it is, but what does it *mean*?

While he buckles Everly in, I get in the passenger seat and put on my seat belt for the short ride home. What happens now?

Austin drives us back to my place, and far too quickly, we're pulling into my driveway.

I turn to look at Everly. "Thanks for taking me out for scream, Everly."

"Scream! Rie!"

I smile at her. "That's right. Rie loved the scream. Have fun swimming tomorrow."

"Pool!"

I love how every word she says has an exclamation mark at the end. Who am I kidding? I love everything about her. "Sleep tight, sweetie."

Leaving the car running and the AC on low, Austin comes around to open my door and waits for me to get out. He keeps the door open a crack so he can hear Everly.

"Thanks for the scream."

"You're welcome. Any chance you can come to the hotel to hang out for a little while?"

"I have to work in the morning."

"I won't keep you too late. I promise."

I'm so torn. On the one hand, I want every second I can get with him. On the other, I worry what'll happen when he leaves, which he'll do eventually. I'm setting myself up for disaster with every second I spend with him, knowing everything about this is temporary.

Then he tips his head and flashes that irresistible grin that creates the groove in his cheek, and I'm dead. "*Please?* Just come for a short time so we can talk?"

"Okay."

"Give me an hour to get Ev down, and then I'm all yours."

I'll be a wreck tomorrow, but I guess I'll worry about that then.

"Valet-park and give them my room number. I moved to my parents' suite, so it's seven twelve." He kisses my cheek. "I'll see you in a bit."

He waits until I'm inside before he drives off.

I pull out my phone and call Carmen.

"Hey," she says, "what's up?"

"So, um, well… Austin didn't go back to Baltimore with the team."

"What? Shut up! How'd you find out?"

145

"When he and Everly showed up at my door and asked me to go out for ice cream."

"Oh my God! This is *huge!*"

"Calm down, will you?"

I hear her catching Jason up on what's happened. "He stayed in town *for her.*"

"Carmen! Stop. He's only here for a little while longer. Nothing has changed."

"When are you going to see him again?"

"He asked me to come to their hotel after he gets Everly down."

"And you're going, right?"

"For a little while. I have to work in the morning."

"Pack a bag so you can go right to work from there."

"I'm not doing that."

"*Why not?*"

"Because!"

"You can't think of one good reason not to do that."

"His daughter is a good reason. She doesn't need to see me there when she wakes up."

"So be gone when she gets up."

"She's up with the chickens, Car. She's three. I'm not staying there."

"But you *are* going, right?"

"For a little while. I guess."

"I hate that you're so dejected about this major development, Mari. There's no way he'd still be in Miami if he didn't want to spend more time with you. Tell me you know that."

"I do, but… What happens after he spends a few more days here? What then? Every minute I spend with him and Everly, I just get deeper and deeper into this thing, and… I just don't know if I should be."

"Well then, I guess you need to make a decision. If you think Austin could be the one for you, are you willing to do whatever it takes to make it work? At the end of the day, that's what it comes down to. You can do whatever you want to do, Maria. Anything at all. If this is the man you want, go for it. The details —and that's what they are, just *details*—will work themselves out."

"You're like the worst kind of enabler," I tell her, laughing. "You make it seem so simple."

"It is. You care about him and his daughter. Go be with him."

"Okay."

"And pack a bag, you idiot."

Carmen has given me permission to feel all the things, and the feeling I have for him is so big, it takes up every ounce of space inside me.

"Are you okay?"

"I think so. This whole thing is terrifying."

"And exciting. It's that, too, right?"

"Yeah, it is. He's just…"

"He's everything you've ever wanted and then some. Go get him."

"I'm going!"

Carmen laughs. "Good, and then call me tomorrow and let me know how it goes."

"I will. Thanks for talking me down off the ledge."

"That's what I'm here for. Love you."

"Love you, too."

I end the call and go into my room to pack a bag because Carmen told me to. I refuse to delve any deeper into the many reasons why it might be a bad idea. I'm well aware of the myriad reasons. Apparently, I no longer care.

CHAPTER 14

CARMEN

I end the call with Maria and do a happy dance around the master bedroom while Jason watches me from bed.

"Big development in the Maria saga," he says.

"A *huge* development! Austin stayed in Miami after the team left! *He stayed for her!*"

"That is huge."

I throw my arms over my head and add some boogie to my dance. "This is the most exciting thing to happen since you pulled up to my hospital in a black Porsche with a blonde riding shotgun."

He laughs. "As I recall, you didn't think it was exciting at the time. I believe the word you used was *predictable*?"

"We got past that, didn't we?"

"Not until I bailed you out of jail."

I continue my dance on the California-king-size bed. "You're not allowed to talk about *jail*." Somehow, we've managed to keep the fact that I landed in jail *twice* on the day we met from my parents and grandmothers. I plan to keep it that way.

He watches my every move, the way he always does. "I can't help that *jail* will always be part of our story."

I love him madly, passionately, eternally. However... "If you keep talking about that, you're going to slip up in front of my parents and grandmothers one of these days."

"Nah. If it hasn't happened yet..." He holds out a hand to me. "Come down here and bring some of that energy to your fiancé."

I land on the bed and crawl on top of him, loving the way his arms come around me and his lips find mine in a hungry, passionate kiss. It's always like this between us, hot and sexy and fun and so, *so* sweet after the years I spent in the pits of grief after Tony was murdered.

Jason has restored my faith in love and life and happily ever after, but that doesn't mean I don't worry about him every time he leaves the house. I do, and I probably always will after having seen how suddenly the one I love most can be taken from me without warning.

"Why did you just get tense?"

"I didn't."

He massages my shoulders. "Yes, you did."

"I was thinking about how much I love you."

"And that makes you tense?"

"When you love someone as much as I love you, it comes with... concerns about something happening, especially when it's happened before."

"Ah, baby, I don't want you thinking like that."

"I can't help it."

"I only want you thinking about happy things, like our wedding and honeymoon and how much fun we're going to have in Turks, not to mention the rest of our lives."

"That's what I'm mostly thinking about."

"Nothing will happen to me."

"You don't know that, so please don't make promises you can't keep."

"I understand where this is coming from, sweetheart, but I don't want you being worried about me all the time."

"I'm trying to keep it under control, but with the wedding coming soon, I'm a little more anxious than I've been in a while."

"What can I do?"

I snuggle into his embrace, experiencing the same feelings of overwhelming attraction that I've had toward him since the day we met. If anything, it's only grown in the fifteen months we've been together. "This helps. It always helps."

"I'm always happy to hold you, but I want to know if the stress is getting to you. Do you promise to tell me?"

"I will."

"Everything will be okay. Think about Maria and keep doing your happy dance."

"I'm trying. I really am."

MARIA

I make myself watch HGTV for thirty minutes so I won't be tempted to get to the hotel too soon. While I keep my gaze fixed on the TV, I refuse to think about anything other than paint, lighting, tile and cased doorway openings. On the way out, I grab the bag I packed at Carmen's direction and the lunch I made earlier for tomorrow from the fridge and take it with me, hoping there's a fridge in his suite.

There's almost no traffic this time of night, and I get to the hotel ten minutes before my allotted hour is up. I turn over the car to the valet, give him Austin's last name and room number and am looking for a seat in the lobby to kill a few more minutes when my phone chimes with a text.

Ev is down for the count. I'm all yours. He includes his room number.

And yes, my overly involved heart skips a beat at the idea of such an extraordinary man being all mine. I type in a reply. *On the way up.*

He responds with all emojis that convey his happiness.

I'm a silly fool on the road to ruin, but what a way to go. I get off the elevator on the seventh floor and follow the signs to his room. I'm about halfway down the hallway when I see Austin standing in the doorway waiting for me.

His smile lights up my world, and I run to him, not caring for a second about the many ways it could go bad, not when he's right here with me and nothing has ever felt better than being with him.

He catches me, wrapping me up in his strong arms, and holds on tight. "There you are."

"Here I am."

Without letting me go, Austin walks us into the room, and the door closes with a loud clunk. He presses me against the wall and kisses me with the same desperation I feel for him. My bag drops to the floor, and my arms end up around his neck, my fingers buried in his hair as my tongue tangles with his.

I lose all sense of time and place and anything that isn't him and me and us and *this*, this amazing thing between us that only seems to become more so every time we're together. But then I remember the things I wanted to tell him. I slowly withdraw from the kiss but keep my lips close to his.

"I brought a bag with my work stuff."

"That's the best news I've had all day."

"Better than winning your twenty-second game of the season?"

"Way better."

"Can I put my lunch for tomorrow in your fridge?"

"My fridge is your fridge, and in case I forget to tell you, you're super cute."

"Because I make my lunch?"

"That and every single other thing about you."

I'm already completely crazy about this guy, and then he has to go and be sweet, too. "I have conditions."

He kisses my neck, and it's all I can do not to whimper from the sensations that spiral through me like an out-of-control fever. "Name them."

"I don't want Everly to see us together in bed."

"She won't. She's got her own room, and she won't stir until about six. I'll move to the sofa before she gets up."

"Okay."

"What else?"

"I want to know how long you're going to be here and what we're doing."

"I'm actually thinking about wintering in Florida this off-season."

I pull back from him to determine if he's being serious. He is. *"Really?"* My voice sounds squeaky and high-pitched.

He grins at my reaction. "Uh-huh."

"Because of me?"

"No, because of the sunshine and palm trees." He kisses my nose. "Of course because of you." Taking my hand, he bends to grab my bag and then leads me into the spacious suite. "Have a seat."

As I sit on the sofa, curling my legs under me, I have so many questions but can't seem to organize my thoughts to ask any of them. He's knocked the wind right out of me with this news.

Austin stashes my lunch in the fridge, brings me a glass of Chardonnay and a beer for himself and sits next to me, turning to face me. With his free hand, he plays with my hair as he stares at my lips. "What do you want to know?"

"Everything. What you're thinking and feeling and planning."

"After the game today, when we found out tomorrow's game was canceled, I felt sick knowing we'd be leaving for Baltimore a whole day and a half earlier than planned. But then it occurred to me that I didn't have to go. Our season is over as of today. I can do whatever I want, and what I want is to be with you—and Everly. So I told Coach I was going to hang here for a bit, said my goodbyes to the guys and here I am, right where I want to be. With you, and my little girl sleeping close by."

"And you, you're going to stay, for the winter..."

"If you want me to."

"Of course I do. I'm just... What about after that?"

"I honestly don't know. I'm keeping all my options open, and right now, it's a waiting game. But here's what I'm thinking... We spend the winter together, as much as we can, dating, hanging out with Ev, doing our thing. And in the spring, we see where we're at and what we want to do."

"You make it sound so simple, like I could spend the winter with you and Everly, and then you guys could leave to go some-where else like it's no big deal."

He cups my face, caressing my skin with his thumb. "It's already a big deal for me. Why do you think I'm still here?"

"I can't believe you stayed."

Leaning in as he smiles, he says, "You can't? Really?" He takes my glass from me, puts it on the table next to his beer bottle and kisses me again. Before I know what's what, we're wrapped up in each other, straining for more. "I know there's so much up in the air and so many things we don't know, but one thing I do know is how much I want you in my life."

"I want that, too. I want you and Everly."

"Come to bed with me, Maria. Be with me."

Recalling what Carmen said about details and how they

work themselves out, I give a subtle but definitive nod. "I assume you have what we need for this?"

Smiling, he says, "You assume correctly." He stands, gives me a hand up and leads me toward two closed doors, pointing to the one on the right. "I want to look in on Ev real quick."

"Could I come with you?"

"Of course." He releases my hand, and we tiptoe into Everly's room where she's sound asleep and cute as a bug in a pink nightgown. Austin pulls the covers up over her shoulder and kisses the top of her head.

I gesture toward her, silently asking if I can kiss her, too.

He steps aside to let me in.

I kiss her forehead and breathe in the baby shampoo scent of her hair. And then I follow her father out of the room and into the room next door.

Austin leaves both doors cracked so he can hear Everly.

"What if she wakes up?"

"She usually doesn't."

"But if she does?"

"I'll hear her. Don't worry."

I'm worried about everything, not that I want to spoil this special moment by telling him that.

But he seems to figure that out for himself as he puts his arms around me. "Don't worry about anything, sweet Maria. We're going to take this one day at a time and figure it out. I know it's a lot to ask of you, to come on this ride with me, but you've become one of the most important people in my life, and I want to be with you. Tell me that's what you want, too."

"It is. Of course it is. It's just what happens later that worries me."

"I know, and all I can do is promise you that I'll keep you in the loop as much as I can, and we'll talk about what's going on and figure it out."

"Okay."

"I'm going to try really hard not to disappoint you."

"I'll try really hard not to disappoint you."

"You never could."

"I probably could."

"But you won't. I know that about you already, and the only way I'll disappoint you is if I end up far away from you for months on end. That's the only thing you have to worry about where I'm concerned."

He's telling me, in no uncertain terms, that he'll never cheat on me.

I appreciate that he knows what that means to me. "Same. And I'd never, ever, *ever* leave your child home alone, either."

"I already knew that, but thanks for confirming. Is there anything else you need to know?"

So many things, but he's given me everything I need to feel good about where we are right now. "Not at the moment."

"I have one other thing I want you to know… Since the first time we talked all those months ago, I felt a connection to you that I've never felt for anyone else."

"I felt it, too. I couldn't wait until we could talk freely at the one-year mark. I kept telling myself not to blow it up into a big deal, but it was far too late for those sorts of warnings."

"I thought about you all the time and would think how crazy it was to be so obsessed with someone I'd never actually met. I didn't know your name yet, and I was fixated on you."

"Same. I wondered if the connection was because of what I did for Everly."

"It was at first, but it's about so much more than that now. You know that, right?"

"I think so."

"It is, Maria. Everly brought us together, but everything that's happened since then is about you and me. And all I want is more of that, of us."

"Me, too." I'm completely lost to this man, and even my

concerns about what might happen down the road can't stop me from fully experiencing this moment with him. I reach up to unbutton his shirt.

He stands perfectly still as I follow the trail of buttons down, allowing my fingers to brush against his chest and muscled abdomen. I push the shirt off his shoulders, and he flinches when my hand brushes against his left shoulder.

"Are you sore from pitching?"

"A little. It's fine."

I place a soft kiss on his left shoulder, and he sighs as his arms come around me. "You should ice it."

"I will. Later." He tugs at my T-shirt, and I step back to let him remove it.

I've always been self-conscious about my extravagant curves, as my mother once referred to them, but the hungry way Austin looks at my full breasts contained by the sexiest sheer bra I own fills me with confidence.

"You're so very beautiful, Maria. I'll never forget the night you sent me your photo. The first time I saw your face... I must've stared at that picture for an hour."

"Same. I was instantly attracted. Although, I'm sure half the women in America are attracted to the sexy ballplayer with the sweet little girl."

"I'm only concerned with one of those women. Her opinion is the only one that matters."

"She thinks you're smoking hot."

He laughs even as he seems embarrassed. "Whatever you say."

Now that I'm allowed to, I want to touch him everywhere. I run my hands over the well-inked muscles of his chest, back and arms, being careful of his tender left arm. "What's with all the ink?"

"Do you hate it?"

"Nope. It's actually rather gorgeous."

"I'm glad you think so. I love to draw, and it seemed like a good way to display some of my work."

"So, wait. You *drew* this?"

He nods as I continue to run my hands over him. "You're making me crazy for you."

"Am I?"

His harsh laugh makes me smile. "You know exactly what you're doing to me."

I kiss his chest and arm, making a circle around him to kiss his back, which is as inked and muscled as the front. While I'm back there, I slide my hands over his ass and give it a squeeze, which has him sucking in a sharp deep breath.

I'm not sure where this temptress is coming from, but being with him makes me feel free in a way I never did with Scott or the other two guys I've slept with. When Austin tells me I'm beautiful, I believe him. I remove my bra, press my breasts to his back and reach around to unbutton his shorts, sliding a hand inside the waistband where I encounter the head of his very hard cock.

"Maria… If you keep that up, this is gonna be fast…" He grabs my hand and spins around to kiss me with a ferocity he hasn't shown me before now. There's a desperate neediness to it that makes my knees feel weak. We come down on the bed without breaking the kiss. His hands are on my breasts, mine are in the back of his shorts. I've never wanted anyone or anything the way I want this man who showed me his heart before I ever saw his face.

He pulls back to look at me. "I want you to know, there hasn't been anyone since Ev got sick. I've been such a mess… This is apt to be over before it starts."

I reach up to frame his face with my hands. "You're not a mess."

"I am on the inside."

"No, you're as beautiful on the inside as you are on the outside."

He drops his forehead to lean against mine. "So are you. Beautiful through and through."

After that, there're no more words, only longing and desire so hot, it burns me inside and out as we pull at clothes until we're naked and wrapped around each other.

In the back of my mind, though, is the fact that his daughter is asleep in the next room. "Could we cover up, just in case?"

"Yeah, of course."

We release each other only long enough to get under the covers, and then we come back together in a tangle of limbs and frantic desire. I'm so carried away by him that I can't bother to think about anything other than how badly I want him and this and us.

He breaks the kiss and moves so he's above me, kissing my neck and along my collarbone and then down to the valley between my breasts. "You have no idea how distracted I've been since I saw you Friday night. I've wanted to kiss you everywhere, touch you, hold you, make love to you. I can't believe that was only two days ago. It feels like a lifetime of wanting you."

His heartfelt words bring tears to my eyes. I never imagined finding someone like him and now that I have, I already can't picture my life without him and Everly as part of it.

He draws my nipple into his mouth, tugging and sucking until I'm half out of my mind and nearly tearing the hair out of his head.

"Easy, tiger, I'm not ready to be bald quite yet." He smiles as he kisses his way down the front of me, his lips setting me on fire even before he adds his tongue and fingers between my legs, giving me the fastest orgasm of my life.

I have to bite my lip to keep from screaming as he goes right back and does it again, leaving me a boneless, quivering shell of the person I was when I walked into his room. I've barely begun to recover when I hear the crinkle of the foil wrapper on the condom and open my eyes to watch him roll it on, my mouth watering at the sight of him fully erect for me. I extend my arms to him, encouraging him to come back to me, and then wrap my arms and legs around him as he comes down on top of me. His lips find mine in another frantic kiss that distracts me from the press of his flesh against mine. But only momentarily.

I gasp and move under him, wanting him right now.

"Easy, sweetheart. Nice and easy. I never want to forget a second of this."

I look up at him, and the way he's gazing at me is something I never want to forget as he enters me, arousing me to the point of madness. It's never been like this, but I've also never felt for anyone what I have for him from the beginning.

When he pushes the rest of the way inside me, I again have to hold back the need to scream from the pleasure of it.

Austin brushes his lips against mine. "Hey," he whispers.

I open my eyes to meet his intense gaze. "Hey."

"You feel so good, but I knew you would."

"Mmm, same." We move together like we've been doing this forever. "So good."

"I want you to know something."

"Right now?"

"Right now."

"What?"

"I was more than halfway in love with you before I ever met you."

"I was, too."

"And now..."

I nod, because I feel the same thing, but it's almost too big to put into words.

He gazes into my eyes as he makes love to me, changing me forever in the span of those minutes when our bodies are joined for the first time. It's almost surreal, as if this is happening to someone else and I'm watching.

It shouldn't surprise me that he's fierce and physical and demanding in bed the way he is on the field, and the next orgasm powers through me like a tsunami, touching every part of me, especially the heart that now belongs entirely to him.

"*God*, Maria..." He thrusts into me, his head thrown back, his muscles tense and his body glistening with sweat as he reaches the peak right after me. He's the most beautiful thing I've ever seen, and I already know I'll love him forever.

CHAPTER 15

AUSTIN

*M*y alarm goes off at five a.m., reminding me to move to the sofa before Everly wakes up. My eyes are gritty from a mostly sleepless night, but it was so, so worth it. The last thing I want to do is pull myself away from Maria's warm, naked body, but I promised her I wouldn't let Ev catch us in bed together, and I happen to agree it's too soon for that.

Not that Everly would mind. She loves "Rie" as much as I do. And yes, of course I love her. How could I not? And no, it's not about what she did for Everly, although that's definitely part of it. Like I told her, it's gone so far beyond that. One email at a time, one conversation at a time, one kiss at a time, she's worked her way so deep into my heart that I can't remember what life was like when she wasn't right in the middle of it.

And after last night, all I want is more of the way I feel when she's in my arms. It's the best feeling I've ever had outside of fatherhood.

I kiss her shoulder and leave her to sleep while I drag myself out of bed, find some shorts, close my bedroom door and head for the sofa to crash until Everly wakes up. I come to sometime later, gasping for air as an impish little face giggles at the reaction she gets to plugging my nose. It works every time, and her delighted belly laughter is a great thing to wake up to, even if it's at my expense.

"You think you're so funny, Miss Everly."

"Dada silly."

I gather her into my arms and hold her close to me, breathing in the fresh clean scent of her hair and giving thanks, as I do every day, for her return to good health. The images of her, pale, listless, hairless, bruised from endless needle sticks, will stay with me forever. But at moments like this, I see only the sweet, healthy little girl she is now, and I'm so thankful to the woman sleeping in my bed that it brings tears to my eyes.

I get to have this moment with my baby girl because Maria gave us the ultimate gift. I'll never forget that.

I turn on the TV for Ev, find some cartoons and doze for a bit, until she gets restless wanting breakfast. I order room service for three and ask Everly to sit on the sofa for a minute while I go in to wake Maria at seven thirty. She has to work at nine, but I sense she might want some time to get herself together. Also, I have no idea how long it'll take her to get to work from here.

Sitting on the edge of the mattress, I kiss her cheek. "Time to wake up, Sleeping Beauty."

She groans and burrows deeper into the covers.

"I'm coming in after you."

"So tired."

"I'm sorry."

"You are not."

"No, I'm really not." I nibble on her shoulder. "I ordered breakfast, and it'll be up soon."

"What're we telling Ev?"

"That you came to visit and slept over. She won't think anything of it. Don't worry."

"'Kay."

"Um, Maria? You have to get up."

"Don't wanna."

"Call out sick."

"I *can't*," she says without opening her eyes. "I did that after we broke up."

"We never broke up."

"I tried to break up with you."

"Don't do that again."

Her lips curve into a smile even as her eyes remain closed. "It didn't work out so well the first time."

"Do you have any vacation time?"

"Some."

I kiss a path from her shoulder to her neck. "Why don't you take a few days so we can hang out? You can help me house hunt."

"I'll see if I can do that. I'm off next Friday for Carmen's wedding." She finally opens her eyes. "Would you like to come with me to the wedding?"

"I'd love to."

"My whole family will be there. They'll be all over us…"

"Okay."

"You say that because you have no idea what you're in for."

"I can handle it."

"I'm sure we can bring Everly, too. Carmen won't care. There'll be other kids there."

"I have to go back to Baltimore and pack for this unexpected winter in Miami at some point. I figure we'll drive back down so I'll have my car."

"You're really going to spend the winter in Miami?"

"I really am. Are you sure you still want me?"

She takes my hand and gives it a squeeze. "I'm sure."

I'm ridiculously relieved to hear that. "Good. Now get up."

"Your bedside manner could use some work."

I raise a brow. "Really?"

She giggles. "No, not really. If it was any better, I'd be completely hobbled today rather than only partially hobbled."

"You're hurting?"

"Just a little. But it's the best kind of hurt."

"Dada!"

"Duty calls. Come out when you're ready. I'll tell her you're here."

"Tell me you ordered coffee."

"Of course I did."

"Thank you."

I kiss her cheek and leave her to return to Everly, closing the bedroom door behind me.

Without taking her gaze off the TV, Everly pats the sofa next to her, in charge as usual.

I sit next to her and put my arm around her. "Hey, so last night after you went night-night, Rie came over to visit, and she stayed over."

She looks up at me. "Rie?"

"Yes, she's here, and she's going to have breakfast with us."

"See Rie?"

"In a minute." I pause for a second before I take the plunge. "You like Rie, right?"

Everly nods.

"That's good, honey. I like her, too." I like her so, so much. Last night was just... I don't have the words for what it was like to make love with her—three times—and then sleep with her in my arms. I've had my share of girlfriends and hookups and the actual "relationship" with Kasey that ended in dramatic fashion with threats and lawyers and enough heartache to keep me single forever.

But I've never connected with anyone the way I have with

Maria, and not just in bed. We were fully connected in every other way before we ever got naked together, and that makes our relationship even more meaningful to me.

Room service delivers our breakfast, and as I wait for Maria to emerge from the bedroom, I find myself breathless with anticipation, knowing she's in there and coming out to join us any second.

I set Everly up at the table with oatmeal and orange juice and pour a cup of coffee for myself. Coffee has never tasted better than it does this morning, nor has the bacon I steal from under one of the catering covers.

"Dada, eat!"

I love how all her sentences end with exclamation marks now that she's finding her voice. "I will, sweetheart. I'm just waiting for Rie."

"Rie! Scream!"

It's all I can do not to crack up. I fear she's going to be dreadfully spoiled because I find her so damned cute, and I'm always so painfully aware of how close I came to losing her. "No scream before dinner."

She takes another bite of oatmeal as she thinks about that. "Why?"

As I celebrate yet another new word, I choose my own words carefully. "Because ice cream is dessert, and we have dessert after dinner."

"Why?"

"Because that's the rule."

Her little brows come together as she ponders the word *rule*.

"And rules are things little girls have to follow so they can grow up to be big and strong."

Because she's seen me lifting weights before, she makes her muscle arms.

Laughing, I tell her, "That's right."

When Maria finally joins us, I'm using a napkin to wipe the

oatmeal off Everly's face. Maria is wearing pink scrubs and white Nikes. Scrubs have never looked so sexy.

"Rie! Scream!" Everly squiggles free of me and runs to Maria.

She picks her up and gives her a loud smooch on the cheek that has Everly giggling.

My heart is on overload watching the two of them together —one with dark hair and eyes, the other blond and blue-eyed, connected to each other forever through a life-saving gift.

"Scream, Rie!"

Maria laughs and tweaks Everly's nose. "No scream until after dinner, pumpkin."

"Rules," Everly says, frowning.

"That's two new words today so far."

"What was the other one?"

"Why."

"Oh yikes."

"Right?" I take Everly from Maria, return her to her seat to finish her breakfast and pour coffee for Maria.

She looks tired, but happy. I hope she is, anyway. I want her to be as happy as I am today after a night that changed both our lives, or so I hope.

"How do you want it?" I ask about the coffee.

"Black is good."

"That'll put hair on your chest."

"Hasn't yet," she says with a meaningful look that takes me right back to having my face buried between her gorgeous breasts.

"I might need to double-check that again later."

Her face flushes as she drinks her coffee and tries not to look at me.

Everly gets up and goes running into her room.

I hold a chair for Maria. "Have a scat."

"Thank you."

"I wasn't sure what you like, so I got a little of everything."

"I feel like Vivian in *Pretty Woman*."

I'm not sure what she means. "Wasn't she a hooker?"

She laughs. "Edward ordered everything the next morning because he didn't know what she liked."

"The only thing you have in common with her is that you're a very pretty woman." Seeing that Everly is occupied in her room, I lean in to kiss Maria. "Very, *very* pretty."

"I'm looking rough this morning. Someone messed with my sleep last night."

"If this is you looking rough, I'm going to mess with your sleep every night."

"You can't. I'll be a monster."

"That's not possible."

"Ask my family what I'm like without sleep."

"I'll do that first chance I get. Better yet, I'll keep you nice and sleep-deprived so I can find out for myself."

Everly comes running out of her room with her bathing suit on—backward—and her swim floats hanging around her neck. She looks like a mermaid after a bender as Maria and I laugh.

"Dada, *swim!*"

Maria's eyes dance with amusement over the rim of her coffee mug. "I bet I know what you're doing this morning."

"Probably all day, which is fine. Whatever my monkey wants to do is good with me. Dada on vacation!"

"B'cation!"

"I'm going to have to watch every word I say now that my baby is finding her words."

"Word."

"And there're two more." I shake my head, because part of me wants to weep at how relieved I am to see her catching up to other kids her age as we get further out from her illness.

Excited to swim, Everly runs around the big room with her floats and flip-flops in hand.

"I heard a doctor say once that if the words are getting in, eventually they'll come out," Maria says.

"We were told that, too. One of us would tell her to do things, like get her shoes, and she'd come back with shoes— maybe not a matched pair, but they were shoes. The doctor said if she was doing that, eventually she'd say the words. I think it would've happened sooner…" Were it not for her illness, but I don't need to fill in that blank for Maria. She gets it.

"She's doing great, Austin. I know it's so hard not to worry, but she's absolutely perfect."

"Keep telling me that?"

"Any time you need to hear it."

She eats half a cheese-and-bacon omelet and a piece of French toast before gathering her bag and lunch from the fridge to head for work.

I call down to the valet for her car. "Everly, come say bye to Rie. She has to go to work."

"Work!" Everly runs over to hug Maria's legs.

Maria bends to kiss the top of her head. "Have fun swimming with Dada."

"Dada, *swim!*"

"We're gonna swim, Pooh." I want to kiss Maria, but I know she won't do that in front of Everly. "Can we see you for dinner?"

"I think we can make that happen."

"Good."

Everly runs off as I walk Maria to the door, where I steal a kiss. "Have a good day."

"You, too."

"We'll miss you."

"I'll miss you guys."

I kiss her again. "Last night was everything, Maria. Every single thing."

"For me, too."

I raise my hand to caress her face. "Hurry back."

CHAPTER 16

MARIA

I drive to work in a fog of sleep deprivation and an overload of bliss. Last night was incredible, right up to the point where I got only about three hours of sleep. I knew at the time I'd pay for it today, and the check is coming due as I stare down a long day running on fumes.

My phone rings, and I take the call from Carmen.

"Well," she says, "how was it, prima?"

"There are no words."

She screams, and I wince. "Easy! I'm sleep-deprived while driving."

"Uh-oh. Gonna be a long day, huh?"

"You know it."

"But worth it?"

"So worth it. So, so, *so* worth it."

"That's what I wanted to hear. Did you invite him to the wedding?"

"I did. Can he bring Everly?"

"Of course."

Carmen is being super chill about the wedding, in stark contrast to her first time around when she micromanaged every detail. She's learned since then, in the worst way possible, that you can't micromanage life. So she's kept her focus on herself and Jason and given over the rest of the planning to her mother and grandmothers, who're in their glory.

"I'm so, so happy for you, Mari. No one deserves a rip-roaring romance more than you do."

"Is that what this is?"

"You tell me."

"It is rather rip-roaring, whatever that is."

"It's the best possible thing when two people who're destined to be together somehow manage to find each other in this crazy world."

"I don't know if we're destined to be together, but I'm getting in deeper with every minute I spend with him and Everly. Get this—he's going to spend the off-season here."

"Shut. *Up!*"

Since she's on the Bluetooth, I can't hold the phone away from my ear, but I can turn down the volume.

"I can't believe you're just now telling me this when we've been on the phone for… three whole minutes! That's the headline!"

"Not the fact that I slept with him?"

"No! That's second to the fact that *he's relocating for you!*"

"Temporarily. Who knows where he'll be by the spring?"

"Who cares? We know where he'll be for the next few months."

"And what happens to me if they end up three thousand miles away for half the year?"

"You go with him."

I moan. "My whole life is here, Car. You know I've never wanted to live anywhere else."

"I do know that, and at some point, you may have to choose.

But that doesn't have to happen today. Right now, the only thing you need to worry about is getting through work so you can see them later. Take it one day at a time and try not to get so far down the road with your worries that you fail to enjoy what's happening right now."

"That's pretty good advice."

"I know! You should listen to me." Carmen pauses before she adds, "I've had it twice, that unmistakable *thing* that can't be described in mere words. It's a feeling unlike any other, and having had it and lost it once, I'll tell you to do whatever it takes to hold on to it for as long as you can, because there's nothing else quite like being in love with the *right* person."

And now I'm in tears. "I hear you." Scott wasn't the right person for me. I know that now. I was in love with him, but I never got back from him a fraction of what I gave him. I already know that won't be the case with Austin. I knew that before we had sex, and I'm even more certain of it now. Never once did Scott make sure I had an orgasm—or *two*—before he got what he wanted. Not once. And that should've been a huge red flag that he wasn't the one for me.

That's one of a hundred ways Austin is different from Scott. It would be foolish to even try to compare the two—the epitome of apples and oranges.

"Are you all right?" Carmen asks.

"I think so."

"Be happy in this moment, Maria. It's all we have."

"I'm going to try like hell to do what my very wise cousin is telling me to do."

"Excellent. Then my work here is finished—for now. Let's do dinner one night this week. We'd love to spend more time with Austin and Everly and get to know them."

"I'd love that. Maybe tomorrow night?"

"I'll check with Jason, but that should be fine. On another

note, I'm hearing from reliable sources that Marcus is in a bad way."

"Dee told me the skank left him."

"I wish it was that simple," Carmen says with a sigh. "From what I've heard, it's because he's realized what a huge mistake he made letting Dee get away."

That is truly shocking. "No way."

"Way."

"Are you going to tell her that?"

Carmen groaned. "I have no idea what to do. You tell me."

"Ugh, I don't know, either. It took her forever to move past him, and then when he got *married*…"

"Sounds like he married her on the rebound. People do dumb stuff like that and then live to regret it."

"Let's talk to her when she gets here next week for the wedding."

"Yeah, that's a good idea," Carmen says. "I don't want her stewing about it for a week in New York where she can't do anything about it."

"For sure. We'll help her figure out what to do. I gotta run. I'm at the clinic, and there's a line out the door."

"Have a good day."

"You, too."

"Love you."

"Love you, too."

I park behind the clinic, gather up my stuff and head inside. My boss, Miranda, is coming out of her office as I walk in. She's our nurse practitioner and the clinic administrator.

"Morning." She's a tall Black woman in her early fifties who started the clinic thirty years ago with her late husband, who was a doctor from Cuba. I've learned so much about community health, nursing, compassion and social justice from her.

"Morning. I see we're already in for a busy day."

"You know it." She takes a closer look at me. "Are you okay?"

I stop short. "I'm fine. Why?"

"You look tired maybe."

"I didn't sleep well last night." Because I was having mad, crazy sex with the hottest guy on the planet, not that I can tell her that.

She squeezes my arm. "I just made more coffee. Help yourself."

"Thanks." I stash my lunch in the fridge and am pouring coffee when my phone chimes with a text from Jason.

Hey, this is officially off the record, but I'm worried about Carmen. She mentioned last night that she's afraid every time we're apart that something will happen to me the way it did to Tony. I wanted someone else to be aware so we can make sure she's well supported ahead of the wedding. Please don't let on that I told you.

It makes me so sad to think of her anxious like that, especially since I haven't seen or heard any sign of that from her. I write back to him. *Thanks for the heads-up, and I won't say anything. I hate that she's got that weighing on her, but I guess it's totally understandable. I think she'll feel better once she gets past the wedding. She's juggling a lot right now.*

I realize I've been caught up in my own situation and not keeping a close enough eye on her as one of her two maids of honor—and the only one who's local.

Yeah, he says. *It's a lot, but I want this to be a happy time for her. Not sure how to reassure her that everything will be okay.*

Just keep telling her that, and I will, too. I'll check in with her later. We talked about doing dinner this week, with Austin and Everly. Maybe tomorrow night?

The act of typing their names makes me happy. That's how far gone I am over both of them.

I heard they were sticking around for a while, and I'm happy for you! Let's do that tomorrow night. It'll be good for Carmen to hang out with you.

I send back a thumbs-up.

My day gets crazy from there with nonstop patients of all ages with a wide variety of health concerns. Many of them have no health insurance, so we're their only source of medical care, which is a responsibility we take very seriously. It's satisfying work to serve this population, and even though I could make a lot more money working at a hospital, I love this job and the sense of accomplishment I feel working with our clientele.

We're so busy that I eat lunch standing up in the break room.

One of my patients in the afternoon is a young mother named Sara, who I suspect is being abused by her boyfriend. We've developed a rapport over a number of visits, and I keep hoping she'll let me help her. She's here for a well-baby visit with her daughter.

I knock on the door and go in to take the baby's vitals before she sees Miranda.

Sara has dark silky hair, tanned skin and big brown eyes. She has a haunted look about her that touches me every time I see her and her baby daughter, Isabella.

"How are you ladies today?"

"Doing good."

Sara sits on the exam table with Isabella, a chubby, well-cared-for three-month-old. While I weigh and measure the baby, I try to think of something I can say to get Sara talking about her home situation, but my brain is scrambled due to lack of sleep.

"I saw you on TV the other day," Sara says.

HOW MUCH I CARE

"Did you? That was kind of embarrassing."

"It's so great the way you stepped up for that little girl."

"I'm just so glad it worked. She's in remission."

"She's a very lucky girl."

"She is, and her dad and grandparents are very devoted to her. Does Isabella have grandparents?"

Sara nods. "We don't see them, though. They don't like her dad, so he doesn't want me to see them."

"What about the rest of your family and friends?"

"They don't like him, either."

"Do *you* like him, Sara?" I ask the question as gently as possible, hoping she'll see me as someone who can help, not make everything worse.

"Not anymore," she says, her eyes filling and her lip quivering.

"Let me help you, honey."

"He said he'll take Isabella if I try to leave him."

"We have access to people who can help. Remember all the times you've come in with bruises and other injuries you said were from falling or tripping?"

As she holds the baby close to her, she nods.

"I've documented every one of them in your file. If he's hurting you, we have proof."

"I'm afraid of him," she says on a sob. "He said he'd kill me if I tried to leave him."

"I'm afraid he'll kill you—or your baby—if you stay. Please let me help you."

She lifts her chin in agreement. The slight movement is all I need to act.

"Stay right here. I'll be back, and please don't call or text anyone." One call or text from the exam room can derail the whole plan. We're so close to being able to get her help, I don't want that to happen.

"There's no one left to tell. He's taken them all away."

I pat her shoulder. "We're going to fix that." I leave the exam room, closing the door behind me, and go into Miranda's office where she's working on charts between patients while drinking soup from a mug. "I've finally talked Sara into letting us help her."

"Thank goodness. What're you thinking?"

"I was going to call Sergeant Ramos." The female special victims detective we've worked with in the past is almost always our first call in these situations.

"Does Sara have family support?"

"He's isolated her, but I think her family would be receptive to hearing from her."

"Let's work that angle, too."

"Okay, I'm on it."

In between checking on other patients, I spend the rest of my day working on Sara's situation and helping her through the reporting of the abuse she's suffered at the hands of her partner. Sgt. Ramos is a pro and knows how to keep victims of abuse safe while extricating them from dangerous situations.

By the time I leave at six, I'm emotionally and physically drained, but relieved to know that Sara and Isabella will be safe in the arms of Sara's family tonight, with an officer assigned to watch the house in case there's any trouble. It's the first step in what will be a long and difficult process, but taking that first step is the hardest part. I made sure Sara knows how proud I am of her for doing it. Now I just pray she won't waver in her determination and go back to him. That happens far too often.

In my car, I check my phone for the first time since this morning and find texts and pictures from Austin and Everly, who had a big day at the hotel pool. As I gaze at their sweet faces and happy smiles, my phone chimes with a new text from Austin. *What do you feel like for dinner? I'll get you anything you want.*

I was going to tell him I'm too tired to do anything tonight, but the second I saw their photos, my resolve disappeared. *Mexican?*

On it. ETA?

Going home to shower and change, and then I'll be over.

We can't wait.

Neither can I.

Bring your suit. Everly wants to show Rie how good she is at swimming.

Will do.

Traffic is bad on the way home, which gives me time to check in with Carmen. Jason's worries have been on my mind all day, even when I was too busy to breathe.

"Hey," she says. "What's up?"

"Just checking in on the bride. It occurred to me today that I haven't been holding up my maid of honor duties by asking what I can do to help with the wedding." She asked us not to bother with a shower since they've lived together for more than a year and already have everything they need.

"There's really nothing to do. Mom, Nona and Abuela are large and in charge, which is fine with me. It's keeping them busy and out of trouble."

"And out of your business."

"That, too."

"I think it's keeping them out of my business, too. They've been pretty chill about everything with Austin."

"You can thank me later, but be ready for them to shift their attention your way after next weekend."

"Yikes. Thanks for the warning."

She cracks up laughing, a welcome sound in light of what Jason shared earlier.

"You know I'm here if I can do anything for you, right?" I ask her.

"Of course. I can't believe it's already next week!"

"That's what happens when you have a three-month engagement."

"True."

"I'm glad you're excited. You deserve every happiness, Car. We all want that for you so much."

"I know you do. Thanks for holding me up for all the years it took to find Jason."

"Always my pleasure to hold you up."

"Likewise. Are you seeing Austin tonight?"

"Yeah, I'm heading to his hotel after I go home to change."

"And pack a bag."

"And pack a bag."

"That's my girl! Call me in the morning and let me know how round two went."

"This'll be rounds four and above, actually."

"*Whoa*, girl, way to get back in that saddle."

That makes me laugh. "I've got the saddle sore to prove it."

Carmen snorts with laughter. "Best kind of sore. Have fun tonight, and call me in the morning."

"Will do. Later."

"Later, love you."

"Love you, too." We say that almost every time we talk since Tony died, because we're now painfully aware that it can always be the last time.

At home, I grab a quick shower and wash my hair to get any germs from the clinic off me before I see Everly, whose immune system is still fragile. I make my lunch and pack a bag to stay with Austin again, but tonight, there's going to be a hell of a lot more sleep.

I realize I forgot to ask Miranda about taking time off later in the week. I shoot her a quick text. *I meant to ask you today if you mind if I take a day or two this week? I have friends in town and would love to spend some time with them if you can spare me.*

I always feel guilty asking for time off because the clinic is busy every day, and whenever one of us is out, it's a grind for everyone else. But Miranda is always preaching self-care, and time off counts.

Sure, no problem. Take Thurs and Friday. Jason is here Thurs, so we should be good.

Great, thanks.

And with that, my workweek just got two days shorter. Filled with excitement, I drive to Austin's hotel and valet-park before taking the elevator to his room. I knock on the door and smile when I hear Everly shriek.

He comes to the door with her in his arms, the two of them sun-kissed from a day at the pool.

Before Austin can say a word, Everly says, "Rie! Scream! Swim!" As she announces our agenda, she leans toward me, and I take her from Austin.

He relieves me of my bags, smiling at the way Everly takes over. "Let Rie come in."

"Rie! In!"

"I'm in!" I hug the sweet little girl until she squirms to be let down. After I put her down, she runs off.

Austin takes advantage of the opportunity to kiss me. "Thought tonight would never get here," he says between sweet kisses. "Couldn't wait to see you."

"Same. *Long* day."

"Are you okay?"

"Yeah, but I'm tired."

He puts his arms around me and presses his lips to the top of my head. "I'll make sure you get a good night's sleep."

"Why do I not believe you?"

Laughing, he says, "I will. I swear."

"Rie! Sleep!"

He laughs at my impression of Everly. "Rie will get to sleep. I promise."

"I took off Thursday and Friday."

His grin lights up his entire face. "That's the best news I've had all day. You can help me decide which house to rent for the winter, and then I'm going to go back to Baltimore on Saturday to pack up and get back here in time for the wedding. Does that sound like a plan?"

"That sounds good, except for the part about you leaving."

"I'll be quick."

"I still can't believe you're staying for the winter."

He kisses me again. "Believe it, baby. There's nowhere else Ev and I want to be than wherever you are."

CHAPTER 17

AUSTIN

*T*hat week in Miami with Maria and Everly is one of the best I've had in a long time. For the first time since Ev was sick, I find myself truly relaxing in a way I couldn't when the fear of losing my daughter overtook my every waking moment—and tortured me on the rare times I actually slept. Living with that kind of fear is debilitating, so it's a huge relief to be regaining the ability to relax and enjoy my life without waiting all the time for disaster to strike.

Of course, a big reason for my ability to relax is Maria. Her calming presence is just what I need, and I want to be with her all the time. I've had her with me since after work yesterday, and we've got until I leave for Baltimore Saturday morning to spend together—three nights and two full days of Maria.

We had dinner with Carmen and Jason last night, which was a lot of fun. Jason is a great dude, and I can see us becoming friends. He promised to hook me up with some golf and cycling when I get back to Miami. And Carmen is awesome. I love the way she and Maria finish each other's sentences and laugh over their own inside jokes.

They speak a language all their own, developed over a lifetime of togetherness. I loved being around them and seeing Maria be completely herself with the cousin she adores.

The only thing Everly has wanted to do this week is swim. We offered her a wide variety of things to do today, but we ended up spending another day at the pool. We've already warned her that we're going to look at houses tomorrow and won't be going to the pool until later. I've let the Realtor know that in addition to two master suites, the house we rent will need to have a pool—with a gigantic fence around it so there's no chance Everly can get near it without one of us with her.

Maria's parents have invited us to their home tonight, but for now, Maria and I are enjoying some time to ourselves while Ev naps.

"What're you thinking about?" Maria asks, tracing a path over my chest with her index finger.

"I'm thinking that being naked in bed with you is my new favorite thing."

"That's not what you were thinking about."

"How can you tell?"

"Because you were tense."

"Just for the record, being naked in bed with you is in fact my new favorite thing."

"Mine, too, with you that is, but you still haven't told me what was making you tense."

"I was thinking about how we have to find a house with a pool for Ev, but it has to have a gigantic fence around it so I don't have to worry about her the whole time we live there."

"That's a good point."

"Thinking about keeping her safe made me tense, but right before that, I was thinking about how I'm more relaxed than

I've been since disaster struck last year, and it's all thanks to you."

"This week has been fun. Are you ready to meet my parents and my brothers?"

"I'm ready. Looking forward to it."

"You say that now... When they're all up in your business, you might be singing a new song."

"They'll be a breeze compared to the baseball media that's been up in my business during the season."

"My dad asked me yesterday where you think you'll end up. I said I didn't know, so he's apt to ask you."

"That's the big question hanging over everything right now."

"When will you know?"

"December, when the winter meetings happen. That's when all the deals get finalized, but there'll be lots of talking and stuff in the meantime, and it really kicks into gear after the World Series. My agent, Aaron, is on it. I told him to keep me posted but let me enjoy the time off."

"Three months is a long time to be up in the air."

"I'm counting on you to keep me very well entertained." Noting the time on the clock on the bedside table, I see that we've got another hour before Ev wakes up. "You can start now." I tip her chin up to receive my kiss. I never get tired of kissing her. In fact, that's my new second favorite thing to do. Like always with Maria, our kisses quickly become desperate and needy as we strain to get closer to each other.

I can never get close enough to her.

Her leg slides between mine, her softness presses against my hard cock, and her sweet scent fills every part of me with fierce desire. I'm completely addicted to her, and it's getting "worse" by the day, which is fine with me. I have no idea how I'll leave her for five days to go home to Baltimore to pack and grab my car. That's going to be a long-ass five days.

I'm so caught up in her, I almost forget to grab a condom. I pull back from her, stunned by how carried away I got. I never take those kinds of chances, especially not after what I suspect Kasey did.

"I'm on birth control." Maria takes my hand to show me the bump in her arm. "Long-term, no pills, no patches, no chance for mistakes."

"I wondered what that was. I thought your family had you microchipped."

Have I mentioned how much I love her husky, lusty laugh? She laughs like she lives, with everything she's got. "They're not quite *that* bad."

"So what you're saying…"

"Is there's almost no chance of me getting pregnant."

I ponder that for a second. Every part of me trusts this woman, but I was so burned once before that I'm not sure I can go there, even with Maria.

Naturally, she knows that, because she's Maria and she gets me. As she places her hands on my face, her expression open, honest and loving, I feel cared for in a way I've never been with any woman. I'm far more accustomed to women who are looking for something from me than I am to someone who seems to want to give me—and my daughter—everything they've got. "I'd understand completely if you want to still use condoms."

"I trust you. Of course I do."

"I know you do, and I know this is an issue for you. I'm just tossing it out there so you know."

"Thanks for telling me."

"Did I ruin the mood?"

"It's not possible for you to ruin my mood when you're soft and sweet and naked in my arms."

She draws me into another of those hot, sexy kisses that make me so crazy for her, and with her breasts pressed against my chest and her legs wrapped around my hips, I decide to see what it's like without a condom. Just for a second...

And it takes only that long to figure out what paradise must feel like.

"Maria... You... I... *God*."

She laughs until I sink deeper into her, and her laugh becomes the best kind of moan.

"This... I was only gonna... For a second..."

Laughter has her shaking under me as I try to get myself together to make this good for both of us. With my hands on her hips, I hold her still and lose all sense of time and place and anything that isn't this, and her, and us. *Fuck*, we're so good together, and I love her, I love making love with her, being with her, touching her, laughing with her. I love talking to her and holding her and watching her with Ev, who adores her Rie as much as I do.

I wrap my arms around her, and she does the same to me.

We come together, holding on tight to each other through the storm. It's the best thing I've ever experienced with a woman, and it's all I can do not to tell her how much I love her, how I want her to stay with me forever so I'll have a prayer of being happy. That's how vital she's become to me. That's how much I need her.

But I don't have time for that conversation now with Everly sleeping in the next room and us due at Maria's parents' home in an hour.

"We need a shower," Maria says after a long period of silence.

"Uh-huh."

She gently pokes my shoulder. "That means you have to move, Austin."

"Can't move. Never been more comfortable."

"Everly is going to catch you bare-ass naked and smothering her Rie if you don't move it."

185

"Only because I don't feel like explaining why I was smothering her Rie will I move." I kiss her. "To be continued later."

We take turns showering, and by the time I hear Everly stirring in the other room, Maria and I are presentable. We've been lucky so far that Ev hasn't caught us in bed together, but I'm not under any illusions that our luck will last. I hope that by the time it happens, Everly will be so used to seeing us together that she won't think anything of us sleeping together, too.

Everly wants us both when she wakes up from her nap, and while Maria helps her pick out a dress to wear to dinner at her parents' house, I work on taming blond curls into a ponytail.

"*Ow*, Dada."

"Sorry, Pooh. You've got some tangles."

"Rie do!"

"Rie is getting you dressed. I'm doing your hair."

"Rie! Hair!"

I look up at Maria, amused as always by my little boss baby. "And we've got another new word."

"Let's switch." Maria is endlessly patient when it comes to Everly and her many demands—and she assures me that Everly isn't turning into a brat who barks out orders to everyone around her, which was my fear. In fact, Maria says, she's becoming a perfectly normal three-year-old.

A perfectly normal three-year-old. Those are the best words I've ever heard, and as I watch Maria efficiently work out the tangles in Everly's hair, I realize how attached Ev is getting to her and how much more so she'll be by the end of the winter. We're going to have to figure this out and make a plan to be together, because living without Maria isn't an option.

MARIA

I'm nervous about bringing them home to meet my family, mostly because my parents will take one look at us together and know I'm in love with him—and Everly—and they'll have tons of questions about what's going to happen. I have the same questions and no answers, yet. I'm going to have to wait like everyone else until Austin finds out where he's playing next year, and we won't know that for certain until December.

I've already realized this relationship is going to change my life, and I'm working on wrapping my head around that. I like things just the way they are—with most of my family and friends nearby, a job that satisfies me and a vibrant community that's been such a big part of my life. I honestly can't imagine living anywhere else, but as I stare down five days without Austin and Everly, my thinking is beginning to change.

And yes, that scares the crap out of me, because after Scott, I promised myself I'd never again rearrange my own situation to fit into someone else's life. I was like putty, so intent on trying to make myself fit in Scott's world, trying to make him happy, trying to make our relationship work that I lost myself. I swore I'd never do that again, but now I find myself wondering what it would be like to live part of the year in Seattle or Chicago or Boston or San Francisco or Los Angeles and spend the off-season in Miami.

It's also occurred to me that Austin will be twenty-nine early next year. This next contract may well be his last one, so it's not as if we're talking about relocating forever. I also know, for sure, that it's probably far too soon to be this far down the road with what-ifs. But I also know for sure that I want this man and his daughter in my life. In that way, it's not too soon at all to be thinking ahead.

Austin drives his rental car as I direct him to my parents' home in Little Havana. He keeps a hand on my leg as he drives, and as always, his touch makes my blood run hot through my veins. In the back seat, Everly is singing a song of her own creation with jumbled words that make sense only to her. The joyful sound of her voice has both of us smiling as we soak in the moment.

Austin's phone rings, and he pulls it from his pocket to hand to me. "Who is it?"

"Kasey."

His expression registers shock as he glances at me. "Decline it."

I do what he asks, but I wonder what it means that she's calling him. "When did you last speak to her?"

"Months ago."

I can't believe she doesn't at least regularly check on her daughter, especially after Everly was so ill. But this is the same woman who left a baby home alone, so why am I surprised she doesn't care enough to check on her? Still, it makes me sad for Everly, and in a weird way, I'm sad for Kasey, because I get to see what she's missing out on by not being present in Everly's life.

"What do you suppose she wants?"

"Who knows?"

I have so many other questions, but I decide not to ask them now. Will he call her back? Will she call again?

We arrive at my parents' home a few minutes later, and seeing Nona's car in the driveway, I direct him to park on the street in front of the two-story yellow stucco house where I was raised. An ornate white metal fence surrounds the house and yard, and my mom has filled the window boxes with colorful flowers.

"Home sweet home," I tell Austin as we walk toward the garage door, which is open.

He's holding Everly's hand as she skips up the driveway. "It's really nice."

"They work on it constantly. Painting, pruning, planting. That's how they de-stress from work."

"The effort shows. It's beautiful."

"They're proud of it." I stop and turn to him. "Don't forget what I told you earlier about how my family is famous for asking inappropriate questions."

He smiles, making me wish I had nothing else to do but stare at his gorgeous face for the next few hours. "It's fine. I'm not worried."

"Well, I'm worried enough for both of us. My Nona is here, which means she's taken a night off from the restaurant, and that hardly ever happens. If she's here, Abuela is probably with her, and they do a double-team like you ain't never seen."

He leans in and kisses my cheek. "I can't wait to see them again. It's all good, sweetheart. Nothing to worry about."

"You say that now..."

"You love them, so I will, too." He puts his hand on my lower back, urging me to move forward so I can introduce him to my family.

We enter through the door from the garage, which takes us right into the kitchen, where my mom has probably been all day in preparation for having Austin over for dinner. My family makes a BFD out of everything, including Thursday night dinner with Maria's new boyfriend and his daughter.

"Lo, they're here!" My mom beckons my dad at the top of her considerable lungs. She zeroes in on Austin, like a laser beam finding its target. "And you must be Austin."

No, he's some dude I found outside on the sidewalk. "Yes, this is Austin and Everly."

Ev hides behind her dad until my mom squats to greet her at her level. "Hi, Everly, I'm Elena."

Mom extends a hand to Ev.

Everly looks up at me.

I squat, too. "This is my mommy. Can you say hi?"

"Hi." She shakes my mom's hand.

"Isn't she just delightful?"

I smile at my mom. "We think so."

MARIE FORCE

Everly steps into my arms, and I pick her up, wanting her to be comfortable with me and my family.

Dad comes into the room, and I introduce him to Austin and Everly, who is very shy with my dad until he kisses my cheek and plays peek-a-boo with Everly.

He has her giggling in no time, which doesn't surprise me. He's a doll, and kids always love him.

"Come in," he says. "What can I get you to drink, Austin? I've got beer and wine and soda."

"A beer sounds good," Austin says.

"Wine for you, love?" Dad asks.

"That'd be great, Dad. Thanks."

"Dinner is almost ready," Mom says. "Go on in before the boys eat all the appetizers."

I lead Austin into the living room where my brothers are sitting with Nona and Abuela, both of whom jump up to greet us with hugs and kisses, as if we haven't seen each other in years when we just saw them last Saturday night.

"It's so good to see you again, Austin," Nona says, hugging him. "And your darling little girl."

"Thanks for having us."

"Austin, Everly, these animals are my brothers, Nico and Milo, who're only here for the food and to meet the famous pitcher."

"Don't listen to her," Nico says when he stands to shake hands with Austin. "We've learned to ignore her." He's the epitome of tall, dark and handsome—so handsome that he's still single at thirty-one and a world-class player, from what I hear. I try not to pay too much attention to his very active social life.

"I could never ignore Maria," Austin says. "She's my favorite person to talk to."

Nico rolls his eyes. "Whatever you say."

I put my arm around my younger brother. "This is Milo. He's much nicer than the other one."

190

He, too, shakes hands with Austin. "Great to meet you. That perfect game this season was freaking *awesome*."

"Thanks. Nice to meet you, too."

At twenty-five, Milo is every bit as handsome as Nico, but he's a little heavier and wears black-framed glasses that give him a smart, nerdy look that Nico is forever mocking. Not that Nico is a bad guy. He's not, but he is a ballbuster.

They make room for us to sit on the sofa. On the coffee table, my mom has put out her famous stuffed mushrooms, some fried mozzarella and olives.

"You have to try the mushrooms," I tell Austin. "They're so good."

"Don't mind if I do."

I bring Everly onto my lap and tear off a piece of fried motz for her. "Try this. My mom made it. I think you'll love it."

She takes a tentative bite and then looks up at me.

"Good?"

She nods enthusiastically and takes another bite.

"What a sweetheart," Dad says as he hands us our drinks. "What can I get for her?"

"We brought her sippy cup with water," I tell him as I get it out of her backpack and hand it to her.

I look up to find my dad, brothers and grandmothers watching me as I tend to Ev, and I wonder what conclusions they're leaping to. Probably the same ones I've already made myself.

CHAPTER 18

MARIA

"So, Austin," Nico says, "it's free-agency time, huh?"

"Yep."

"I read online how you could command up to a *hundred million*. That's freaking insane!"

I'm mortified that Nico brought that up and a little freaked out by the number. *A hundred million?* Seriously?

"I don't know about that," Austin says. "We'll have to see what happens."

"You must be losing it," Nico says, undeterred. "I'd be picking out my Lambo if I were you."

"You can't put a car seat in a Lambo," Austin says, making me adore him even more. "I'm more of an SUV kind of guy these days."

"Where do you think you'll end up?" Dad asks.

"I honestly don't know. We'll be talking to quite a few teams as soon as the World Series is over. By November, we'll be narrowing it down, and I expect to know more by the winter meetings in December."

"An exciting time for you," Dad says.

Austin glances at me and smiles. "It is, but for much bigger reasons than baseball."

I feel my face get warm as he makes a rather public declaration. There's nothing he could've said that Dad, Nona and Abuela would want to hear more than that. It'll matter to them that Austin has his priorities straight—and he basically just told them I'm high on his list of priorities.

Mom calls us into the dining room a short time later and feeds us a feast of delicious chicken piccata with lemon sauce, pasta carbonara, risotto balls, a huge antipasto and freshly baked bread.

"You went crazy, Mom," I say when I see the spread and realize she must've taken a rare day off to have done all this.

"It looks and smells delicious, Mrs. Giordino," Austin says.

"Call me Elena, honey, and dig in. Is there something Everly will eat?"

"She'll love the chicken and the risotto," I reply.

My mom raises a brow, which means I'm in for a full grilling on all things Austin and Everly in the near future.

Over dinner, we talk about the wedding, who's picking Dee up from the airport on Wednesday and Austin's plans for the off-season.

"Everly and I are planning to spend the winter here," he says as he accepts a third helping of chicken from my mom, who loves nothing more than feeding people to the point of explosion.

My family goes silent, which doesn't happen very often.

"You're spending the winter in Miami," Mom says, her brow lifted. "Well, that's an interesting development."

"We love it here," Austin says with a meaningful look my way.

He may as well have said, *I'm in love with Maria and planning to marry her,* because that's the leap my parents and grandmothers will take from that perfectly innocuous statement. I'll have to do some damage control after this, but that's okay. There's simply no way to prepare a newcomer for my family, as Carmen discovered when she first brought Jason home and they swarmed the pediatric neurosurgeon like buzzards on fresh roadkill.

They mean well, and they're the best people I know. They do so much for so many. Nona and Abuela are always organizing fundraisers at the restaurant for someone in need, to the point that Uncle Vincent jokes that he's going to be the one in need by the time they're finished. But he doesn't really mind, because he, too, has the biggest heart.

Take Sofia at the restaurant. When Jason diagnosed her son Mateo with a malignant brain tumor that he then removed, Nona and Abuela made Sofia their personal project, holding fundraisers, giving her a job and doing anything they could to help her through the most difficult time in her life. They made her part of our family and continue to support her and Mateo more than a year after the surgery that saved his life. That's how they are, and I wouldn't trade them for anything.

"Did I blow it by saying I like it here?" Austin asks when we're on the way back to his hotel two hours later.

"You picked up on that, huh?"

"I thought it was a safe way to say that I like you, but when they all went silent…"

I laugh at the grimace he directs my way. "It's okay. You didn't do anything wrong. They're jumping to all the big conclusions, but they were going to do that anyway."

"It's okay with me if they jump to all the big conclusions. I'm jumping to them myself."

I look over at him. "Are you?"

"Hell yes. I'm spending the winter in Miami so I can see you every day, not because I care about fun in the sun. Although, that is a nice side benefit. Winter in Baltimore is cold."

"And here I thought it was all about the sun."

"You know better." At a stoplight, he looks over at me. "I couldn't help but notice you seemed a little shocked when your brother started talking money."

"I was a little shocked. *A hundred million?* That's like Lebron- or Jordan-level money."

He laughs. "They might make that in a year, but for me that would be the value of a multiyear contract, not my annual take. And it could end up being a lot less than that."

"But it's going to be in that ballpark, no pun intended."

"Yeah, I guess. I don't know."

He seems exquisitely uncomfortable, so I drop it, even if the thought of him making that kind of money makes me a bit queasy. Although, he's not exactly a pauper now…

We return to the hotel, drop the car with the valet and spend the next thirty minutes getting Everly ready for bed and reading her two stories—one by Dada and one by Rie! And yes, I love how she can't say my name without the exclamation mark. It's quite possibly the cutest thing ever.

She's tired from swimming and being in the sun and falls asleep before I finish my story.

"Psst," Austin whispers. "She's out."

"I want to know how it ends."

"The lion mommy ends up being friends with the zebra mommy and the tiger mommy, and all the little babies are happy."

"Okay, then. Now I'll be able to sleep."

We sneak out of Everly's room, and Austin leaves the door cracked so he can hear her if she wakes up.

"Can I interest you in one more glass of wine?"

"I could be talked into that."

He pours wine for me, grabs a beer for himself and suggests we take them outside to the patio, where the night is warm but not humid.

"This is my favorite time of year here," I tell him when we're snuggled up to each other on one of the lounge chairs. "It's warm and sunny during the day, warm at night, but hardly ever crazy humid."

"What's the winter like?"

"A little chillier, but you never really need more than a light jacket. Every once in a while, we'll have a real cold snap, but that doesn't usually last longer than a few days."

His cell phone rings ,and he manages to pull it out of his pocket without disturbing me or spilling his beer. "Fuck, it's Kasey again. Do you mind if I take it?"

"Of course not. Go ahead."

He gets up and takes the call. "What's up?" There's not an ounce of warmth or anything other than pure annoyance in his tone.

I wish I could hear what she's saying.

His shoulders are tense, his posture rigid. "Get to the point, Kasey. What do you want? Because you always want something." After another long pause, he says, "Nope. Not happening. And don't give me that bullshit about how you *gave me* Ev. The court gave me Ev because you were negligent. I don't owe you shit. Don't call me again." He ends the call, jams his phone into his pocket and continues to stare off into the darkness.

I put down my glass, get up and go to him, sliding an arm around his waist and resting my head on his shoulder.

"Sorry," he says. "I should've ignored it."

"It's okay. Better to take care of it."

"She's never going to go away."

"What did she want?"

"What she always wants—money. She thinks I owe her a steady stream of it because she gave birth to my daughter and then 'gave' me full custody."

"Austin..."

"It's fine. It is what it is. I'm used to it by now. I made the mistake of giving her money when I first got full custody, and she keeps coming back for more. And she never asks about Everly, not even when she was sick."

"God. That's unbelievable. I'm sorry you have to deal with that."

"It's my own fault. I knew she was shallow when we were dating. I was actually about to end it with her when she was suddenly pregnant. I think she knew I was checking out, and that's why I think she messed with the condoms. She wanted a gravy train, not a family."

"I hate that she hurt you that way, that she continues to hurt you."

"It only hurts me in relation to Everly. How do you call your child's father for the first time in months and not ask how your daughter, who was battling leukemia this time last year, is doing?"

"I don't know. I can't imagine that."

"No, you can't, and that's why I'm spending the winter in Miami and trying to figure out a way to keep you in our lives forever."

"Is that what you're trying to do?"

He tucks a strand of hair behind my ear. "I asked Aaron to put the Marlins in the mix."

I'm stunned by this news. "You *did*? Really?"

"Yeah. I didn't want to say anything because it's a bit of a long shot, but I want you to know I made the request and we're talking to them."

"Because of me?" I cannot believe he's making career decisions based on me.

He kisses my nose and then my lips. "It was definitely more about the sun and the fun than you." Then he laughs and kisses me again. "I'm joking. Of course it's all about you. Everything is about you and Everly and us and having more of this." He draws me into his embrace. "I loved you before I ever met you, and not because you saved my daughter's life, although that's definitely part of it. I loved you for *you*, for who you are and your big heart and the way you care so much about everyone in your life. You made me want to be one of the people you care about. And I wanted that for Ev, too. I wanted you for both of us."

"I… Wow, you've rendered me speechless."

"You can't be surprised to hear me say I love you."

"I'm not, and of course I love you and Everly. I love you both so much. The two of you have become the center of my world from the time we first talked. It was so weird to feel such a connection to someone when I didn't even know your name yet."

"I felt the same thing. I couldn't wait to be able to actually talk to you."

"Want to hear something I've never told you?" I ask him.

"Always."

"In the six months from the time I first heard from you until the one-year mark when we were allowed to talk freely, three different guys asked me out."

"Who are they, and how can I have them killed?"

"Easy, tiger," I say, laughing at his vehemence. "I said no to all three of them. After the first time I talked to you, I didn't want to go out with anyone else. I didn't want to talk to anyone else. I just wanted to talk to you."

"What does it say about me that I'm jealous of three dudes I've never met?"

"You have no reason to be jealous of anyone."

For the longest time, we stand there wrapped up in each other's arms as the warm South Florida breeze washes over us.

"Things are going to get crazy for me in the next couple of months."

"I know."

"No matter what happens, you and I are going to talk about it, and we're going to decide what's best for all of us. I don't want you hearing things and wondering what's going on or obsessing about big numbers or thinking about anything other than this, right here. This is what matters, and this is where my focus is."

"You need to give your career some of your attention while you figure out this next move."

"And I will, but I don't want you to worry about it. Whatever I do, whatever happens, you'll be part of the conversation."

"Is it surreal to you?"

"What?"

"All of this with us and how it happened."

"It's the best kind of surreal. Just when I'd given up on ever finding you, there you were, saving my daughter's life, and mine by extension, because without her... I don't know if I would've survived losing her."

"You would have, but you'd never be the same."

"No, I wouldn't, so you saved both of us." He nuzzles my neck, giving me goose bumps that make me shiver. "You didn't drink your wine."

"I don't care about the wine."

"No? What do you care about?"

I reach for him and draw him into a hot, sexy, tongue-twisting kiss that quickly has us clinging and straining for more, like always.

"Let's go to bed," he whispers against my lips.

He takes my hand and leads me inside, where we laugh and moan as we undress each other and come down on the bed in a rush of need and desire so sharp, it blots out anything that isn't him and me and *this*. I want him to know how much I love him, how much I want him, how much... well, everything. It's all for him and his beautiful daughter.

With my hand on his shoulder, I direct him to lie on his

back, and when he's where I want him, I start with kisses to his lips, his chest and rippled abdomen. I've never been up close and personal with an actual six-pack until his, and I'm fascinated by the way the muscles come together, the way they ripple under my tongue and how his hard cock gets even harder with every passing second.

Mimicking Everly's emphatic tone, he says, "Rie! *Now!*"

Laughing, I kiss the tip, the shaft and add dabs of tongue until he's making inarticulate sounds that thrill me. I love knowing I've got him basically babbling as I pleasure him. Moving so I'm between his legs, I bend over him and take him into my mouth.

His hips come up off the bed, and his hands end up tangled in my hair as I set out to give him a ride he'll never forget.

"*Maria…*"

I hear the warning in the tense way he says my name, but I ignore it and continue to lick and suck until he's shouting as he comes. I stay with him through the storm and ease him down gently, kissing my way up his body until I'm stretched out on top of him, his arms around me, his eyes closed and his chest heaving from deep breaths.

His eyes pop open, his gaze connecting with mine. "Wow."

I smile, pleased with the one-word review. "Yeah?"

"Oh yeah."

"You were all stressed. I couldn't have that."

"I might need that service a lot over the next few stressful months."

I laugh at his shameless comment. "We'll see what we can do to keep you relaxed."

He tightens his arms around me and turns us over so he's on top, looking down at me with a fierce expression on his sinfully handsome face. "I love you. I want this forever. You and me and Ev and more kids and lots of laughs and fun and everything. Tell me you want that, too."

"I do. Of course I do."

"Then let's make that happen, okay?"

"Okay."

CHAPTER 19

MARIA

*A*fter last night with Austin, I'm filled with euphoria as he drives us to check out houses to rent for the winter. Even though we warned her that today we'd be looking at houses, Everly is cranky about not swimming first thing like she has all week. Austin told her if she's a good girl while we look at houses, he'll take her to the pool as soon as we get back to the hotel.

He's so good with her, and in my mind, there's nothing sexier than a man who's ruled by a tiny girl who has him wrapped tightly around all her fingers. He's firm but loving with her, determined that she's not going to be completely spoiled and unmanageable, although I can't imagine her being either.

She's so sweet and funny. I melt every time she screams my name, and not spoiling her is going to be a huge challenge for me.

My euphoria lasts until I realize where we're going—Indian Creek Island, only the most exclusive neighborhood in all of

Miami, where the houses probably start around fifteen million. From what I've heard about it, there're only thirty or forty properties on the island, and it's almost impossible to buy anything out here because the turnover is so low.

"Uh, what're we doing out here?" I ask Austin.

"Looking at a house."

"To rent?"

"Temporarily. A friend of a friend owns it and isn't coming down this winter. He said it's available if we're interested. So I'm going to check it out."

"Oh."

He looks over at me. "Is that okay?"

"If you want to live in the most bougie neighborhood in Miami."

"It's not about the bougie. It's about the house having what we need—two master suites, a good-sized room for Ev, a pool, a view and a yard where I can throw. I also want single family versus a condo or townhome so we have plenty of privacy. This one checks all the boxes."

He pulls up to a mansion. There's no other word for it, and for a second, I can't do anything but stare at the massive contemporary home that sits right on the water. I mean... Wow.

"Come on," he says. "Let's take a look and see what we think."

"What's there to look at? Who wouldn't want to live here?"

"It could be hideous on the inside for all we know."

I give him a withering look and get out of the car with a sinking feeling that sucks all the remaining euphoria from last night right out of me. Naturally, he'd want to live in a place like this. Who wouldn't? I don't begrudge him his ability to afford a house like this, but it's a stark reminder of our vastly different economic situations.

He punches in a code on a keypad that gets us inside. After putting Everly down to explore, he holds out his hand to me. "Don't look so freaked out. It's just a rental for the winter."

That may be true, but it's also a firsthand look at what life with Austin would be like, and I'm not sure how I feel about it. Most of my life takes place on the opposite end of the spectrum, working with the neediest people in our community. How can I reconcile this house with that reality? I can't, and I shouldn't even try.

I take that unsettling realization with me into the most extraordinary house I've ever seen anywhere, even in magazines or on TV. The rooms are huge, the views exceptional, the decorating clean and contemporary and simply gorgeous. There's a wine locker and a media room and six bedrooms, six and a half bathrooms, two enormous master suites, a stunning pool and a dock out front with a sexy speedboat tied up to it. In addition, there's a grassy area between the pool and the dock that includes a huge sandbox and swing set, all of it surrounded by palm trees and lush landscaping.

Everly sees the swing set and lets out a squeal. "Dada! *Swing!*"

"Let's go check it out, baby girl." Austin lets her drag him outside to look at the pool and to swing while I hang back, trying to wrap my head around this.

The furniture on the patio and pool deck alone are worth more than I'll make in ten years.

I swallow hard as a feeling akin to hysteria overtakes me. This is too much. It's obscene and beautiful and luxurious and...

He's worked hard for everything he has and deserves to spend his money any way he chooses. I know all that, and I admire what he's accomplished with his talent.

But this... This might be too much for me. Try as I might, I can't imagine myself spending the night in this palace and then commuting to my job at a free clinic in Little Havana, where I experience breathtaking poverty and overwhelming need every day. We're constantly struggling to make ends meet at the clinic, to provide the most basic of health services to our clients on a shoestring budget that gets tighter all the time.

I sit on the end of a cushy lounge chair on the patio and watch Austin push Everly on the swings, the two of them laughing and smiling. I love seeing them together and watching their undeniable bond. I love everything about them both, except for this... I don't love that he's so staggeringly rich that he can afford to live in a place like this, and I have no idea what to do with those feelings.

Austin gives Everly ten minutes on the swings before collecting her to check out the rest of the house.

I follow him, bringing the dead feeling inside as I view huge bedrooms, marble bathrooms with fixtures I've never seen before and the most amazing kitchen in the history of amazing kitchens.

We leave there a short time later and a Realtor takes us through two more houses in equally exclusive areas—Hibiscus Island and Star Island—before concluding our tour in Gable Estates at yet another mansion, this one on the Intracoastal Waterway. Not one of the houses we look at would sell for less than ten million dollars.

I can tell that Austin likes the last one in Gable Estates the best. It's not quite as huge as the others but still has all the other features he's looking for and is in a secure, gated community.

"What do you think?" he asks me as we stand in the spacious great room in the center of the home while Everly runs circles around us.

"It's beautiful."

"Tell me what you really think, Maria. I want to know."

"Um, well, it's a bit obscene."

"Huh. Really?"

I nod.

"Well, okay. Hey, Ev, come on. Let's go."

"Dada! Swim!"

"Soon, Pooh."

I follow him out of the house and get in the passenger seat

while he straps Everly into her car seat. We're both quiet as he drives us back to the hotel, and I can't help but notice that he doesn't hold my hand the way he always has when we're in the car.

After starting the day on such a high note, I try to reconcile that feeling with the one that's overtaken me during our house tour. As we pull up in front of the hotel, I decide I need a break to process what I'm feeling before I say something that can't be unsaid.

"I think I'm going to run home for a bit," I tell him after he turns the car over to the valet. I'm fishing for the ticket for my own car in my purse when his hand encircles my arm.

"Don't go. Let's talk about it."

"We will. I just need…" I force myself to look up at him. "I need a minute. Go to the pool and have some fun. I'll see you later."

Everly puts her hands on Austin's face. "Dada! Swim!"

"We're going to swim, Pooh," he says, but he never looks away from me. "We'll see you later?"

Nodding, I hand my ticket to the valet.

Austin kisses my forehead and walks into the hotel with Everly in his arms.

I turn to watch them go, my heart feeling broken for reasons I can't begin to comprehend. The valet stand is busy, and it takes fifteen very long minutes for my car to arrive. I have to fight the urge to run after Austin and Everly for every one of those long minutes. They're leaving tomorrow for five days. What am I doing running away?

I get in the car and sit for a second, trying to figure out what I want to do. And when I pull out of the hotel parking lot, I head toward home in late afternoon traffic that gives me far too much time to think. My phone chimes with a text, but I don't check it. Not yet.

I find myself at the restaurant, wanting to see my Nona. All my life, she's been the one I go to when I need someone to help me make sense of something. Why should now be any different? I park in the back and duck in the kitchen door, the scents of Italian and Cuban food making my mouth water the way they always do.

Uncle Vincent is coming out of the kitchen. "Hey, hon. Are you working tonight?"

I rarely work on Fridays, but sometimes I'll cover for one of the other waitresses. "Nope. I was looking for Nona. Is she around?"

"She's upstairs in the banquet room. We've got a rehearsal dinner tonight."

"I don't want to bother her if she's busy."

"Go on up, sweetheart. You know she's never too busy for you or any of her grandchildren."

"That's true."

"Are you okay?" Vincent asks, giving me the same look my dad gives me when he can tell something isn't quite right.

"I'm fine, but thanks for checking. I'll see you before I go."

"I'm here all night," he jokes, since he's there just about every night.

As I go up the stairs to the function rooms, I think about the comfort I've always had in knowing where to find these particular people any time I need them. I love my own parents very much, but in times of turmoil, it's Nona and Abuela I turn to most often.

Nona is supervising the final details of the setup for the dinner that'll take place in the banquet room tonight. She watches over the staff with a finely tuned eye for the kind of details that make Giordino's such a destination. Flowers, place settings, candles and first-rate food. The banquet rooms are often booked a year in advance. They're closing the restaurant itself for Carmen's wedding reception because the rooms upstairs were already booked.

When she turns toward the stairs, Nona sees me there, her face lighting up with a delighted smile. Carmen, Dee and I often talk about how no one will ever love us the way our grandmothers do, and even though they're in perfect health, we worry about the day when they're no longer around to ground us.

"This is a nice surprise," she says when she hugs and kisses me the way she always does, as if we haven't seen each other in months. "I thought you were with Austin and Everly tonight."

"I was. I am… I, uh, do you have a minute?"

"For you? Always." She takes me by the hand and leads me to the bar that serves both banquet rooms. "Drink?"

"Some water maybe."

She pours ice water for both of us and sits next to me on one of the barstools. "Ah, feels good to sit."

"You're not doing too much, are you?"

"Probably, but it sure beats sitting around doing nothing."

I laugh at her frequent refrain on the perils of retirement, which is a dirty word around here. Neither she nor Abuela have any desire to be retired, or "put out to pasture," as they say. Nona's dark hair is shot through with gray these days, her face lined with a wrinkle here and there, but her mind is as sharp as it's ever been.

"What's wrong?"

"It's the dumbest thing."

"Usually is," she says, her lips curling and her eyes lighting up with amusement.

"He's *obscenely* wealthy."

Her brow rises in a comical expression. "You're just finding that out?"

"I knew he had money… I mean, all professional athletes make a lot of money, which is something I've always thought was so strange."

"Nurses and teachers should be the millionaires."

"Exactly!" We've had this conversation before when I've

ranted about the pay inequities for such important jobs. "I've sat at the ballpark with my dad and talked about the overpaid ballplayers and all the things we could do to help people if we had their money."

"And now that you're dating one of them, your perspective has changed."

·"It hasn't, though. I still think it's obscene that they get paid what they do to play a game."

"Fair enough, but it's not his fault that his profession commands that kind of money. Society is to blame for placing a higher value on what he does than what you do, even if we all know what you do is far more important."

"It's not about what I do versus what he does."

"Isn't it?"

"Not specifically."

"What brought this on?"

"We went to look at houses today on Indian Creek Island, Hibiscus Island, Star Island, Gable Estates."

"Ah…"

"Nona, the houses were mansions on steroids. I've never seen anything like them."

"And it left you feeling unsettled."

"Yes! I was thinking, how do I spend time in this place with him and then get in my car and drive to work at the clinic where people have nothing?"

"I can totally understand why you'd have those thoughts and feelings, but let me ask you this. Do you love him?"

"Yes. God, yes, I love him so much. Him and Everly both."

"Do you think it matters to him that you make a very modest salary?"

"No. I'm sure he doesn't care about that."

"And yet you're here with me rather than with him because you can't handle that he makes a big salary."

"They're saying he could make *a hundred million* as a free agent."

"I saw your face when Nico said that the other night. You hadn't heard that before?"

"No! I had no clue. I mean I knew it would be a big payday, but a hundred million is just..."

"Think about what he could do with that kind of money. What you could *help* him do."

"What you mean?"

"Your clinic is always operating on a wing and a prayer. If you told Austin that, I bet he'd personally fund the clinic going forward, not to mention local food banks, pantries, homeless shelters. If you were to end up married to him at some point, perhaps that could be your mission in life. To help him spend his money on worthwhile causes."

"Why is it that you can always cut through to the heart of a matter in a way that never occurs to me?"

"It would've occurred to you eventually, sweet girl. You're just having trouble seeing the forest for the trees because you're falling in love with a man whose life is very different from yours, and those differences are going to present challenges. No question about that."

"A *hundred million*, Nona," I say on a sigh. "I have no idea what to do with that info."

"There're far worse problems you could have than to be falling in love with a rich man."

"And I know that. Please... Of course I know that."

"I know you do, honey. Your heart has always been so big toward people who have less than you do. It's not lost on any of us that you could make much more by taking a job at a hospital or private practice."

I've had numerous offers over the years to upgrade my career and salary and have turned them all down because I love what I do at the clinic so much. I have no doubt I'm making a

HOW MUCH I CARE

huge difference for people who need what we provide. Even my
Saturday nights at the restaurant are part of that effort. I
supplement my income by waitressing so I can afford to work
at the clinic. "I could never leave the clinic because of money."

"And I love you so much for that attitude."

"My need to help others comes right from you and Abuela.
You lead by example."

"You make us proud every day with the work you do. But
that doesn't mean you're not allowed to love a man who makes
an obscene amount of money. My mother used to tell us it's just
as easy to love a rich man as it is to love a poor man. Not that
we listened to her."

"Pardon me, Livia," one of the banquet captains says when he
approaches us. "Could I borrow you for just a minute?"

"Duty calls." Nona pats my knee. "Don't run away. I'll be
right back."

"I'll be here." I take a sip of my water and check my phone to
find a long text from Austin.

Dear Maria,
I miss writing to you. As much as I love seeing you every day
and spending time with you, I loved writing to you and having
you write back to me. Let's never stop doing that, okay?

And I'm already in tears.

I know you're freaking out about the houses we looked at. I get
why. You may not realize that I come from humble beginnings.
We were solidly middle-class growing up in Wisconsin. We
always had what we needed, took fun vacations and had
wonderful holidays and birthdays and played Little League
and hockey. But we weren't rich by any means.
It's taken me years to come to terms with my new circum-
stances, and I give generously to a number of different organi-

zations, including the Big Brothers/Big Sisters of Baltimore, several organizations that help underprivileged kids play Little League Baseball, and I also give to the American Cancer Society because both my grandfathers died of cancer, and to St. Jude's because of the great work they do for kids with cancer. I understand that my situation will be an adjustment for you, but I'm willing to do whatever it takes to help you fit into my world if you'll help me fit into yours.

If there are causes you want to support, all you have to do is tell me about them and it's done. I'm a few years ahead of you in coming to terms with what it means to have the kind of money I earn playing a silly game. I know it's obnoxious. But I'm not about to give it back. Instead, I'd rather use it to make life beautiful for the people I love and to help others who are less fortunate.

You were right—the houses are bougie, but they're pretty awesome, too, right!?? I loved the one in Indian Creek Island with the pool and the swing set, but the one in Gable Estates would be closer to work for you, so I'm leaning in that direction because I want you there with us whenever you're able to be, and I don't want you battling hideous traffic to get there. I want us to spend as much time together this fall and winter as we possibly can. I'm spending the winter in Miami so I can be with you. If you're not happy with my plans, then I'm not happy, either.

Come back. Let's talk.

I love you.

Austin (and Everly)

CHAPTER 20

MARIA

*N*ona returns to find me dabbing at tears with a cocktail napkin. "What happened?"

I hand her my phone so she can read the text. She pulls reading glasses from the top of her head and puts them on the end of her nose, her expression softening as she reads what he wrote.

"I like this young man very much."

"I do, too."

"So then why are you here with me instead of with him?"

"Because I needed my Nona."

She wraps her strong arms around me and hugs me tight. "Your Nona is always right here for you, my love."

"You'd better be."

She kisses the top of my head. "Go see your guy and figure this out with him."

Nodding, I kiss her cheek. "Thank you."

"Any time."

"I may not say it often enough, but I appreciate you so much.

I appreciate that I can dump my stuff all over you and know it'll never go any further. In our family, that means so much."

"Nothing in my life has ever brought me more pleasure than my grandchildren. And you, my sweet, are one of my favorites."

I roll my eyes at her because she says that to all of us.

"Drive carefully. Love you."

"Love you, too." I head back downstairs and run into Abuela at the hostess station for the Cuban side of the house. She is Nona's opposite in every way. Abuela is petite, with snow-white hair. But like Nona, she's ageless and tireless.

"I heard you were here," she says, giving me a careful once-over. "Everything okay?"

"It is now. Your partner in crime upstairs fixed me right up."

"Then I'll just give you a hug, tell you I love you and send you on your way."

"Love you, too, Abuela. See you tomorrow night."

"See you then."

I wave to my uncle at the bar on the way out the back door. Once I'm back in my car and headed out of the parking lot, I face a decision. Go right toward home or go left toward Austin and Everly and his millions of dollars and his loving heart. I fell in love with his words and his heart before I understood the full extent of his resources. And once again, his words have me taking a left toward him rather than running away.

I loved what he said in his text, how he homed right in on what was causing me to freak out and assuaged my concerns so perfectly. The idea of being able to fully fund the clinic and support other worthwhile causes in my community is a heady notion and something I hadn't considered before he and Nona mentioned it.

That he would actually fund things that matter to me is just another reason to love this man who's turned my world upside down. I can't get back to the hotel fast enough, especially in bumper-to-bumper Friday night traffic. It takes forty minutes to get downtown, and when I turn the keys over to the valet, I decide to go upstairs first rather than check the pool.

He's big on keeping Everly on a schedule, and it's getting close to dinner, bath and bedtime.

Outside the suite, I ring the doorbell.

A full minute later, the door swings open.

Austin is holding Everly, who is wrapped up in a bath towel. His expression is full of relief when he sees me there. "Come in."

"Rie! Scream!"

"We thought you might be room service. Someone is more excited about her scream than she is about her dinner."

Everly is leaning toward me so I take her from Austin. "Scream is so much more fun than dinner."

Everly nods enthusiastically. "Rie!"

"Everly!"

Her giggle is my favorite thing. "Rie!"

"Everly!"

She snuggles into my embrace, and a profound sense of homecoming overtakes me as I glance at Austin watching us together.

"Glad you came back."

"Me, too."

AUSTIN

I've never been so happy to see anyone. While Everly splashed in the kiddie pool, I sat next to her and composed the text to Maria, pouring everything I feel for her into that message out of the fear I'd never see her again after taking her house shopping. I have to confess it never occurred to me that she'd freak out about the luxury of the homes we toured. Every other woman I've ever known would've freaked out because they would've wanted to live there.

Not my Maria. She's special and unaffected and thoughtful

and so many other things, it'd take me a year to list them all. In fact, I may start making that list and watch it grow as I discover new things about her.

We sit with Ev while she eats her mac 'n' cheese and then the vanilla ice cream with chocolate sauce she's had every night we've been here. I fear she's going to expect the room service waiter to show up with her favorite things long after we leave the hotel, a thought I share with Maria.

"You may need to get a white shirt and bow tie." She wipes the chocolate from Everly's face. "So you can keep her in the style she's used to."

Watching the tender way she cares for Ev, I realize she already cares more about my little girl than the child's mother ever did.

"I was wondering if you might be willing to read the books tonight so I can return the rental car. I'm not sure I can juggle the car, Ev and the bags myself in the morning."

"I could take you."

"It's crazy early. We'll get an Uber if you don't mind staying with her while I drop off the rental."

"Sure, we can do that, can't we, baby girl?"

"Rie!"

"And the people have spoken," I say, laughing. To Everly, I add, "Dada will be right back. Rie is going to read your stories, okay?"

"Rie! Read!"

I squeeze Maria's shoulder. "I'll be quick." I call down to the valet stand for the car and am on my way to the airport drop-off fifteen minutes later. I can get an Uber with a car seat in the morning, and it'll be easier to get dropped off outside of Departures than have to deal with the rental car. I'm eager to get back to Maria, so I drive faster than I probably should, and as I'm getting gas, I think about what happened earlier and what I want to say to her when I get back to the hotel.

Thanks to traffic and a line at the rental car drop-off place, I end up being gone an hour. When I get back, I find Maria outside on a lounge, drinking a glass of wine. She's changed into pajama pants and a tank, which is a relief because that means she's planning to spend the night.

I look in on Everly, who's out cold, and bend over to kiss her cheek. Then I change into basketball shorts in the other bedroom, grab a beer and join my love on the patio to make things right between us. I'll do whatever it takes to put her mind at ease.

"You got room for me?"

"Of course." She scoots over to make a space for me to join her on the lounge.

I put the beer on a table and reach for her, bringing her into my embrace. I breathe in her distinctive scent and kiss the top of her head. "I'm sorry today was weird for you. I never intended for that to happen."

"I know. It's just a bit of an… adjustment for me."

"I'm sorry to hit you over the head with it. I didn't mean to do that. I guess I figured you knew…"

"I did. I mean, I do, but it's still… It's a lot."

"It's crazy money, and at times, it's been embarrassing to me to make so much when so many people have so little. I've been really focused on giving back since my first year in the majors."

"And knowing that only makes me love you more than I already did."

"You tell me what's important to you, and I'll do anything I can. All you have to do is point me in the right direction."

She drops her head onto my chest and puts her arm around me. "My Nona and Abuela are all about giving back, and they raised us to keep an eye out for those less fortunate. The clinic where I work… We serve people who have no insurance, no hope of ever having insurance. Many of them are here illegally, so they fear being reported if they go to a hospital. There's so much need, Austin. And that's why I'm still there six years after I graduated from nursing school when I could make triple the money at a hospital or private practice. That's why I waitress on Saturday nights, so I can afford to work at the clinic during the week."

"I admire that so much."

"It's because of what I see there every day that I had a freak-out over the houses we looked at today."

"I get it. I asked the Realtor to find me something less bougie."

"Don't do that. Get what you want, and I'll adjust."

"I want you to be happy."

"Being with you and Everly makes me happy. You spending the winter here makes me happy. I don't want you to feel you have to change yourself for me."

"I would. I can't bear the idea of you being unhappy or thinking I'm revolting because of my bougie house."

"You're not revolting. You're just filthy rich, and it's going to take me a minute to wrap my head around that."

"Do you know how fucking refreshing it is to be with someone who isn't looking for a sugar daddy? Someone who's a bit appalled by the money rather than seduced by it? To know that you're with me for me and not for what I have?"

"So that's been an issue, then?"

"From the second I signed my first contract, I've had to question the motives of almost everyone in my life, except my own family. They've never asked me for anything. I had the biggest fight ever with my parents when I wanted them to retire early, kick back and enjoy life after all they did to get me to where I am. They weren't having it, but eventually, my brothers and I ganged up on them, and we talked them into it."

"It's so sweet of you to want to do that for them."

"They did everything for me, and continue to make it possible for me to do what I do, so why wouldn't I? And you…

Anything you want, my sweet Maria… All you have to do is tell me. I'll fund your clinic and all your causes, your grandmothers' causes…"

She draws in a deep breath and lets it out slowly. "Thank you."

"Please don't thank me for using my embarrassment of riches to help others. That should be a no-brainer for anyone in my position."

"Get the house in Gable Estates. It has the fence around the pool that we need, and it won't take me two hours to get there."

"Will you be able to be comfortable there?"

Her low, husky laugh is the best sound. "*Anyone* would be comfortable there, Austin."

"My sweet Maria isn't just anyone. She's *everyone*. If she can't be comfortable there, I'll find something else."

"I'll be fine. Get the house, and make your little girl happy."

"When I get back from Baltimore, can I come see your clinic?"

"Sure. I'd love that, but it'll take about five minutes to show it to you. It's not much to look at."

"But it's everything to the people you serve."

"Yeah, it is, and we're always struggling to make ends meet."

"Not anymore. You've got yourself a benefactor, my love."

"You have no idea what that'll mean to our community."

"That's the upside of having money. You can do things like fund a clinic in Little Havana that does so much good for so many people. There's tremendous satisfaction in that, and I want you to feel that satisfaction, too. If you see a need, we can address it any way you see fit."

"That's gonna take me a minute to process, too."

"Take all the time you want. I'm not going anywhere."

"You're going to Baltimore," she says, sounding glum.

"We'll be back so fast, you won't have time to miss us."

"I'll miss you the minute you leave." She tips her head to look up at me. "Your text earlier was so sweet. You made me cry."

"I'm glad you liked it and that you came back. I felt so bad that you were upset by something I did."

"It wasn't what you did. It was just me trying to wrap my head around some things."

"Do that with me next time, okay?"

"I will. I'm just so used to running to my Nona." She laughs. "Old habits die hard."

"And did your Nona help?"

"She always does. She told me there are worse things than falling in love with a rich man."

I laugh at that and fall a bit in love with her Nona. "This is true. So you told her you're falling in love with me, huh?"

"She already knew. Nothing gets by her." Maria's hand is flat against my chest, where she has to be able to feel the rapid beat of my heart. That happens any time she's close to me this way. "I want you to know that it'll always be important to me to help others, to do work that matters to people who have less, to take care of people in need. That's who I am, Austin, who my family raised me to be."

"I know, and I love that about you so much. Look at what you did for Everly without blinking an eye or with hardly a thought to what it would mean for you. I've known who you really are since the first second you made that donation for my daughter, and everything I've learned about you since then has only reinforced my first impression. I'd never ask you to change who you are for me, Maria."

"I wouldn't ask that of you, either. You've worked hard for what you have, and you should be able to enjoy the money without being worried about offending me. I'll get over it. I promise."

"We're going to figure all this out together, okay?"

She nods, and I let go of the fear I experienced earlier that maybe I'd driven her away by taking her to those houses.

"And yes," she says with a soft sigh, "let's never stop writing to each other."

"You've got yourself a deal, sweetheart."

MARIA

I wake the next morning when Austin brushes a kiss over my cheek. "I'll be right back," he whispers.

"Be safe."

"Rie!" Everly comes bombing into the room and jumps up on the bed. "Fly!"

I sit up to hug her. "Yes, my sweet girl. You're going to fly in the sky. Be a good girl for Dada, and come back to see me soon, okay?"

"Rie! *Scream!*"

Austin and I share a laugh.

"I fear my name will always be associated with scream."

"There're worse things you could be known for. Come on, Pooh. Let's go so we can get back to our Rie."

I give Everly one more squeeze. "Love you, pumpkin."

"Rie! Love!"

"Add another new word to the list." Austin takes her from me and leans over to kiss me. "Hang out, have room service, take a swim. The room is ours until noon."

"It won't be any fun without you guys."

He kisses me again. "Do it anyway. Love you."

"Love you, too. Text me when you land."

"Will do."

"Hey, Austin?"

He turns back.

"I already miss you guys."

Smiling, he says, "We miss you, too."

I watch them go, and when the hotel door closes behind them, I fall back onto the pillows and listen to the silence that echoes through the space that's become lifeless without them. The silence is a metaphor for what my life would be like if they were no longer part of it. I think about what happened yesterday and how we worked it out like rational, sane adults.

That's not what would've happened with Scott. We would've gone days without speaking, after which we'd get tired of fighting and move on without ever solving the issue that started the fight in the first place.

I reach for my phone to compose a text to Austin and find one from him.

I ordered room service for you because I know you won't do it for yourself. Enjoy. Love you and miss you so much, and we only just left!

Dear Austin,
Thank you for breakfast. That's so nice of you—and you're right. I wouldn't have ordered it for myself. LOL! I miss you and Everly so much, and you only just left. It feels wrong to be in this city where I've lived all my life without you guys close by. How did you two manage to change everything for me so quickly? How did you manage to make yourselves so much a part of my life that everything feels wrong without you here with me?
I wanted to tell you how much I appreciated the way we worked out our differences yesterday. It meant a lot to me that you understood what was happening without me having to spell it out for you and that you made an immediate effort to right what was wrong between us. I've never had that in a relationship before, and it's refreshing—to say the least—to have that with you.
It helps me to know that underneath all the flash of your

current situation, you come from humble beginnings, too, and understand how much need there is in our world. Thank you for offering to support the organizations and causes close to my heart. That means so much to me. And for the record, I love you for YOU. I love your heart and your smile. I love the way you love your little girl and take such tender care of her. I love your sexy body and the way you hold me and kiss me and treat me like one of the most precious things in your life. I love to watch you pitch and walk and breathe and smile and laugh. I love that you knew I wouldn't order breakfast for myself and did it for me. I love you for YOU, not for what you have. I'd love you even if you weren't a wildly talented pitcher, but I love that you have such an amazing talent. I just wanted you to know that.

Hurry back, but drive safely. I'll be counting the days.

Love,

Maria

He responds a few minutes later. *About to go through security, but you ARE one of the most precious things in my life. Don't ever doubt that. Will write more later. Enjoy your breakfast. Love you.*

Swoon! He makes my heart race with his words the way he has from the first messages he sent me. I get out of bed, take a quick shower and get dressed before breakfast arrives. I'm running a brush through my wet hair when the doorbell rings.

The room service waiter rolls in a cart that has a vase with a red rose in it and a note with my name on the front.

"Do I need to sign?" I ask the waiter.

"No, ma'am. It's all set."

"Thank you so much."

"You have a nice day."

"You, too."

I go right to the table and open the note. *Maria, I heard every-*

thing you said yesterday, but you're going to have to let me spoil you a little bit. Sorry not sorry. We love you. Austin & Everly.

My smile stretches across my face as I pour coffee and dive into the bacon-and-cheese omelet he ordered for me along with the fried potatoes I raved over yesterday and a bowl of fruit. Two mornings ago, I told him the fruit made me feel less guilty about eating the rest. He pays attention. That's another thing to love about him.

I drive home an hour later, still on cloud nine from the breakfast and the note and the last week with him and Everly. I unpack my bag, do a couple of loads of laundry and make a grocery list for after-brunch shopping tomorrow.

My phone chimes with a text from Austin. *Landed BWI. Will be back ASAP!*

I write back. *Glad you're safe, and can't wait to have you back. xoxo*

I spend the afternoon reading, watching TV and trying to relax before my shift at the restaurant. I text Carmen. *Are you guys coming in tonight?* They come in most Saturday nights, and we've fallen into the habit of hanging out after I get out of work.

We are! See you in a bit.

Good!

Wearing the starched white dress shirt and black skirt that make up the waitstaff uniform, I head to work around four thirty, all the while wondering what Austin and Everly are up to in Baltimore.

CHAPTER 21

AUSTIN

*M*y dad picks us up in my black BMW SUV, and as I buckle Everly into her car seat, I notice her cheeks are rosier than usual, which has me brushing a hand over her forehead. She's warm and that's all it takes for me to go rigid with complete panic. There's simply no other way to describe it. She was listless and out of sorts on the plane until the descent when she cried uncontrollably for twenty minutes. I chalked up the listlessness and crying to being overly tired from a busy week, but now I can't deny that she looks and feels feverish.

I close her door and get into the passenger seat. "Take us to Hopkins."

Dad looks over at me, shock etched into his expression. "What? Why?"

"She's feverish."

"Come on. She is not."

"She is, Dad. Drive. Please?"

After taking another tentative look at me and at Everly in the rearview mirror, he shifts the car into gear and takes off.

I send a text to Ev's oncologist. *Just arrived back in Baltimore after a week in Miami, and Ev's running a fever. Bringing her to Hopkins ER right now.*

The doctor, a godsend named Jai Anand, responds immediately. *I'll meet you there.*

He's amazing, and I credit him with helping to save Everly's life. But the fact that he feels the need to meet us at the ER on a Saturday does nothing to calm my out-of-control anxiety. My blood pressure has to be in the danger zone, and I can barely breathe from the fear that has my throat feeling tight and closed off.

I should text Maria and tell her what's going on, but she's got to work tonight, and I don't want to worry her until I know more.

"You should call Mom," Dad says, his tone grim.

I don't want to have to say the words out loud, even to my own mother. But Dad is right. The three of us have been on this journey together from the beginning, and she has a right to know what's going on. I put through the call.

"Hey! Did you guys land?"

"We did. We're with Dad now, and, um, well, Ev's a bit feverish, so we're going to run by Hopkins real quick just to, you know, make sure."

Her gasp comes through loud and clear. "Austin. No."

I can't breathe or talk or do anything other than panic.

"I'll meet you there."

"Okay."

"She's fine. She's completely *fine.*"

"Yeah."

"I'll be right there."

"Thanks, Mom." To my dad, I say, "She's meeting us."

He reaches over to squeeze my arm. "Try to stay calm, son. A fever can be a sign of lots of things."

I nod and try to heed his advice, but I won't be able to breathe normally again until I know what's going on. And if the cancer is back...

No. It can't be. It just can't be.

Dr. Anand must've called ahead, because we're taken right back when we check in at the Hopkins ER. A nurse comes in a few minutes later and takes her temp. It's 102.

I'm about to lose my shit. Where in the fuck did that come from? The smell of this place takes me right back to the most terrifying time in my life. It's my least favorite place in the entire world, despite what they did here to save my daughter's life.

Another nurse comes to take blood from Everly. She remembers this process and recoils from the nurse. I hate myself as I hold her still while she screams and cries from the needle stick and then after when she sobs softly into my neck.

Thankfully, Ev dozes off, and I hold her while she sleeps, trying not to notice the heat coming from her tiny body.

Mom comes rushing in a short time later, hugs and kisses me and Everly, and looks at me with the same wild-eyed expression she wore that first night when I walked into a nightmare after flying cross-country to get to them.

My dad puts an arm around her, and they stay nearby during the interminable wait for information. I don't say a word in the two hours that pass, but every minute feels like a fucking year to me. I go over the last few days in my mind, looking for signs of impending doom that simply weren't there. She was *fine*. I kept her on a good schedule, she got plenty of sleep and good food and sunshine.

I have no idea what I'm going to do if it's back.

By the time Dr. Anand comes in, I fear I'm about to have a stroke from the pressure building inside my head.

"She's fine," the doc says.

At first, I'm not sure I heard him correctly. Did he really say, *She's fine*, or do I want to hear that so badly, I'm hearing things?

"All her counts are within normal range, and she's still in remission. Let me give her a quick exam to make sure, but whatever this is, it's not leukemia."

There's nothing else he could say that would mean more to me than that. I force myself to breathe, to swallow around the massive lump in my throat, to lay my sleeping child on the exam table so he can check her.

She awakens with a cry, until she sees Dr. Anand, whom she loves.

In a matter of minutes, he has her smiling and chatting. He's very thorough, as always, and after looking in her ears, he says, "Her ear canals are red and swollen."

"She's been swimming a lot this week."

"Swimmer's ear might be our culprit."

"*Seriously? That* can cause a fever?"

"Sometimes."

I can't believe it could actually be something so simple, probably because I'm now predisposed to expect the worst.

He prescribes an antibiotic and drops for her ears and signs discharge paperwork a short time later. "Give her some Tylenol when you get home, and keep it up for the next twenty-four hours. If she's not much better tomorrow, let me know. And let's use earplugs for swimming."

I shake his hand, this man who saved my child's life and who came running when we needed him today. "Thank you."

"Any time." He playfully taps on Everly's chin, making her giggle. "Anything for my girl Everly."

"You're the best."

"Go have a stiff drink, Dad. Everything's fine."

"You may have to tell me that a few more times."

"Let me know how she is in the morning."

"I will. Thanks again, Doc."

"You got it."

Mom and Dad walk out with us. I've got Everly in my arms, her head on my shoulder. I'm so filled with gratitude that I want to cry. I've cried more since Ev got sick than I had in my entire life before.

"I'll pick up the prescription," Dad says. "You guys get our baby girl home to rest."

"Thanks, Dad."

Mom sits in the back seat with Everly while I drive us home.

I'm a fucking wreck. My hands are shaking, my stomach hurts, and every part of me feels like it's been sent through a shredder. I park in the garage under our building and carry our bags while Mom carries Everly. The first thing we do when we get in our place is give her the Tylenol, which she takes without protest.

She puts her hands on my face, forcing me to look at her. "Rie?"

"She's still in Florida, Pooh, but we'll see her very soon."

"Dora!"

I settle her on the sofa with her favorite blanket and find *Dora the Explorer* on the TV. She snuggles in to watch, and I inhale the first deep breath I've taken in hours.

Mom comes over to hug me. She doesn't say anything, but then, she doesn't have to. She gets it because she lived through every second of hell with me. "I'll make something for dinner."

"What would I do without you guys?"

"No need to worry about something that isn't going to happen."

"Thank you."

"We love you both. You don't have to thank us." She starts toward the door. "By the way, I took the liberty of packing Ev's things for Florida, so you only have to worry about yourself. I figured that might get you back to where you want to be that much quicker."

"You're the best, Mama."

"How's Maria?"

"She's amazing, fantastic, beautiful, delightful." Just thinking about her makes me feel better after the last few horrific hours.

"You light up when you talk about her."

"Because I love her."

"Oh, Austin... That's wonderful. She's a lovely person."

"You have no idea how lovely she is." Thinking about Maria loosens the tension inside me and fills me with a feeling I never had before I had her. It's a level of joy that can't be described in words. I tell Mom about taking Maria to see houses yesterday and her reaction to them. "We worked it out, but it was kind of refreshing to realize she was put off by the money rather than turned on."

"Which is what you're used to."

"Yeah. Not to mention, Ev just adores her—and vice versa."

"I couldn't be happier for you all."

"I'm heading back there the second Everly is feeling better."

"We'll be right behind you. Dad has a doctor's appointment on Tuesday, so we're planning to leave Wednesday."

"How do you feel about babysitting next Saturday? Carmen is getting married."

"We've got you covered. I'll text you when dinner is ready."

"Sounds good. Thanks again."

"No problem."

I check on Everly, see that she's dozed off again and sit next to her on the sofa, wanting to be close by if she needs me. I put my head back and try to force myself to relax, to let go of the panic and gritty fear. *She's okay. She's okay. She's okay.* Maybe if I think it enough times, it'll actually register.

I send a text to Maria. *I know you're working, but give me a call if you take a break.*

The phone rings two minutes later, and I get up to take the call in the kitchen so I won't disturb Ev.

"Hey," she says. "We're not busy yet. What's up?"

"Everly spiked a fever on the flight home."

"*What?* Is she okay? Did you get her checked?"

"I did. She's fine. But I'm a wreck." I try so hard to keep my emotions in check, but hearing Maria's voice and her concern is my undoing.

"Oh God, Austin... I wish I could hug you."

"Freaked me out." I wipe tears from my face, wishing I could control out-of-control emotions, but I know by now there's no fighting the tsunami when it hits.

"Of course it did. I'm so sorry. Did they say what they think it is?"

"She's got red, swollen ear canals, probably from all the swimming. He gave her an antibiotic and drops in addition to the Tylenol for the fever."

"And they ran her blood?"

"Yeah. All good."

She breathes out a deep breath. "Thank God. You must've been beside yourself."

"You have no idea."

"I have a small idea. I'm beside myself for you after the fact."

"Sorry to bother you when you're working."

"Please, don't worry about it. Of course I wanted to know about this."

"Call me when you get home?"

"I will. Are you okay?"

"I will be. Eventually. I'm all triggered and shit."

"Maybe you should check in with the therapist?"

"Yeah, probably. That's a good idea."

"Do whatever it takes to feel better, Austin. There's no shame in any of it."

"Talking to you helps." I take a deep breath and release it

slowly, trying to sort the wild thoughts running through my mind. "When we were first talking to each other, I felt stupid for telling you about the PTSD and the therapy and all that, but now I'm glad you know."

"You should never feel stupid about how you feel. And knowing you were so deeply affected by Everly's illness only makes me love you more, not less."

"I miss you so much. How can it only be eight hours since I last saw you?"

"Feels like a week."

"I, um… I'm having second thoughts about moving Ev away from her oncologist."

"Which is also perfectly normal, but if anything happens, we can get her top-quality care here in consultation with her doctor there. I'm a nurse and you can bet I'll be keeping a very close eye on our girl."

"Our girl… I've never wanted to share her with anyone until you."

"I love her so much, it's ridiculous. I worry I'm going to spoil her rotten."

"It's okay if you do. I want her to have everything, including you and your love."

"She's got both. I'm all hers, and I love her madly."

"Guess what?"

"What?"

"My mom packed up Ev's stuff for Miami, so I only have to pack for myself and get her feeling better. We might be back sooner than I thought."

"I can't wait, and just keep telling yourself she's fine, everything is fine, and we're going to have so much fun this winter."

"I'll do that. Call me later?"

"As soon as I get home."

"Have a good night at work."

"I will. Love you."

"Love you, too, babe." I end the call and think about what Maria said regarding my therapist. I've cut back from weekly appointments to an as-needed basis as we got further out from the bone marrow transplant, but Maria is right. I need to check in with Lois after what happened today. My reaction to what turned out to be a simple fever proves I'm not as "recovered" from the trauma as I'd like to believe.

I send her a text asking if she can fit me in at some point in the next few days.

She writes back twenty minutes later. *I'm booked solid this week, but I have thirty minutes right now if you want to give me a call.*

I check to make sure Everly is still asleep on the sofa and go into my bedroom to make the call.

"Hi there," Lois says when she picks up. She's in her mid-fifties and recently became a first-time grandmother. I credit her with putting me back together after Everly was ill and helping me learn to function with crippling anxiety. "I was thinking of you the other day. Congrats on the perfect game. That was thrilling to watch."

"Thank you."

"How's Everly?"

"She's been doing great until a fever today sent me spiraling."

"Is she okay?"

"She's fine. All her blood work came back normal, and she's still in remission. They think the fever came from an ear infection."

"Thank goodness that's all it is. You must've had a frightening few hours."

"It was awful, and thus my text for an appointment."

"I'm sure it took you right back to the trauma of her illness."

"It did. I keep telling myself she's fine, but..."

"The anxiety is telling you otherwise."

"Yeah."

"It's perfectly normal to overreact to a fever after what you've been through, Austin. Tell me you know that."

"I do. It just... It took me back."

"Of course it did."

"Things have been so much better lately. Ev is thriving, and I... I met someone."

"Did you? That's great."

"Believe it or not, she's Everly's bone marrow donor."

"Wow, that's amazing."

"It's been pretty great. She's the sweetest person. Once we were allowed to finally talk freely, we haven't really stopped since."

"Does she live near you?"

"No, she's in Miami, so Ev and I and my folks are going to spend the winter down there, but after today, I'm anxious about being so far from her doctor."

"They have doctors in Miami, Austin."

"That's what Maria said, too. She's a nurse. She said she'll keep a close eye on Everly."

"Then it sounds like you have all your bases covered, no pun intended. Remember how we've talked about Everly and her illness and how her journey is going to play out regardless of what you do or don't do?"

"I remember." Letting go of the notion that I could control any aspect of this situation has taken time and effort on my part.

"We talked about the things you can do every day to keep her safe and healthy, and I'm sure you're all over that."

"I am."

"The rest is simply out of your hands."

"Intellectually, I know that. Emotionally, however..."

"She's your little girl, and the thought of her being sick again is unbearable."

"Right." I'm furious at the tears that fill my eyes, threatening to suck me back into the undertow of helplessness I lived with for months during the worst of Everly's illness. There is, literally, nothing worse than watching your child suffer and being powerless to fix it for them.

"She's not sick again. She has an ear infection, and in a day or two, she's going to be right back to herself.

"Thanks for the reminder."

"I know it's very difficult to pull yourself out of these spirals once they take hold, but keep thinking about all the positive things in your life. Everly is healthy. You've got this exciting new relationship that's making you happy. Your career is thriving. Everything is good, Austin. It's better than good. It's wonderful. Keep your eye on the positive things even when the negative is calling to you."

"I'm trying."

"I feel for you. You've been through hell, and it's going to take a while to get over waiting for the sky to fall on you. Be kind to yourself."

"Thanks for taking the time today. I appreciate it."

"I'm here any time you need me."

"I appreciate that, too."

"Keep me posted on how you and Everly are doing, and best of luck in the off-season. I'm hoping you get everything you deserve."

"Thanks." Her comment reminds me of messages from Aaron that I need to deal with at some point.

"Take care."

"You, too." I end the call and take a few minutes to try to find my chill, which has been missing since I realized Everly was feverish earlier. Lois has been such a great source of help and sanity to me while Everly was sick and since she's recovered. I can't imagine where I'd be without her, my parents, my brothers, my friends and teammates who surrounded me and Ev with so much love and support during the best and worst of times.

Lois is right. Things are going my way again. The months of hell are behind us, and only good things are ahead. Despite the fever and ear infection, Everly is healthy and thriving, and that's all that matters. I can handle anything else as long as she's okay.

My mom texts that Dad is back with Everly's prescription and dinner is ready.

I go to the sofa to rouse Everly with kisses to her cheek, which feels cooler than it did an hour ago. When her eyes pop open, the first thing she says is, "Rie?"

Smiling, I tell her, "Not yet, Pooh. But soon. Very, very soon."

CHAPTER 22

MARIA

I'm off my game at work after the call from Austin. I mess up two orders and spill a cosmopolitan down the front of me, leaving my white shirt stained. As soon as things die down a bit with the dinner rush, I take a break, go into the ladies' room and wash my hands, which are sticky from the sugary drink.

Carmen comes in after me.

I've been so busy, I haven't been able to talk to her or Jason while they eat dinner at the bar with my parents.

"Dude, you're a hot mess tonight. What's going on?"

"Everly spiked a fever on the flight to Baltimore, and Austin was losing it when I talked to him. She's fine, but it's left us both rattled."

"Understandably so. What can I do for you?"

"Nothing. She's okay, so I'm okay. How are you? One week until the big day!"

"I'm all good, just concerned about you."

"I love her so much," I whisper. "So, so much."

Carmen hugs me. "She's wonderful and sweet, and she loves her Rie, too."

"It's all so big." I pull back from her and place my hand on my heart, which feels too large for my chest lately. "With her and with him."

"I know that feeling. It's kind of scary, right?"

"Terrifying, but also the best thing ever."

"That sounds about right."

"How do people survive falling in love like this?"

"I asked myself that question when I was first with Jason and beginning to realize what he was going to mean to me. It's always such a big risk to open your heart to feelings as big as what you're experiencing for Austin and Everly. But I've found the payoff to be worth the gamble, twice now."

The pager on my belt buzzes to let me know I have food up in the kitchen. "Duty calls. Thank you for checking on me."

"Let's have a drink after your shift."

"Sounds good. And let me know what I can do for you this week."

"I will."

I finish my shift, cash out with nearly four hundred dollars in tips and join my family for a quick drink at the bar before I head home. I can't wait to talk to Austin and check on Everly and just be with him, even if being with him isn't the same when he's not here. I wish they were still at the hotel and I could sleep with his arms around me.

After a quick shower, I put on a robe and check my phone to find an email from him, sent an hour ago.

Dear Maria,

Today has been a really, really long day. I feel like it's been a month since I left you this morning. I'm glad you enjoyed the breakfast, and thanks for letting me spoil you a little. You deserve it!

*Ev is doing much better. The fever is down to 99.9 from 102
earlier, and she's much perkier than she was. Hopefully, the
antibiotic will kick in overnight and fix her right up. I'll admit
that I've been hitting the whiskey tonight. Sometimes that's the
only thing that takes the edge off the anxiety. Hearing that
she's still in remission after fearing a relapse was such a relief,
but the sick feeling of dread and fear is hard to shake. I'm
working on it, though!*

*I hope you had a good night at work. Hit me up on FaceTime
when you get home.*

I miss you. I love you. I can't wait to get back to you.

Austin

Moved to tears by his heartfelt words, I put through the
FaceTime call.

He comes on the screen, smiling and happy to see me, but he
looks exhausted. "Hey."

"How're you doing?" I take in the sight of his bare chest and
the handsome face that just does it for me.

"I'm okay, and Everly was much better by bedtime."

"I just read your email. I'm so glad the fever is down and
she's perked up. We need her full of beans."

"Right? I talked to Lois, the shrink, had dinner with my
parents and Ev and talked to my brothers. I'm better than I was.
But I still wish you were here."

"I do, too. I'm sorry you had such a rough day."

"I suppose it's bound to happen. All that matters is that she's
still in remission."

"Right, but you matter, too, and I know this was awful for
you."

"I'm coping and staying focused on the positive, including
getting back to you as soon as I possibly can. I packed all my
stuff tonight, and if Ev is better tomorrow, we'll head out
Monday morning, first thing. I looked online. It's sixteen hours."

"That's a long time in the car with a three-year-old."

"We'll be okay. I loaded a bunch of her favorite videos and shows on the iPad, and she's got her books and music." He takes a sip from a glass full of amber-colored liquor. "How was work?"

I hold up my ruined uniform shirt. "This is how it was."

"Whoa! What happened?"

"I was off my game tonight." That's putting it mildly.

"How come?"

"I was worried about Everly and you and just... everything."

"I'm sorry we messed with your game."

"I'm not sorry. I always want to know what's going on with you guys."

"I hate being away from you, and it's only been one very long day."

"Same."

"I pulled the trigger on the Gable Estates house. It's all ours as of this coming Friday."

"You guys can stay with me if you get back before then."

"We'll be back before then."

We chat for two hours, until we're both yawning our heads off and have no choice but to say good night.

I power through the next few days—brunch with the family on Sunday and work on Monday. Everly is still a bit droopy on Monday, so Austin decides to give her one more day before they hit the road. By Tuesday, she's much better, and they leave Baltimore early that morning, making it to Georgia before stopping for the night. I'm giddy at work on Wednesday, knowing they'll be here sometime today.

After work, I hit the grocery store and go home to make dinner while I wait for them. The last time I talked to Austin, they were in traffic in West Palm Beach, and the GPS was showing ninety minutes to my house. That last hour and a half goes by so slowly, I'm about to crawl out of my skin.

A light knock on my door has me flying across the room and letting out a happy scream when I see Everly there, holding a bunch of flowers in her pudgy little hands.

"Rie! Flowers!"

I'm so happy to see her, I weep. I pick her up and swing her around, nearly crushing the flowers that I manage to rescue at the last second. I put them on the counter and hug her as Austin comes in after her with two bags hooked over his shoulder and Everly's backpack in hand.

I've never in my life been so glad to see anyone. They were gone for five days, but it felt like a lifetime. In those five days, something became very clear to me: I'll follow him—them—to the ends of the earth if it means I get to be with them every day. At some point, I probably ought to tell him that.

I put Everly down and walk into Austin's outstretched arms.

"There you are," he says, sounding as relieved as I am to be back together.

I cling to him. "Was it really only five days?"

"Felt like a hundred." He pulls back to kiss me—a light caress of lips against lips in deference to our little audience, but it makes me shiver with pleasure. "To be continued later. Everly, quit running around."

"It's fine. She's probably thrilled to be out of the car."

"We both are. That was a long-ass drive."

"Rie! Ass!"

I rock with silent laughter as Austin looks at me with horror. "Don't say that, Pooh. Dada said a bad word."

"Rie?"

"No, the other one."

"Ass, ass, *ass!*"

I'm beside myself, trying to hold in the laughter, the joy, the love. They're back, and everything in my world is right again.

AUSTIN

After dinner, we take Everly to a park to play and run off some of her pent-up energy from being in the car for two days. We bring her back to Maria's around eight, give her a bath and read four stories to her before she finally falls asleep in Maria's bed around nine. We'll move her to the sofa when it's time for us to go to bed.

For now, we sneak out, leaving the door propped so we can hear her if she wakes up.

"Phew," I say when we're in the living room. "I thought she'd be with us until midnight."

"She's the cutest thing on the entire planet."

"I agree. Come to me, hug me, kiss me, put me out of my misery."

She walks into my arms, and we hold on to each other for the longest time. I have no idea how long because time ceases to exist when I'm with her. It's just her and me and us and the perfection we've found with each other.

"I couldn't wait to get back to you. Every mile of that drive was torturous."

"I've been on pins and needles for days, waiting for you to get back." She pulls back and looks up at me. "I realized something while you were gone."

"What's that?"

She draws me down so she can kiss the furrow between my brows. "Nothing bad. It's actually something really good."

Taking her hand, I lead her to the sofa, and we sit together, arms and legs intertwined. "Tell me."

"I don't care where you end up. I'm going with you."

This is the best news she could've given me. "Really?"

She nods. "I can't be away from you guys for months on end. I just can't."

"That's really great, because I can't stand to be away from you, either, and neither can Ev. She drove me mad asking for

Rie the whole time we were away from you, even though she talked to you on FaceTime every day."

"It wasn't enough for me, either. I just love her so damned much."

"She loves you, too."

"When she started with the 'ass' business earlier... I'm going to be a terrible influence on her, because I can't stop the laughter."

"That was funny. And horrifying."

"Your face was so priceless."

"My little girl was swearing like a sailor!"

"We have to watch everything we say around her going forward."

"I know." I curl a strand of her long hair around my finger, fascinated by her curls and the silky texture. Hell, I'm fascinated by every single thing about this amazing woman. "What've you got going the rest of the week?"

"My sister gets here tomorrow, and the bachelorette party is tomorrow night. Rehearsal and rehearsal dinner on Friday night and then the wedding on Saturday. It's going to be a crazy few days."

"It'll be fun, though, right?"

"Oh yeah. I'm super excited to celebrate with Carmen and Jason."

"My parents will be here by Friday, so we're set with babysitters for the weekend."

"This is very good news. I'm looking forward to having you all to myself."

"Don't make any plans for after the wedding," I tell her.

"What're you up to?"

"You'll find out." I kiss her because I can't wait another second.

She responds with equal ardor, and we end up stretched out on her sofa, arms around each other, trying to get closer the way we always do. I can never get close enough to her. "I think it might be time to move Everly and go to bed. I'm wiped out after that long drive."

Smiling, Maria presses against my hard cock, making me whimper. "I can tell how worn out you are."

"Flat-out exhausted." I flash a dirty grin as I pull myself up and off her to relocate Everly to the sofa.

Maria covers her with Everly's favorite blanket and tucks her in with tender care before kissing her.

We go into her room, pulling off clothes as we go, and come together on her bed with an urgency I've never felt so strongly, even with her. I need this woman the way I need air and food. I need her so badly, we skip all the preliminaries and go right to the main event.

"Yes, *Austin*... Yes."

Being inside her feels like coming home to the safest, happiest, most secure place I've ever been. I wrap my arms around her and hold on tight to the best thing to ever happen to me. She's right up there with Everly, and I can't wait to see what's ahead for us as we go forward together.

"I love you," I whisper in her ear. "I love you so much. Being away from you was hell."

"Same, same. I love you, too."

"Marry me, Maria." The words are out before I take even a second to consider what I'm saying, but I don't regret it. That's what I want. She's what I want. I've known that since the first time I ever talked to her, before I knew her name or had seen her face or experienced her love firsthand. I want us to be a family.

She gasps, her eyes fly open, and she goes still under me. "What?"

I press deep inside her and gaze down at her, so lovely and sweet and sexy and perfect. "I love you. Everly loves you. Marry us. Be our family. Be our everything."

Blinking rapidly, she tries to contain tears that spill down her cheeks. "I, ah... Are you really asking me that?"

I push even deeper into her, making us both gasp from the intensity of what we feel when we're together this way. "I'm really asking." Bending my head, I draw her nipple into my mouth, giving a gentle tug that has her internal muscles clamping down on my cock. It's all I can do to hang on when that happens. "Marry me, sweet Maria. I'll give you the world."

"I only want you and Ev."

"Is that a yes?" I can barely breathe as I wait for her to say the only word I want to hear.

"Yes."

I squeeze her so tightly. "Best word ever."

"We can't tell anyone until after Carmen's wedding. This is her big week."

"I can live with that. Are you really going to marry me?"

"Yes, Austin, I'm really going to marry you."

"Can I come see your clinic tomorrow?"

"Sure."

"Good, now what do you say we finish what we started here?"

"Mmm, I say yes to that, too."

"Yes is my new favorite word." There's nothing quite like finding that one person who completes you, who loves your child as much as you do, who makes you feel like you're the king of the world when you're with her, as if anything is possible. I know without any doubt that I'll be safe with this woman, that my child will be safe with her. At the end of the day, what else matters?

CHAPTER 23

MARIA

"*I* probably shouldn't have done that while we were having sex."

I turn my head so I can see him. "It was perfect. As long as you meant it."

"Hell yes, I meant it. Did you mean it when you said yes?"

"Hell yes."

His smile lights up his face as he turns on his side to face me, his arm around me. "It's going to be so great. *We're* going to be so great."

"We already are."

"I talked to my agent, Aaron, today." He combs his fingers through my hair. "What do you think of Seattle?"

"As in the Seattle that's on the other side of the country Seattle?"

"Yeah, that's the one."

"Um, well… I haven't really thought much about it, to be honest."

"Would you be willing to consider it for roughly half the

year for the next six or so years? We could spend the off-season here."

As I rest my head on his chest and run my fingers over the elaborate artwork on his pectorals, I try to imagine life without regular time with my family and friends and what that would be like.

"You'd be able to come home any time you need to for any reason. No questions asked. Your Nona's birthday, your sister's home for the weekend, your cousin is having a Tupperware party… Whatever it is, if you want to go, you go."

I'm rocking with silent laughter. "No one has Tupperware parties anymore. With my family, it's more likely to be Pampered Chef."

"Whatever it is, if you need to be there, you'll be there."

"You're very sweet to understand how connected I am to my family."

"I've seen that firsthand, and I'd never want to keep you from them. But selfishly, I need you with me and Ev. I know this is a big ask."

"It's not that big. Yes, it'll be hard to be away from my life here, but I'll have you and Ev to make it worth the sacrifice."

"We'll make it worth it—and the Mariners are making it worth it, too. Aaron says they're offering a hundred twenty million for three years with all sorts of options and incentives."

"Holy. *Shit.*"

"Right?"

I look up to catch his gaze. "Can I ask you something else?"

"Anything you want."

"Do you want more kids?"

"Absolutely. I'd have ten kids. I love being a dad."

"We're not having ten kids."

"You're no fun."

"Yes, I am, and you know it. I'd consider two more with possible negotiations for a fourth, but that's it."

"I'll take that deal."

"Are we really doing this? Are we talking about our life together?"

"That's what I'm talking about. What're you talking about?"

I smile at the way he says that and snuggle into his warm embrace. "I'm so excited."

"So am I. What kind of wedding should we have?"

"The only kind of wedding my family is capable of—an extravaganza. You'll see this weekend."

"I want you to have whatever you want. Anything you want."

"All I want is you and Ev and your family and my family. That's all I need." I pause and let out a laugh. "I can't believe I'm getting married."

"Believe it, baby. We're going to have it all. Every single thing."

I'm not sure what time it was when we finally fell asleep, but it was late, and I'm startled awake when I can't breathe. I open my eyes to find Everly hovering over me, plugging my nose to get me to wake up.

"Rie!"

Austin comes to with a gasp as we realize we've been caught in bed together for the first time. "Pooh, don't do that to Rie. It's bad enough when you do it to Dada."

"Dada! Rie! Bed!"

I'm dying, and I can't stop the gurgle of laughter that erupts from deep inside me.

"Rie! Silly!"

We never did get around to putting clothes back on, so not only has she caught us in bed together, but we're also bare-ass naked.

"Pooh, go on out to the sofa. Dada will be right out."

"Rie!"

"I'm coming, too, pumpkin." As soon as I can stop laughing, that is.

Everly jumps off the bed and goes running out to the living room.

Austin gets up, pulls on a pair of underwear and shorts and then leans over to kiss me. "We're busted."

"Looks that way. Are you okay with that?"

"She needs to get used to seeing us sleep together. And you know what's great?"

"Besides everything?"

He smiles. "She'll never remember life before you. You'll be the only mother she ever knows." After dropping that emotional bomb on me, he kisses me and goes to see what Everly is doing while I lie in bed and marvel at how I'm now a fiancée and the mother of a three-year-old.

MARIA

I float through the morning at the clinic, in the best mood I've ever been in. My future is set. I've found my one, and that he comes with the most wonderful little girl is a delightful bonus. In the break room between patients, Miranda asks me what's got me smiling from ear to ear.

"You'll meet them around noon when they come in for lunch."

"Them?"

"My boyfriend and his daughter." It pains me to call him that when he's my fiancé now, but I can't do anything to take the spotlight off Carmen this week. There will be time enough to celebrate my news after her wedding.

"Ah, so it's all official, then?"

"It is. I can't wait for you to meet them, and you should know he's interested in funding the clinic."

She pauses mid-sip. "Seriously?"

"Yep. I told him what we do here, what it means to me and the community. He's excited to be part of it."

Miranda blinks a few times, and I realize she's trying not to cry. "This is a miracle," she says softly. "I haven't wanted to say anything, but our funding is really low. I've been praying to the Blessed Virgin for relief…"

I go to her and hug her, filled with love for her and the man who will ease her burden. "I'm sorry you've been so worried. You could've told me."

"I didn't want you to be worried, too."

"You need to prepare yourself… When Austin goes all in, he doesn't hold back."

She fans her face as she tries to contain her tears.

I hand her a tissue from a box on the counter. "I should tell you that it's possible he's going to sign with Seattle."

Her smile falters. "That's awfully far from Miami."

"I know, and I'll probably be going with him."

"Ah, mi amiga, you're in love."

"Very much so."

"I'm so happy for you—and for him. He's a lucky man."

"We're both lucky to have found each other."

"And in the most special way. You were a perfect match for his child, and he's a perfect match for you. What a lovely thing that is."

Our receptionist, Angie, comes to the break room door. "Maria, there's a hot-as-F dude here with the cutest kid ever, and they're asking for you."

"That'd be her boyfriend and his daughter," Miranda says.

Angie's eyes bug. "Legit?"

"As legit as it gets." They're early, but I don't care. I follow Angie to the reception area, where Austin is holding Everly and a big shopping bag.

"Rie! Lunch!"

"There's my pumpkin." I take her from him and give her a squeeze.

"Rie! Bed! Dada!"

While Austin, Angie and Miranda crack up, I gently cover Everly's mouth. "Shhh, don't tell my secrets at work."

"I'm Austin," he says. "You must be Angie and Miranda."

As they shake hands with him, both women seem a little dazzled. I can't blame them. He has the same effect on me.

"So this is the clinic I've heard so much about."

"It's not much, but it's our home away from home," Miranda tells him. "Come take a look."

While I hold Everly, Miranda shows him our two exam rooms and the break room. "And that concludes our five-minute tour."

"How many patients do you see here in a week?"

"It varies, but on our busiest week, about two hundred fifty."

"That's a lot."

"We can never accommodate everyone in a given day," I tell him. "But we give them numbers so they can come back without having to wait again."

"If you had a bigger place and more staff, would that help?"

Miranda stares at him. "Uhhh…"

"It would make a huge difference for our community," I tell him.

"Then let's do that, shall we?"

"Holy F," Angie says. "Is he for real?"

"He is," I tell her, bursting with pride. He's all mine, and I love him for doing this. "He's as real as it gets."

Over the lunch that Austin brought, we discuss his intention to fund the clinic going forward, to provide whatever is needed, up to and including a new, larger facility.

"You're going to have to give me some time to catch up," Miranda says. "I can't believe this is happening."

Austin covers her hand with his much larger one. "It's an absolute pleasure to be able to do this, Miranda. I get paid a ridiculous amount of money to play a game. Being able to do some real good with that money is important to me—and this place is important to Maria. That makes it important to me."

"*Girl,*" Angie says.

I send her a smug smile. "I know, right?"

"We were really, really lucky when Everly got sick to have access to the best health care money could buy. I can't take care of everyone who needs it, but I can do this."

"Thank you so much," Miranda says. "So, so much."

Jason comes in and stops short when he sees us gathered around the table with Austin and Everly. I almost forgot that today is his afternoon at the clinic. "What's up?" he asks.

"We've got ourselves a new benefactor," Miranda tells him.

"Is that right?" Jason smiles at Austin. "That's awesome and so badly needed."

"So I've been told." He gestures to the sandwich makings on the table. "Have something to eat."

"Don't mind if I do. I was running late and didn't get to eat."

We make room for him at the table.

"Are you getting excited?" I ask him.

"So excited. I never knew getting married was so much fun."

"It's only fun when you get it exactly right," Miranda tells him. "Which you did."

"I sure did."

"How's the bride holding up?" Austin asks.

"She seems good, although I know it's not the same for her as it is for me. I'm trying to be mindful of that."

"When you marry a widow, you don't just get her," Miranda says. "You get her late husband and his family, too."

Jason nods. "I know, and I love Tony's family and how devoted Carmen has been to them and vice versa. They're her family."

"You'll be just fine because you get it," Miranda says. "And with that, we need to get back to work. Austin, thank you for lunch and everything else. I'm looking forward to working with you."

"Same. You have my number. Let's talk again soon."

"After the wedding. This week is about celebration. We'll take care of business next week."

"Sounds good. I'll look forward to hearing from you."

"Oh, you'll hear from me," she says over her shoulder as she leaves the room.

"It's so, so amazing what you're doing," Angie says. "You have no idea…" She spontaneously hugs him. "And you're hot AF."

She scurries out of the room while the rest of us laugh.

"So that's Angie for you."

"She's funny."

"It's amazing what you're doing here, Austin," Jason says. "The need is so great."

"It's very satisfying to be involved in something like this. Thank you for what you do, too."

"Like you said, it's very satisfying work. And with that, thank you for lunch. I need to get to it."

"There's always a line out the door when Dr. Jason comes in," I tell Austin after Jason leaves the room.

"We need some of our own Dr. Jasons on staff," he says.

"No matter what happens from here on out, I'll never forget that you did this. You've earned *years'* worth of husbandly get-out-of-the-doghouse-free cards with this."

His grin is potent, sexy and satisfied. "Then it's money very well spent."

Austin makes dinner while I get ready for a night out with my girls. This feels so domestic, like what being married will be like. When I come out of my bedroom wearing a black dress, sky-high heels and more makeup than Austin or Everly have ever seen on me, he stares at me with a look of pure desire that makes me wish I didn't have plans tonight.

"Rie pretty!"

I pick up Everly so she can get a closer look at the makeup.

"Rie is so pretty," Austin says. "So, *so* pretty."

"You guys are good for a girl's ego."

"Your ego should be very, *very* healthy." He steals a quick kiss and then gets busy serving up chicken and mashed potatoes and stuffing that Everly apparently loves better than scream, if her father is to be believed.

Austin not only makes dinner, he cleans up afterward, too, while I go brush my teeth, reapply my lipstick and run a brush through my hair.

He comes up behind me, wraps his arms around me and kisses my neck. "It's not fair that you're going out looking so fucking hot, and I don't get to go with you."

"I'm sorry."

"We need a real date."

"We've got the rehearsal and the wedding."

"Which will be awesome, but after that, I want just us. A lot of just us."

"We'll have plenty of that."

"You promise?"

"Absolutely." My phone chimes with a text from my sister. "Dee is here, and she wants to meet you guys." I turn and kiss him. "Don't wait up."

"I will wait up. Don't let some other dude take off with my girl."

"I'm not going anywhere with anyone but you, and you know it." I take him by the hand and lead him to the living room, releasing him to open the door to Dee.

She shrieks and launches herself at me, like always when we see each other for the first time in weeks or months. She's only a year younger than me, and we've always been close. We never fought the way other sisters we knew did, and along with Carmen, she's my closest friend. She's about two inches shorter than me, but otherwise, we could be twins. The only real difference is her curly dark hair isn't as long as mine. "You're looking hot, mama!"

"I was just saying the same thing," Austin says.

"Speaking of hot, you must be Austin."

"Nice to finally meet you."

"You, too." Dee hugs him and then bends at the waist to speak to Everly, who's hiding behind Austin's leg. "And you must be Miss Everly. I've heard so much about you."

"This is Rie's sister, Dee," I tell her. "Can you say hi?"

"Hi."

"She's much chattier when she gets to know you better."

Dee plays a cute game of peek-a-boo that has Everly giggling in no time.

"Rie! Dee!"

"That's right, pumpkin. Dee is Rie's sister."

"Sister."

I look up at Austin. "Another new word!"

"Add it to the list." Austin picks her up so they can walk us out to the limo that's backed into the driveway, waiting for us. Dee and I splurged on the car so none of us has to worry about driving tonight. "You ladies have a blast."

"We will." I kiss him and Everly. "Love you guys."

"Rie! Love!"

Austin's grin makes me again wish I could stay home. "Love you, too."

When we're in the limo, I look back and see them waving to us as we leave.

"Um, wow?" Dee says. "You *love* him? He loves you? What the fuck? I don't talk to you for a couple of days, and *love* has happened?"

"It happened a while ago, actually." I'm dying to tell her the rest, but I literally bite my tongue so I won't be tempted to blurt it out. Carmen's big week. Not the time. *Keep biting your tongue.* "He asked me to marry him."

She screams so loud, the driver startles.

"Sorry," I tell him while shushing her. "You can't tell anyone. This is Carmen's week. I'd never want to steal her thunder. You have to promise."

She hurls herself at me, hugging me so hard, she nearly breaks my ribs. "This is so awesome, Mari. He's gorgeous, and that little one… Dear God, she's *adorable!*"

"Is he gorgeous? I hadn't noticed."

"Shut up. You have to tell me everything. How did he ask?"

"Um, well, we were… you know…"

"Oh my God! No way! Right in the middle of it?"

"Yep."

"That's so amazing. Does he know yet where he's going to play next year?"

"Maybe Seattle."

"Ugh, Mari… That's so far away!"

"Believe me, I know, but as he said, it's only half the year, and his contract will probably be six years. I can do anything for half the year for six years. We'd spend the winters here."

"Until you have kids in school, and then it's not quite so simple."

Her comment has the same effect as a pin hitting a balloon. "How did I not even think of school? Everly is already three…"

"School is coming soon."

"So I guess we'll spend next winter here. After that, we won't be able to." That realization is devastating. "But he said he's fine with me coming home any time I want to."

"It'll still be hard," Dee says. "You've never wanted to live anywhere else for a good reason. This is where your heart is."

"That's true, but if they're in Seattle, that's where my heart will be. He went to Baltimore for five days to pack and drive back down for the winter, and I almost went mad from missing them."

"Sigh," she says, making the sound to go with the word. "That's so incredible, Mari. You've waited so long for this. I couldn't be more thrilled, except for the part about you moving to Seattle."

"Don't tell anyone that. Nothing is finalized, and it won't be for a while yet."

"How're we going to keep this from Carmen?"

"I shouldn't have told you."

"As if you could hold this in for two full days."

"I couldn't hold it in for two full minutes."

"You should just tell her. She's not the type who'd care about sharing the limelight."

"I don't want to tell her until after the wedding."

"It's your news, and she won't hear it from me. I'm just saying… She'd want to know."

"Speaking of things people would want to know, she and I want to talk to you about Marcus."

Dee goes perfectly still. "What about him?"

"We heard some things…"

"What things?"

"I should probably wait for Car. She's the one who heard it."

"Why didn't you guys tell me?"

"We were waiting until you were here, because there was nothing you could do from New York."

"About what?"

"So you know how he broke up with the skank, right?"

"Yes."

"Well, Car talked to Bonita, and she said he's a mess."

"What's that got to do with me?"

"Apparently, he's not a mess over the skank. He's a mess because he's realized that letting you go was the biggest mistake of his life."

Her face goes blank with shock. "He did not say that."

"If you believe his sister, he did say it."

"I can't hear that."

"We thought you'd want to know."

"And now I do."

"What're you going to do?"

"I'm not doing anything. That was over a long time ago."

"Was it? Really?" I've never known her to date anyone else in all the years since she broke up with Marcus. If she has, she hasn't told me, and she would have. We tell each other everything.

"Yes, really. Let's talk about something else. How has Car been this week?"

Though I'm concerned by how shocked she seems by the Marcus news, I follow her lead. "Good, from what I can tell." I shared Jason's concerns with her. "She hasn't said anything that leads me to believe she's anything but thrilled."

"You guys are lucky. You've got it all figured out."

"Not everything."

"The big things."

The limo glides to a stop outside the building where Carmen and Jason live in Brickell. They're outside waiting for us, and when Dee steps out of the limo, Carmen runs to her on spike heels and jumps into Dee's arms.

"Jeez, woman," Dee says. "You almost took me down."

"I knew you could handle it."

After putting Carmen down, Dee hugs Jason.

"Welcome home," he says.

"Thanks. It's always good to be here."

No one else, except for Carmen, would notice that Dee is reeling from what I told her about Marcus. She'll try to hide it, but I know her too well, and so does Car.

"You ladies have a good time and be safe," Jason says before laying a hot kiss on Carmen. "If you end up in jail, call Austin, not me."

"Haha," Carmen says, poking his belly. "No one is going to jail. Not tonight, anyway."

She gets in the car, and we follow her.

Jason stands on the sidewalk to wave us off.

Carmen looks back, watching until he's safely inside their building before she turns to find us watching her. "What?"

"What's that about?" Dee asks.

"Nothing. I was just making sure he's okay."

"He's fine, Car, and he's going to *be* fine," Dee says.

"I know."

"Do you?" I ask gently, because God knows I get where she's coming from. Losing Tony was one of the worst things to ever happen to any of us. That she moved past that and got to the point where she could take a chance on love again is nothing short of a miracle. For a time, we wondered if we'd lose her, too.

"I worry about him. I suppose that's to be expected."

"Sure," I say, "a little healthy concern is to be expected. Is that what this is?"

"Might be a little more than that, but I'm handling it. I don't want to talk about that tonight. Tell me everything, Dee! What's new?"

"I told her about Marcus."

"And?"

"And nothing," Dee says. "That's over."

Carmen raises a brow, which says it all. She doesn't believe her any more than I do.

"And Mari is engaged."

"Dee! *For fuck's sake!*" I ought to be pissed, but she saved me from the extraordinary effort it would've taken to keep the biggest news of my life a secret for two more days.

Carmen whirls around to look at me. "Are you?"

"Yes, but I was waiting to tell you until after the wedding."

"Shut up! That's crazy!" She hurls herself at me, and we hug and scream and cry and do what we always do when one of us has big news. "I'm *so* happy about this. I love him *so* much, and Everly… This is the best thing since me and Jason."

"I'm pretty damned happy about it." And relieved that my two closest friends in the world know, even if I'm going to punch Dee the first chance I get for being such a big mouth.

"He asked her while they were doing it," Dee adds, sticking her tongue out at me.

Carmen laughs and claps her hands. "That is amazing. I *love* it. There is no need for you to keep this a secret, Maria. Tell the world."

"It's your week."

She leans across the opening between the seats, takes my hand and holds on tight. "It's *our* week. The best week ever."

CHAPTER 24

AUSTIN

$\mathcal{A}$t the rehearsal and the dinner that follows, I start to get an up-close-and-personal view of the family I'm joining, and I have to say, I'm impressed. They're warm, funny, loving, loyal and not afraid to shower their love on everyone around them, including me. We were going to keep our big news a secret until after the wedding, but apparently, Dee spilled the beans, and now everyone knows.

My parents, Everly and I moved into the house in Gable Estates today, settling in for a winter of fun in the sun. I can't wait to spend as much time as possible with Maria and her family.

At the rehearsal dinner, I ask for a moment alone with Maria's dad, Lorenzo. Everyone calls him Lo, but I call him Mr. Giordino.

The rehearsal dinner is at Jason and Carmen's place, and Mr. Giordino and I take drinks to the huge patio that overlooks Biscayne Bay.

"Quite a place," he says, seeming impressed.

"It's beautiful."

"You didn't bring me out here to talk about the view, though, did you?"

"No, sir. I wanted the chance to apologize to you."

"For what?"

"For not talking to you before I asked Maria to marry me. I know I should've done that, but the proposal was somewhat spontaneous, and so here I am, after the fact, asking for your blessing."

"I should make you suffer, but you're catching me in a good mood."

Laughing, I say, "Well, thank goodness for that. I want you to know—I love Maria very much, and not just because she saved my daughter's life. Of course that was how it started, but I love her for everything she is and for her big heart."

"It'll be hard for her to live anywhere but here."

"I know, and I've told her that she should come home any time she wants or needs to. We'll spend as much time here as we possibly can."

He seems a little sad, which touches me.

"I try to imagine what it would be like to have some guy come along and take my little girl away from me, and I can't for the life of me picture that."

"It's sad for us, but exciting for her. She glows with happiness around you and your daughter. We've all seen that. But like you said, she cares so much for others, which means she's also easily hurt."

"My only goal in life will be to make her happy. You have my word on that."

"Then you have my blessing."

I shake his outstretched hand, relieved to be forgiven for failing to take care of this detail before I asked her.

Carmen comes out to the patio and walks over to us. "I was looking for you," she says to me. She's gorgeous in a white off-the-shoulder dress. Her hair is down and curly, and her smile is so big.

"Uh-oh," Lorenzo says. "What'd you do?"

"Haha, Uncle Lo. You're very funny. Could I borrow Austin for a minute?"

"Of course." Lorenzo kisses his niece and heads inside.

Once we're alone on the patio, Carmen says, "Did you get a ring yet?"

"As a matter of fact, Everly and I did that today."

"That's great, because this is what I think you ought to do…"

MARIA

The wedding is incredible, from Jason's reaction to Carmen in her dress, to Uncle Vincent and Aunt Viv in tears as they give her away, to having everyone we love together in one place for one perfect day of love and celebration and second chances.

Jason and Carmen bring everyone to tears with their heartfelt vows.

"I never imagined anything like this would happen for me again," Carmen tells her handsome groom. "I thought I'd had my one great love. Imagine my surprise at finding a second one. Thank you for being my perfect second chance, and for allowing me to bring my sweet Tony with me into our marriage and for always respecting his place in my heart. I was doing fine before we met, but since then, I've discovered there's a lot of joy to be found between fine and truly happy. I love you so much, and I always will."

Carmen reaches up to wipe the tears from his face as the rest of us battle our own tears.

I'm standing next to Carmen with Dee to my right and Carmen and Jason's friend Betty, who was there the day they met, on the other side of Dee. Tony's parents are seated in the front row with Carmen's parents, Nona and Abuela, which is such a sweet way to honor them. Jason's brother, Ben, is his best man, and two of his friends from medical school are groomsmen.

Jason takes her hand and kisses it. "I was at the lowest point in my life when I met you, and after a few hours with you, I felt better than I had in weeks. That's how quickly you changed my life. It happened in one day. And every day since then has been like something out of a dream as it just got better and better. I love you, I love the way you love Tony and his family, I love the way you love everyone who matters to you, and I feel spectacularly lucky to be loved by you. I can't wait to spend forever with you, my sweet Rizo, mi amor."

Rizo means *curly* in Spanish, which is his perfect nickname for her.

Hours later, after we've taken a million pictures and enjoyed the delicious meal of tenderloin and lobster tail with a variety of Italian and Cuban side dishes, it's time for the speeches. Dee and I flipped a coin, and I lost, so I get to give the maid of honor speech for both of us. Not that we aren't both happy to do it. It's just that public speaking makes us nervous.

"For those of you who don't know me, I'm Carmen's cousin Maria. My sister, Dee, and I are her maids of honor, but don't worry, you're only going to hear from one of us."

"Thank God for that," Nico says, as only a brother can.

"Shut up, Nico."

Everyone laughs and claps because no one deserves to be put in his place more than my brother does.

"This has been such an amazing day of celebration, and, Carmen, you have to know how much it means to all of us to see you happy and smiling and in love with such a great guy. I have no doubt at all that Tony is here with us today and that he loves Jason as much as you do, as much as all of us do. Jason, you showed me your heart early on, when you came to work at the clinic and then kept coming back long after we could do anything to help you. I know I don't have to tell you how much Carmen means to all of us, so please take good care of each other and give us lots of babies to love." I raise my glass to them. "To Carmen and Jason, may you have a long and happy life together full of love and all good things. We love you both."

Carmen and Jason dance to "Unchained Melody," and I cry my eyes out watching them as the lyrics about "God speed your love to me" touch my heart with their poignancy. I have to believe that God and Tony and lots of prayers and tons of love delivered Carmen to her happily ever after with Jason. After that, my maid of honor duties are finished, and I'm ready to dance with my sexy man, who's sexier than usual today in a gray suit.

He's removed the suit coat, and I run my hands over the vest he's left on. It's a good look on him, but a brown bag would look good on him.

"Sexiest bridesmaid I've ever seen," he whispers in my ear. "That dress is *fire.*"

"This old thing?" The rich, navy silk leaves little to the imagination.

"I have to keep reminding myself I'm not allowed to let my hands go anywhere they want."

"Not yet. But later, they can."

"And they will." He holds me as close as he can get me, and it's not enough. "Everything about this day was perfect, especially you in that dress. I almost swallowed my tongue when you came down the aisle."

"Don't do that! It's one of my favorite parts of you."

"What are some of your other favorite parts?"

Though we're surrounded by people, I feel like we're in our own bubble. "Your lips, eyes, smile… Your hands… Your heart."

"How long do we have to stay?"

"Awhile. I'm the maid of honor."

He presses his erection against me. "Don't forget this part."

"As if I ever could."

We dance all night, and I can tell I impress him with my moves on the dance floor, especially when Dee, Carmen, my brothers and cousins join me, and we bust loose the way we always do when we're together. Austin takes a step back and watches me move, and I put on a show just for him.

I'm wiping sweat from my face when Carmen takes the microphone from the DJ. "Hope everyone is having a great time!"

We applaud and cheer for the bride, who's positively glowing.

"So I'm not the only one around here with big news this week. My sweet cousin Maria got *engaged!*"

While the guests applaud, I can't believe what I'm seeing when Everly comes walking toward me, wearing a pretty party dress, her hair up and tied with a bow. I bend to hug her and pick her up as I catch Austin's smiling parents looking on. What is happening?

She hugs me tightly with her chubby arms around my neck.

"You look so pretty, pumpkin."

"Ric! Pretty!"

"Yes, you are," I say, laughing. "What're you doing here?"

"Maria thought she could keep this big news a secret until after my wedding," Carmen says, "but we all know how secrets work in this family."

I turn to find Austin and gasp to realize he's down on one knee and now holding the microphone. "Beautiful Maria… With Carmen's help, I had this all planned and everything I wanted to say to you memorized. But now that the moment is here, and you're holding my little girl, whose life you saved before you saved mine, all I know is that I want you in our lives forever. Everly and I love you so much. Will you please marry us?"

He produces a velvet box with a sparkling diamond ring inside.

"Rie! Marry!"

I'm laughing and crying and nodding. "Yes, I'll marry you guys."

The place goes wild as Austin stands to hug us both before pulling back to kiss me and slide the ring on my left hand. "Now it's official."

AUSTIN

Carmen's idea was perfect. Just about everyone we love was there to see our big moment. My mom took video for my brothers, who sent their congrats. They can't wait to meet Maria, and I can't wait for that, either. They're going to love her as much as I do.

We introduce my parents to the rest of Maria's family and let Everly stay for a bit to dance with us before sending her home to bed.

Maria's Nona invited them to join the family for brunch tomorrow, which I suspect is going to be part of our weekly routine while we're in Miami. That's fine with me. I love being around Maria's family.

After we finally leave the wedding, I ignore everything other than my beautiful fiancée and the private after-party I've planned for us.

"Where are we going?" she asks as we head north on I-95.

I quit drinking hours ago so I'd be able to drive. "You'll see soon enough, my love." I reach for her hand and bring it to my lips, placing a kiss right below her new ring. "The ring is good?"

She snorts out a laugh. "Ah, yeah, Austin, the ring is 'good.'"

I might've gone a little overboard with a nearly three-carat square-cut diamond surrounded by other smaller diamonds. "Is it too much?"

"Probably, but I love it anyway. Thank you for pulling off such a great surprise."

"It was all Carmen's idea. She wanted to celebrate you."

"I love her so much. Seeing her happy like she was today is the best thing after everything she's been through."

"They're a great couple." A short time later, we arrive at the Ritz-Carlton Bal Harbour, located on the northern part of Miami Beach. I'd told Maria to pack a bag to stay somewhere tonight, and after turning over my car to the valet, I carry both our bags inside and go directly to the elevator.

"We don't have to check in?"

"I took care of that earlier."

"Look at you, planning ahead."

"I wanted tonight to be special for you."

"It's special for me because I'm with you. I hope you know I don't need anything else."

"I do know that, which is why I want to give you everything."

She leans her head against my chest. "I only need you."

And that, right there, is one of many reasons I know for certain that I'll love this woman for the rest of my life. In the elevator, I keep my arm around her as we go to the sixth floor, where I've booked an oceanfront suite. We'll get to enjoy the view tomorrow.

"This is awesome!" she says of the room.

I was hoping it would be okay to bring her here. I'm a little unsure of myself when it comes to surprising her with anything luxurious after her reaction to the homes we toured, but tonight demanded something special.

I follow her onto the patio, where we can hear the ocean crashing against the beach and breathe in the scent of sand and salt water. "How about some champagne?"

"In a minute." She wraps her arms around my waist and gazes up at me. "I just need this first."

"I'm always happy to provide this." I kiss her the way I've

been dying to since the second I first saw her in the sexy dress. There's nothing in the world that can compare to the high I get from kissing her. "I need to talk to you about this dress."

"What about it?"

"You made me hard in a church, Maria. If I go straight to hell, it's completely your fault."

She giggles helplessly. "That did not happen."

"It did, too! I was afraid I'd be struck by lightning or something." I nuzzle her neck and bury my face in her fragrant hair. "You were so, so, *so* stunning today. I mean, you always are, but today was just *wow*. And watching you dance... Mmmm, so hot."

"Do you ever think that this is all just a dream? That any minute now, we're going to wake up and discover it was all a very lovely dream?"

"That's how it feels to me, too, like how can something this amazing actually be real? But it's so real. It's the realest thing ever."

She flashes a big smile. "Is realest a word?"

"If it isn't, it ought to be." I take her hand. "Let's check out the rest of this room, shall we?"

"Lead the way."

I grab the bottle of champagne that's chilling on one of the tables and lead her into the bedroom. After I pop the cork, we both drink right from the bottle.

"Look at us. Bringing the class."

I laugh and take another drink. "Why put it in a glass when it comes in one?"

"Good point." She takes another sip and then burps.

We crack up laughing. It feels so good to laugh with her, to be completely myself with her and vice versa.

"Here's to you and me and Everly and forever together."

"I'll drink to that." She hands the bottle back to me. "Austin, do you think maybe, at some point, I could adopt her?"

"That'd be…" My throat tightens around a lump of emotion. "Yeah, baby. Let's make that happen."

"Only if it's what you want, too."

"Of course it is. You're already her mother, Maria. You're the one she loves."

"I'm so happy," she says on a sigh. "Happier than I've ever been in my entire life."

"I am, too. I never knew this kind of happy existed." I kiss her shoulder, along her collarbone and up her neck before capturing her lips in another of those sweet, sexy kisses that have become so necessary to me. "How do I get this stunning dress off you?"

She lifts her arm to show me the zipper that runs down the side.

"I'm going to need lots of pictures from today so I never forget how you looked in this dress."

"I can make that happen. I know people."

Underneath the dress, she's wearing only a low-cut strapless bra and matching thong.

"I just want to look at you forever."

"I can make that happen, too." She reaches out to unbutton my vest and the dress shirt under it. "Give me that sexy chest, and hurry up about it."

I pull off clothes as fast as I can, popping off one of the buttons on my shirt in the process, which makes Maria laugh.

"I'm handy with a needle and thread. I can fix that for you."

"Least of my worries at the moment."

"You have worries? What are they?"

"For one thing, I'm worried I won't be able to last long after being hard for you since the church."

"We're not talking about you being hard in church. I'm not going to hell with you."

"Oh, come on! It won't be any fun without you."

"What else are you worried about?"

"Truthfully?"

"Always."

"That you can be happy anywhere but here with your people. I saw you in your element today, and it just... It gave me pause. The last fucking thing in the world I want to do is anything to make you unhappy—and I worry that taking you away from them will make you unhappy."

"I love you so much for being concerned about that, but I've been doing some research on Seattle, and it looks like a really fun place to live. I think it'll be good for me to live somewhere else for a while and to experience life outside Miami. I'll miss my family, but we'll get home to visit, and when you're done with baseball, maybe we can move back here?"

"We can. Absolutely. Give me six to ten years elsewhere, and I'll give you forever here."

"That's a pretty good deal."

"I want you to be happy, Maria."

"I promise I can be happy in Seattle if you and Everly are there."

"Will we be enough?"

"God, Austin, *yes*. You guys are everything to me. You have to know that by now."

"We're not everything. Your family is such a huge part of your life."

"And now you guys are, too. It'll be okay as long we're together." She draws me into a kiss that has me forgetting about everything other than what's happening right here and now, which is pretty damned awesome.

I release the clasp of her bra and take in the sight of her spectacular breasts and the nipples that tighten before my eyes. I love her unreasonably, and the only thing that matters to me is that she always knows that. I worship every inch of her delicious skin, her tight nipples, her flat belly, which quivers under my lips. With her legs on my shoulders, I kiss and caress and coax her to a series of orgasms that leave her panting and me desperate to get in on the action as I slide into her.

She wraps her arms around me and holds on tight as we move together in the kind of perfect harmony that had eluded me until I found her. Nothing has ever been like this, like her.

"God, Maria… I love you. I love you so much."

"Me, too. Love you." She's breathless and flushed, so fucking sexy and all mine forever.

I'm so high on the magic we create together that I'm under the mistaken belief that nothing could ever come between us.

I'll find out soon enough how wrong I am about that.

CHAPTER 25

MARIA

*M*y parents want to see me and my siblings after brunch and won't say why. The cryptic text from my dad asked that we come by the house—just us—after brunch.

Dee texts me right after. *Um, what the hell?*

No idea.

Are they getting divorced?

No! If there's one thing I'm sure of, that's it. My parents are solid. Always have been, always will be. I refuse to believe anything other than that.

I wish I had nowhere to be and nothing to do today so I could loll around in bed with Austin all day, but today's brunch is the end of the wedding weekend, and everyone will be there to see Carmen and Jason off on their honeymoon to Turks and

Caicos. They're staying in some super-cool resort, and I'd be green with envy if I wasn't so thrilled for both of them.

But now this thing with my parents is hanging over me as Austin drives me home to pick up my car. I'd planned to spend the whole day with him and Everly at their house, swimming and chilling by the pool. And now I have no idea what this day will bring, and that's left me unsettled.

"I'm sure it's nothing horrible," Austin says. "They were both in good spirits yesterday."

"I know. I can't imagine what this is about."

"You'll find out soon enough."

"It won't be soon enough for my liking." Brunch, which is usually the highlight of my week, is going to be torturous today.

At my house, he waits for me to run in and grab my keys, and then I follow him to the restaurant where his parents and Everly are meeting us. I get caught up in introducing them to people they didn't meet yesterday and manage to forget, for a minute, the family meeting that's cast a pall over a day that should be all about celebration.

Nico and Milo corner me when I come out of the ladies' room.

"What's up with Mom and Dad?" Nico asks.

"I have no idea. I know as much as you do."

"You always know what's up," Milo says.

"Not this time."

"Are you freaked out?" Milo asks.

"Kinda."

"That doesn't make me feel any better," Nico says.

"Sorry."

He squeezes my shoulder. "Dee thinks they're getting divorced."

"They are not. That's one thing I'm not worried about."

"Let's get them out of here soon," Milo says. "I can't deal with worrying about what's going on."

"Agreed."

It's after two by the time we arrive back at my parents' house. I was so wound up that I could barely eat at brunch, but my stomach is upset anyway. There's no way they'd do this to us unless something is wrong, and part of me doesn't want to hear whatever it is, especially when everything has been going so right for me lately.

We gather in the family room, my parents sitting next to each other on the love seat, which I take as further proof they're not getting divorced.

"Sit, Maria," Dad says.

"I'd rather stand. What's this about? You've got us freaking out."

Dad glances at Mom, and she nods as he takes hold of her hand.

"We wanted to wait until after the wedding to tell you that your mother has been diagnosed with breast cancer."

As if someone has opened a trap door beneath me, the world seems to tilt on its axis as I listen to him say words no one ever wants to hear associated with someone they love: triple negative, stage three, mastectomy, reconstruction, chemotherapy, radiation.

My brain shuts down, and my heart shatters. I know enough to be seriously concerned about the battle that looms ahead for my mother, and one very clear thought occurs to me—I won't be going to Seattle, or anywhere, for that matter.

Dee is sobbing as Nico and Milo stare blankly at my parents, who're making a big effort to be strong for us.

"We've got the best doctors, and we feel very confident that we're going to beat this," Dad says as Mom weeps silently next to him.

"I'm so sorry to do this to you kids," she says.

We all move at the same instant, going to her, hugging her, reassuring her.

"We'll be with you every step of the way, Mama," Nico says. "Don't worry about anything."

"I'll move home," Dee says. "I'll stay here and help with everything."

"I don't want you to upset your lives for me," Mom says.

"Too late," Dee replies. "It's already done."

"I'll go to every appointment, every treatment, everything," I tell her as I try not to break inside at the thought of Austin and Everly in Seattle without me. "You'll have your own private-duty nurse." It's all I can do not to sob all over her, but she doesn't need that right now. She needs us to be strong for her and to support her as she fights for her life.

"We're not telling the rest of the family until Carmen gets home from her trip," Mom says. "We don't want to do anything to ruin this happy time for her. Please promise me you'll keep it between us for now."

We all agree to her wishes and hang out for another hour, until Mom says she's feeling tired and would like to lie down for a bit.

The four of us walk outside, numbed by shock and the bone-deep fear that always accompanies a cancer diagnosis.

"How bad is it?" Dee asks me.

"It's not great. Stage three means it's already spread to the lymph nodes, and triple negative is a bitch. No way around it."

My sister breaks down again at that news.

I wrap my arms around her, and our brothers join the group hug. "We'll get her through it. We'll get them both through it." I tell them what they need to hear, what we all need to hear, even as I spin with despair on the inside. Everything was perfect.

Until it wasn't.

Because our parents urged us to carry on with our plans for the day, Dee decides to go meet her high school friends as planned, and my brothers head to a local park to play pickup basketball with a group they play with almost every Sunday.

I get in my car, intending to drive to Austin's home, but instead end up back at my place, needing some time alone. I crawl into bed and sob into my pillow, heartbroken and terrified for my mother, but also a little heartbroken for myself and Austin, too. It was too good to be true. That's all I keep thinking. Just when everything was falling into place for us, this bomb goes off in my life that'll keep me in Miami—and that's not even the most upsetting part of it. Thinking about what my mom will endure breaks me.

My cell rings in the other room, and I'm sure it must be Austin, but I can't bring myself to move or do anything other than weep. In a matter of a few hours, I've gone from as high as I've ever been to as low as I hope to ever be. Though I know I'll lose them both at some point, I simply can't picture life without my parents at the center of it. She's fifty-two. This can't be happening.

But it is, and I'm simply devastated for her, my dad, our family and for myself, too. I'd begun to wrap my head around the idea of Seattle, to picture myself there with Austin and Everly. And now...

I hurt like I've never hurt before.

AUSTIN

It's been three hours since I left Maria after brunch, and I expected to hear from her by now. I'm starting to get worried, especially since she's not picking up her phone. Everly's down for a nap, and my parents are watching golf on TV to avoid the afternoon heat.

"Do you guys mind listening for Ev?" I ask them. "I'm going to check on Maria."

"Of course," Mom says. "I hope everything's okay."

"I do, too." It's very strange that she hasn't texted or called or come to the house like we planned. She can't still be with her family hours after they left the restaurant, can she?

I take a guess and decide to try her place first, and when I see her car in the driveway, my anxiety spikes even further. What the heck is going on? I take the stairs to her place two at a time and knock on the door.

There's no answer, so I take a chance and try the door. It's unlocked, and that worries me because she once told me no one leaves their door unlocked in Miami. Concerned, I step inside. "Maria? Babe, are you here?"

Her purse is on the floor next to a chair, her keys on the floor next to it, sending a trickle of unease down my back. I head straight for her room, where I find her on the bed asleep.

Relief floods through me when I see that she's okay, or at least I think she is. Why is she here and not with me at my house like we planned? I sit on the edge of the mattress, and gently place my hand on her shoulder, careful not to startle her.

Her face is puffy, as if she's been crying.

"Maria, honey." I kiss her shoulder and then her cheek.

Her eyes open, and I see they, too, are red and swollen.

"Baby, what's wrong?" I brush the hair back from her face and notice new tears filling her eyes.

"My mom has breast cancer."

"Oh no. Maria…"

"It's pretty bad. Stage three and an aggressive form. She didn't want to tell us until after the wedding."

"I'm so sorry to hear that." I kick off my shoes and stretch out next to her, putting my arm around her and wishing there was more I could do besides hold her. "Does she know yet what the treatment will entail?" I can't deny that my own PTSD surfaces at this news.

"Mastectomy, reconstruction, chemo, radiation. A long and complicated ordeal."

I hear what she doesn't say, loud and clear—she's not going to Seattle. She can't be anywhere but right here with her mother and family. "We'll figure it out, sweetheart. Don't worry."

"What will we figure out? You're going to be in Seattle for at least three years but probably longer, and I'm going to be on the exact opposite side of the country, unable to go anywhere."

"I haven't signed with anyone yet. Anything can still happen."

"You've worked so hard for this moment, Austin. You shouldn't let anything get in the way of the best possible deal for you and your daughter."

"And not my fiancée, too? What about what's best for her?"

"It's not about me. This is about *you* and your career and this exciting time."

"Don't you know by now that without you, there's nothing exciting about anything?"

She breaks down into heartbroken sobs that crush me. If she hurts, I hurt.

Just last night, we were floating on air, and now we're being brought back to earth in the cruelest way possible.

"I don't want you to make decisions based on me, Austin. That'd be crazy. You have such a huge opportunity to get everything you deserve. That's what I want for you. It might be best if we, you know, take a break—"

"No. That's not happening."

"Please, Austin. Don't make this harder than it already is. I have to be here, and your career is going to take you far away from me. It would make everything worse if I thought I kept you from realizing your full potential."

"Do you honestly think I'll be capable of realizing my full potential without you? I don't want to hear any more about taking breaks or going forward without you. Not to mention how bad your mom will feel if she thinks she caused us to break up." Desperation has me playing every card in my hand.

Sobs continue to echo through her body, but she doesn't say anything else. I'm filled with dread just the same, knowing the conversation has only been postponed, not finished. If she thinks she can get rid of me when shit goes sideways, she's going to find out otherwise. I'll fight for her and us with everything I've got. After having found my soul mate, I can't fathom life without her.

MARIA

It's funny how life goes on all around you when you're living your own private hell. The sun rises and sets, the days go by, you go to work, take your mom to doctor's appointments, cook food, eat food that has no taste, take care of your parents and patients and see Austin and Everly, and through it all, you're just numb. You feel nothing other than dread. It hangs over every breath you take, everything you do, every moment you're awake.

I have a whole new appreciation for what Austin went through when Everly was sick. As bad as it is to see my mom go through this, I can't for the life of me know how much harder it must be when your child is the one who is sick. My mom is suffering, and despite the support of our wonderful family and friends, there's not much we can do for her except pray the treatment works.

Her surgery is scheduled for right after the first of the year, and we should know more about her prognosis by March, which is an interminable wait.

Austin officially becomes a free agent on Halloween, but stays focused on Everly that day as she tries to decide between dressing up as a mermaid, a unicorn or Elsa from *Frozen*. In the end, she chooses Elsa, and we take her trick-or-treating in Gable Estates and in my parents' neighborhood. They make a big fuss over her and treat her like a grandchild, which is so sweet. I try not to think about whether my mom will live to see other grandchildren.

In early November, we find out Austin is a finalist for his fourth American League Cy Young Award, which goes to the best pitchers in both leagues.

When free agency officially begins in early November, Austin spends most of each day on the phone with Aaron, taking meetings with general managers and representatives from a variety of teams that're interested in him.

I can't keep it all straight, but from what he tells me, it's still looking like Seattle will make the best offer and give him a great chance at playing for a championship team. There's all kinds of other stuff happening behind the scenes, but Austin has told me nothing will be decided for certain until the middle of December, when the winter meetings are held and Aaron can talk to the general managers face-to-face to reach a deal.

So I try to tune it all out until it's decision time, but the process only feeds the pervasive feeling of dread that hangs over me all the time. What does it matter where he ends up? He and Everly will be living so far from me that I'll never get to see them.

In mid-November, Austin wins the American League Cy Young, while Joaquin Garcia with the Marlins is the National League winner. The award is a great boost for Austin at a time when the negotiations are really heating up. Aaron is apparently thrilled, because the award gives them even more firepower in the negotiations. I'm so proud of Austin and try to work up the required amount of enthusiasm, but even that falls flat.

As he has since I learned about my mother's illness, he's unwavering in his support of me and my family through these difficult times. He and Jason have taken over the yard work at my parents' home and spent an entire recent Saturday replacing some sagging planks on their back deck.

He's officially become the clinic's chief benefactor. Miranda is beyond excited as she shops around for a larger building to house the new facility that Austin has promised to build for us. I'm thrilled for Miranda and the community we serve, but like everything else right now, I can't work up the proper enthusiasm for even that.

Ridiculous numbers float around the baseball media and in conversations I overhear, but the one that keeps coming up is a hundred and twenty million for three years from Seattle.

As a longtime baseball fan, I've tried to picture making millions of dollars to work six months a year. But having spent time with Austin and witnessed how hard he works in the gym and the light throwing he does in the yard with his dad catching for him at least once a day to keep his arm limber, I believe he deserves whatever largesse is coming his way.

I'm well aware that our relationship has been different since the day I found out my mother is sick. I've been pulling away from him, preparing myself for life without him and Everly, and he knows it. He's been super patient with me, and of course, that only makes me love him more.

By mid-December, I've slipped into my new routine of working, checking on my parents, cooking for them, spending time with Austin and Everly whenever I can and generally feeling as if I'm running in fifty different directions at the same time. Having Dee home has made a huge difference, as she's staying with my parents, but I try to help as much as I can, too, so it doesn't all fall to her. She's the only reason I ever get to see Austin at all.

I'm on my way home from checking in on my parents after a frantically busy day at the clinic. Thursdays are always our busiest days because Jason is there in the afternoons. My goal tonight is to finish the laundry I started last night, do some cooking so that my parents and Dee are covered for the weekend and go to bed early.

I've got my radio tuned to Power 96, and I'm zoned out as

I always am when battling Miami's rush-hour traffic. An announcer comes on between songs and gets my attention when he says, "There's big news for Miami Marlins fans! Cy Young Award-winning pitcher Austin Jacobs has just inked a four-year, eighty-million-dollar deal to play for the Marlins! As one of the most sought-after free agents in this off-season, no one saw this coming. When asked why Jacobs chose Miami, his agent would only say he has personal ties to the city. On behalf of all Marlins fans, let me be the first to welcome Austin Jacobs to Miami! With two Cy Young Award winners in the pitching rotation, look for Miami to be on fire next season!"

I'm so shocked, I nearly drive off the road. He was supposed to go to Seattle for a hundred and twenty million! What the hell is he doing?

The first chance I get, I make a U-turn and head for Gable Estates.

AUSTIN

So the deal is done, and Aaron is absolutely *furious* with me. He even threatened to drop me as a client if I took the Miami deal. I told him to do what he needs to, which is what I did. Maria needs to be in Miami, I need to be with Maria, so really, there was no decision to make. I did what was best for our family, the new family she and I are going to create together.

Only my parents and brothers knew ahead of time what I was planning to do, and having spent time with Maria and her family, my parents wholeheartedly approved and understood what I was doing and why. They sold it to my brothers, who were more skeptical at first. They came around when they understood that I love her too much to live without her, even for half the year. And with Everly two years from starting school, spending winters in Miami soon won't be an option.

This was the only way I could have everything I want and need, and I'm very pleased with how it worked out.

After I get Ev down for the night, I plan to go over to Maria's and talk to her about it. For now, I'm completely focused on Everly, while ignoring my incessantly ringing phone. Every baseball reporter I've ever talked to is trying to reach me, along with Miami media and others who want more info about why I took a lesser deal to play in Miami.

They'll know soon enough.

Everly and I are playing tea party in the living room after dinner when Maria comes in hot. *Uh-oh.* It appears she's already heard the news and doesn't seem happy. That's okay. I'm ready for her. For now, I stare at my gorgeous nurse in the light blue scrubs she wears to work. She makes scrubs look almost as sexy as that bridesmaid dress was.

"Rie! Tea! Party!" Everly runs for her, like she always does.

Maria picks her up and gives her a hug and kiss. "Hi, pumpkin."

"Play tea, Rie!"

"We're graduating to sentences," she says, keeping her attention on Everly.

"But the exclamation mark is still in full effect."

She rubs noses with Everly, who is delighted by her, as per usual. "We wouldn't have it any other way."

Though I can tell Maria is pissed with me, she sits and has tea and cookies with Everly before I tell my daughter it's time for bed. While she runs off to say good night to my parents, who are out by the pool, I take a long leisurely look at Maria.

She's glaring at me, and I love her madly. "What the *hell* did you do?"

"I'll tell you all about it after we get Ev to bed."

Everly comes back inside, and we oversee the brushing of teeth and the reading of stories and the bedtime snuggling we all love so much.

We tiptoe out of Everly's room nearly forty-five minutes after Maria first arrived. I take her hand and lead her into my bedroom and close the door. "First things first." I put my hands on her shoulders, noting they're tight with tension, and kiss her. "Hi."

She turns away from my kiss. "Start talking. Right now."

"I signed with Miami."

"I know that! *How could you do that?* You were going to make *a hundred and twenty million* with Seattle!"

I shrug, which only further infuriates her. "What's the difference between eighty and a hundred and twenty?"

Her gorgeous eyes shoot fire at me. "*Forty million!*"

I smile at her outrage. "That's how much you're worth to me, my sweet Maria. I don't need the forty million, but I *do* need you, and so does Everly. The thought of being three thousand miles from you was simply unbearable. And if anyone understands the need to be close by while a loved one battles a serious illness, it's me. In the end, Miami was the only team I considered."

"Aaron must be pissed."

"He threatened to dump me as a client if I took the Miami deal. I told him to do whatever he needs to."

She drops her head to my chest. "I cannot believe you did this."

"Really? You can't? You must have no idea how much I love you if you can't believe I want to be wherever you are."

"You could've gotten a much bigger deal! This is your season..."

"And *you* are my reason. Mine and Everly's. She loves you as much as I do. How could I take her away from her Rie, the only mother she'll ever know?"

She breaks down into sobs as I tighten my arms around her.

"Hang on to me, sweet Maria. I've got you. I'm here, and I'm not going anywhere." I run my fingers through her long curls.

"We're going to get married and live in this ridiculous house that I'm going to buy for us and make a home and a family and a life right here in your town. I'll still have to travel with the team during the season, but maybe you guys can come with me."

She shakes her head.

"You don't have to if you don't want to."

Raising her head, she looks up at me, her eyes red and puffy from crying. She takes my breath away. "I do want to."

"Then what?"

"I still can't believe you gave up *forty million dollars* for me."

"I did it for me, too, and for Ev. I did it for all of us, Maria. Before I took this deal, I already had everything I need, everything I'll ever need. I've been smart with the money I've already made. If I never play another game, I'm set. We're set. Eighty million is a king's ransom. Twenty million a year to do what I love while living with the woman I love? Sign me up."

"You should've talked to me about it first."

With my hands framing her face, I gaze down at her. "So you could talk me out of it or break up with me in some misguided attempt to do what was best for me? No, thanks. *You're* what's best for me. *Miami* is what's best for me. In case you haven't noticed, I love it here. I love being with your family. I love Sunday brunch at the restaurant and visiting you there when you're working. I love the clinic and the important work we're doing there. I love the golf and the sun and the pool and the beach. I even love the palm trees. But more than anything else, I love *you*."

"You signed with Miami."

Smiling, I nod. "I signed with Miami."

"You're *insane*."

"Maybe so, but insanity has never felt so good."

"You could've been the ace in Seattle."

Again, I shrug. "Who cares about that? Joaquin will force me to up my game and not get lazy and slovenly."

"You'd never do either of those things."

"Still, it'll be nice to have healthy competition for the top spot on the roster, and the Marlins are thrilled to have both of this year's Cy Young Award winners in their rotation. That greatly improves our chances of going deep into the off-season, which was another of my goals for choosing a new team. It's all good, babe."

She releases a deep breath. "I can't believe you did this."

That makes me laugh, as I realize it's going to take her a while to wrap her head around what I did and why I did it. That's fine. We've got all the time in the world to spend together and with Everly, and that's what makes me happier than anything else.

"Let's get married this winter. We'll go somewhere awesome. Take everyone with us. What do you think?"

"I, uh..."

I kiss her. "You're cute when you're speechless. But then again, you're always cute." I help her out of her scrubs, pull off my T-shirt and shorts and follow her into bed. When we're wrapped up in each other, I brush the wild curls back from her face. "I know these last few weeks have been awful for you. Between your mom's illness and waiting for me to figure out my plan, you've been caught in the middle of it all."

"I've been trying to prepare myself for you guys to leave."

"I know, and you have no idea how often I wanted to put your mind at ease and tell you I was negotiating with Miami, but until it was a done deal, I didn't want to say anything. I was afraid it would fall apart at the last minute or something."

"I can't believe you did this."

Smiling, I kiss her. "Believe it. I'm here to stay, and the only thing that's ever made me happier than I am right now was hearing that Everly was in remission."

"You aren't going to hate me someday for costing you forty million, are you?"

"Never." I kiss her some more, and for the first time in weeks, she kisses me back like she used to before her world imploded. "Want to know something else?"

"I'm almost afraid to ask..."

"I would've signed for sixty."

288

EPILOGUE

MARIA

$\mathcal{M}$y mom has her surgery in January. It's a long day because she had a double mastectomy and reconstruction at the same time. That's a bitch of a surgery, but she wanted to get it over with all at once rather than, as she said, dragging it out indefinitely. Her fortitude and courage have been inspiring to everyone who loves her. She refuses to wallow in self-pity and has put all her energy toward a return to full health.

I stay at my parents' house for the first two weeks she's home so I can tend to her personally while working as much as I can at the clinic. Dee helps with everything, and my brothers are in and out every day, bringing groceries, wine, prescriptions and anything else we want or need. It's been a team effort, and our family has more than risen to the occasion.

Austin and Everly come to visit me every day, but we don't get much time alone together because the house is always full of relatives and friends, who bring food and much-needed good cheer. Despite being surrounded by loved ones, I've never been lonelier as I yearn for time with Austin and a return to normalcy.

I keep telling myself it's not about me, it's about whatever my mother needs and my dad by extension. It's about using my nursing skills to make her as comfortable as possible and to care for her the way she's always cared for me.

However, even though I see Austin every day, I miss my love and our time alone together desperately, not to mention how much I miss Everly.

When she's not sleeping, the only thing my mom wants to talk about is my wedding. She quickly scuttled our plan to go somewhere this winter to get married. "I don't want to look sick in the pictures," she said, and that was that. I don't want that for her, either. So we set a date for early November, when Austin's season will be over and my mother will hopefully be through the worst of the treatment.

I spend much of every day with Dee, which has been a bright spot in an otherwise difficult time. We haven't had this much time together in years, and it reminds me of how much fun we had growing up thick as thieves, as Nona would say. Dee refuses to talk about Marcus or whether she's spoken to him, so we avoid that topic studiously, even if I can tell that something is up with her.

She's not talking about it.

The family brought brunch to our house today so Mom could participate without having to go anywhere. They just left a short time ago, and after we clean up the kitchen, Dee and I escape to the patio for some sun, fresh air and sister time.

"Are you going to move in with Austin?" she asks between sips of wine.

"I suppose I already have since I was there more than home before Mommy's surgery."

She looks over at me. "Can I have your place?"

Her request surprises me. "What about New York?"

"New York was going south before I came south. I got laid off from the doctor's office when he retired in August, and I haven't been able to find anything even close to that, which means I can't pay the rent. Dom has been floating me, but he needs to get a new roommate who can actually pay their share."

"You never said anything!"

She shrugs. "I was embarrassed. I didn't want to come home a failure."

"No one would've thought that."

"Yes, they would have. You wouldn't, but others would. So Mommy's illness gave me an out, and as soon as I can go back to New York, I'll pack up my stuff and let Dom get a new roommate. I talked to Uncle V, and he said he'll put me on the schedule as soon as Mommy feels better."

"I hate that you're sad about New York, but I'm so glad to have you home."

"I'm glad to be here. I think I was ready to come back, even before Dr. Tillis retired. There's no place like home as long as I don't actually have to *live* at home."

"You don't. Of course you can have my place." I look over at her. "Can I tell you a secret?"

"Duh. You'd better."

"I'm still really mad at Austin for settling for less than he could've gotten with another team, but I'm *so glad* I don't have to move away from here. I would've done it for him, but it would've killed me."

"Yes, it would have. You've always been such a homebody."

"And you've always been the adventurer. I'm so jealous that you got to live in New York for six years."

"Don't be. I have absolutely nothing to show for it but massive credit card debt. I don't even have a car."

"You can use Mommy's until she's back on her feet."

"That's what she said, too."

"So you told them you're moving home?"

Dee nodded. "Mommy cried. She said she never wanted me to know how much she worried about me when I was there."

"Aw, that's so sweet. No one will ever love us the way she does. Well, except for Nona and Abuela."

Dee laughs. "Right."

Dad comes out through the sliding door. "I love to hear my girls giggling together. It's like old times when I'd have to go in your room twenty times every night to tell you to go the hell to sleep."

"We never did," Dee says.

"I know! I could hear you whispering every night. I miss that now that you're grown up."

He takes a seat facing us. "We never would've gotten through this without you two. Thank you so much for everything."

"You don't have to thank us, Daddy," Dee says. "There's nowhere else we'd be when you and Mommy need us."

"And we appreciate that so much, but we want you to go back to your lives. We're okay, and I'll be working from home until she's getting around better. Everything is good, and we're ready to be on our own again. You girls have to be ready, too."

Only because my mom had her drains removed on Friday do I even consider leaving, my heart racing at the thought of being back with Austin and Everly for longer than a quick visit here or there. According to Austin, Everly has been super cranky without her Rie. "Are you sure?"

"Positive. We have the best kids ever, but we already knew that before this happened."

I have to admit I'm a tiny bit thrilled at being released from duty. "As long as you're sure, I think I'll go see what Austin and Ev are up to."

"Go," Dee says. "I'll be here if anything comes up."

Dad stands and hugs me. "Thank you, Maria. Thank you so much. We're so, so proud of what a compassionate, competent nurse you are."

"Thank you, Daddy. I love you both."

"We love you, too."

"Tell Mommy I'll check on her after her nap?"

"I will, honey. Go enjoy your new family. They must be missing you."

They are, even though they'd never add to my burden by saying so too often. I run upstairs, throw clothes and toiletries into a bag, find a clean pair of scrubs for work tomorrow and in my haste nearly forget the sneakers I wear to work. I'm in the car and headed for Gable Estates ten minutes later. I decide to surprise them rather than tell Austin I'm on the way.

I can't wait to be there, to see them, to help put Ev to bed and to sleep wrapped up in Austin's arms for the first time in weeks. I've missed him so much, which seems silly since I've seen him every day. It just hasn't been the same.

I'm relieved to see Austin's car in the driveway when I arrive and park behind him. I grab my bag and go in through the open garage door that leads into the kitchen, where Deidre is standing watch over something on the stove. They didn't come to brunch today since they were concerned about over-whelming my mom.

"Hi, honey," she says. "How's Elena?"

"She's doing much better."

"Thank goodness. You'll be shocked to hear that Austin and Everly are in the pool."

That makes me laugh, because they're always in the pool. "I'll find them." I drop my bag and keys in the living room and wander out to the massive patio and pool deck. I'm still trying to wrap my head around living in a palace, but as long as Austin and Everly are there, it doesn't matter where we live.

She sees me first and lets out her trademark scream. "Rie! *Swim!*"

Austin, who has his back to me, whirls around and lights up with a big smile. "Hey, babe. You're home. This is a nice surprise." He guides Everly to the steps and follows her out of the pool, leaning in to kiss me without getting me wet.

Everly has no such care as she hurls herself at me.

Wet clothes are the least of my concerns when I'm back with my loves. "Hi, pumpkin." I pick her up and kiss her sun-rosy cheek. She gives me a wet, noisy kiss back as I help her remove the plugs she wears since the ear infection.

"How long do we have you?" Austin asks.

I make sure to look right at him when I say, "Indefinitely."

His eyes go wide with delight. "Really?"

"Yep. I got sprung from private duty."

"Until tomorrow?"

"Nope, for good. My dad said they're all set and thank you very much and—"

Before I can finish the sentence, he's kissing me, working around Everly to get to me.

"Dada! Kiss! Rie!"

We break apart, laughing, and engage in a three-way group hug that's full of relief and happiness to have our little family back together.

Much later, after we've had dinner with his parents and Everly, given her a bath and read her four stories, we're wrapped up in each other in his bed. Nothing has ever felt better than being back with him does.

"I missed this so much," he whispers as he kisses me like he hasn't seen me in a year. "So, so, so much."

"I did, too. I kept wondering how I could be lonely for you when I saw you every day."

"Same, babe. It was brutal to not be able to hold you and love you and be with you this way." He is so sexy and sweet and hot and just everything as he makes love to me for the first time in weeks. "You're going to have to travel with me during the season. I won't be able to stand being away from you."

"I'll go on the long trips."

"You will?"

"Any time I can." Thanks to him, Miranda is going to be able to hire two more full-time nurses and a full-time doctor. She said I can fill in whenever I'm in town and sit on the board of directors that's being formed to oversee our newly expanded program so I can still be involved with the clinic. It's taken some time to adjust to the change in circumstances that my life with Austin will provide, but I'm relieved to have found a way to stay involved with the clinic and be able to travel with him any time I want. We'd also like to have some babies before too long so they'll be close in age to Everly.

"That'd be so great. Then I never have to miss you."

We're absolutely ravenous for each other, and by the time we collapse into a sweaty mess on the bed, I'm exhausted and elated and full of excitement for everything we have to look forward to.

He turns on his side and puts his arm around me. "I love you so much. Even more than I did before I had to sleep without you for two weeks."

I turn into him, relieved to have his arms around me again, and pepper his chest with kisses. "I love you, too. More than anything."

It's so good to be home.

DEE

An hour after Maria leaves, my phone buzzes with a text from the one person I do *not* want to hear from.

What's up?

I should've blocked him. The only reason I didn't is because he's one of Jason's good friends, and I don't need it getting back to Jason and Carmen that I blocked him. So now I have to put up with him texting me.

I did a bad, bad thing after the wedding, and now I'm paying the price. The only reason he has my number in the first place is because of too much champagne and the fiery rage that burned inside me for days after hearing my ex was pining over me after he broke my heart by marrying the skank.

Champagne and rage are a bad combination. I had no idea *how* bad until Carmen's wedding, when I ended up in bed with one of Jason's groomsmen, who now wants to know what's up.

I stare at the screen for a long time, trying to decide whether or not I should answer him, but before I can, he texts again.

Wanted to tell you I'm coming back to Miami for an interview at M-D General next week. Staying with J and C and hoping to see you again.

I startle like I've been hit by a taser. He's *interviewing at Miami-Dade*? He's supposed to be in Phoenix and nowhere near Miami! This can't be happening.

I'm in the throes of a full-on meltdown when my phone chimes with yet another text. I'm actually afraid to look, but curiosity wins out.

Marcus: *Are you ever going to talk to me?*

Shoot me right now.

Preorder Dee's story, *How Much I Love*, at *marieforce.com/howmuchilove* to read it early next year!

Thank you for reading *How Much I Care*! I loved Austin and Maria so much from the first minute I had the idea for this story to the last seconds of the epilogue. They just jumped off the page for me and I hope for you, too! I'm super excited to be writing this new series set in Miami and to be continuing it next year with Dee's story in *How Much I Love.* Join the *How Much I Care* Reader Group at *facebook.com/groups/howmuchicare* to discuss Austin and Maria's story with spoilers allowed and also make sure to join the Miami Nights Series group at *facebook.com/groups/MiamiNightsSeries/* and like the Miami Nights Series Page: *facebook.com/MiamiNightsSeries/* to keep up with news about upcoming books.

Many thanks to the wonderful team that supports me behind the scenes every day: Julie Cupp, Lisa Cafferty, Tia Kelly, Nikki Haley and Ashley Lopez. Thank you to Dan, Emily and Jake for always supporting my author career, and thanks to my fantastic editorial team of Linda Ingmanson and Joyce Lamb, and my beta readers Anne Woodall, Kara Conrad and Tracey Suppo.

Huge thanks to Sarah Hewitt, family nurse practitioner, for always checking me on anything medically related.

And a big thank you to my Miami beta readers for all their help: Miriam Ayala, Angelica Maya, Dinorah Shoben, Stephanie Behill, Mona Abramesco, Isabel Acevedo, Gwendolyn Neff, Emma Melero Juarez and Carmen Morejon.

Thanks for your support of this new series and all my books. I appreciate my readers more than you'll ever know!

Much love,
Marie

ALSO BY MARIE FORCE

Contemporary Romances Available from Marie Force

The Miami Nights Series

Book 1: How Much I Feel (*Carmen & Jason*)

Book 2: How Much I Care (*Maria & Austin*)

Book 3: How Much I Love (*Dee's story*)

The Gansett Island Series

Book 1: Maid for Love (*Mac & Maddie*)

Book 2: Fool for Love (*Joe & Janey*)

Book 3: Ready for Love (*Luke & Sydney*)

Book 4: Falling for Love (*Grant & Stephanie*)

Book 5: Hoping for Love (*Evan & Grace*)

Book 6: Season for Love (*Owen & Laura*)

Book 7: Longing for Love (*Blaine & Tiffany*)

Book 8: Waiting for Love (*Adam & Abby*)

Book 9: Time for Love (*David & Daisy*)

Book 10: Meant for Love (*Jenny & Alex*)

Book 10.5: Chance for Love, *A Gansett Island Novella* (*Jared & Lizzie*)

Book 11: Gansett After Dark (*Owen & Laura*)

Book 12: Kisses After Dark (*Shane & Katie*)

Book 13: Love After Dark (*Paul & Hope*)

Book 14: Celebration After Dark (*Big Mac & Linda*)

Book 15: Desire After Dark (*Slim & Erin*)

Book 16: Light After Dark (*Mallory & Quinn*)

Book 17: Victoria & Shannon (Episode 1)

Book 18: Kevin & Chelsea (Episode 2)

A Gansett Island Christmas Novella

Book 19: Mine After Dark *(Riley & Nikki)*

Book 20: Yours After Dark *(Finn & Chloe)*

Book 21: Trouble After Dark *(Deacon & Julia)*

Book 22: Rescue After Dark *(Mason & Jordan)*

Book 23: Blackout After Dark

The Green Mountain Series

Book 1: All You Need Is Love *(Will & Cameron)*

Book 2: I Want to Hold Your Hand *(Nolan & Hannah)*

Book 3: I Saw Her Standing There *(Colton & Lucy)*

Book 4: And I Love Her *(Hunter & Megan)*

Novella: You'll Be Mine *(Will & Cam's Wedding)*

Book 5: It's Only Love *(Gavin & Ella)*

Book 6: Ain't She Sweet *(Tyler & Charlotte)*

The Butler, Vermont Series

(Continuation of Green Mountain)

Book 1: Every Little Thing *(Grayson & Emma)*

Book 2: Can't Buy Me Love *(Mary & Patrick)*

Book 3: Here Comes the Sun *(Wade & Mia)*

Book 4: Till There Was You *(Lucas & Dani)*

Book 5: All My Loving *(Landon & Amanda)*

Book 6: Let It Be *(Lincoln & Molly)*

Book 7: Come Together *(Noah & Brianna)*

The Treading Water Series

Book 1: Treading Water

Book 2: Marking Time

Book 3: Starting Over

Book 4: Coming Home

Book 5: Finding Forever

Single Titles

Five Years Gone

One Year Home

Sex Machine

Sex God

Georgia on My Mind

True North

The Fall

The Wreck

Love at First Flight

Everyone Loves a Hero

Line of Scrimmage

The Quantum Series

Book 1: Virtuous *(Flynn & Natalie)*

Book 2: Valorous *(Flynn & Natalie)*

Book 3: Victorious *(Flynn & Natalie)*

Book 4: Rapturous *(Addie & Hayden)*

Book 5: Ravenous *(Jasper & Ellie)*

Book 6: Delirious *(Kristian & Aileen)*

Book 7: Outrageous *(Emmett & Leah)*

Book 8: Famous *(Marlowe & Sebastian)*

Romantic Suspense Novels Available from Marie Force

ABOUT THE AUTHOR

Marie Force is the *New York Times* best-
selling author of contemporary romance,
romantic suspense and erotic romance.
Her series include Gansett Island, Fatal,
Treading Water, Butler Vermont and
Quantum.

Her books have sold nearly 10 million
copies worldwide, have been translated into more than a dozen
languages and have appeared on the *New York Times* bestseller
more than 30 times. She is also a *USA Today* and *Wall Street
Journal* bestseller, as well as a Speigel bestseller in Germany.

Her goals in life are simple—to finish raising two happy,
healthy, productive young adults, to keep writing books for as
long as she possibly can and to never be on a flight that makes
the news.

Join Marie's mailing list on her website at *marieforce.com* for
news about new books and upcoming appearances in your area.
Follow her on Facebook at *www.Facebook.com/MarieForceAuthor*
and on Instagram at *www.instagram.com/marieforceauthor/*.
Contact Marie at *marie@marieforce.com*.